BURIED IN BEIGNETS

A Selection of Titles by J.R. Ripley

The Tony Kozol Mysteries

STIFF IN THE FREEZER
SKULLS OF SEDONA
LOST IN AUSTIN
THE BODY FROM IPANEMA
BUM RAP IN BRANSON
GUNFIGHT IN GATLINBURG

The Gendarme Trenet Series

MURDER IN ST. BARTS
DEATH OF A CHEAT

The Maggie Miller Mysteries

BURIED IN BEIGNETS *

* *available from Severn House*

BURIED IN BEIGNETS

J.R. Ripley

Severn House Large Print
London & New York

This first large print edition published 2016
in Great Britain and the USA by
SEVERN HOUSE PUBLISHERS LTD of
19 Cedar Road, Sutton, Surrey, England, SM2 5DA.
First world regular print edition published 2015 by
Severn House Publishers Ltd.

British Library Cataloguing in Publication Data
A CIP catalogue record for this title is available from the British Library.

ISBN-13: 9780727894489

Severn House Publishers support the Forest Stewardship Council™
[FSC™], the leading international forest certification organisation. All
our titles that are printed on FSC certified paper carry the FSC logo.

Typeset by Palimpsest Book Production Ltd.,
Falkirk, Stirlingshire, Scotland.
Printed and bound in Great Britain by
T J International, Padstow, Cornwall.

ONE

My husband always wanted to own a beignet shop. Always talked about opening a beignet and coffee shop. Ever since our late June honeymoon trip to New Orleans over a dozen years ago, and our even later breakfast that first sunny morning at the world famous Café du Monde that sits beside the muddy – and muggy – Mississippi River on Decatur Street, across from Jackson Square and the Saint Louis Cathedral. The charming café has been a New Orleans institution for over one hundred and fifty years. I was certainly feeling charmed that morning.

With the scent of chicory flavored coffee rising from the table and powdered sugar tickling our now married tongues and noses, my husband leaned back and said, 'Hey, wouldn't it be a great idea, Mags, if we opened up a place like this of our own back home?'

I agreed. I was a newlywed bride reveling in the glow of the first morning after our first night together as husband and wife. Of course I was going to agree. He was my husband now.

And now that Brian was dead, I was honoring his wishes and opening a beignet shop on one of the lesser-travelled downtown streets of Table Rock, Arizona. Population five thousand or so humans and another twenty thousand or so extra-terrestrials – if one was to believe all the New

1

Age mages living and operating from our odd little red-rocked corner of the world. According to the mages, aliens outnumbered Arizonans four-to-one.

And those mages should know – they were in nearly daily contact with the extraterrestrials, after all.

I should mention that Table Rock is up in Coconino County, Arizona. Not far from Sedona, a New Age capital in its own right. Not that you'll hear that from a Table Rocker, though. Table Rock is where folks move to who feel that Sedona is too 'mainstream.'

I moved here about six weeks ago because it's where my little sister, two nephews and Mom live. And no, I'm not a glutton for punishment. Though if you set a big bowl of chocolate ice cream, plate of chocolate cake or bag of French fries in front of me, I am, without a doubt, a glutton of the first order. And maybe Brian wasn't literally dead, but he was dead to me. That counts, doesn't it? I was telling everybody that inquired about him that he was dead. That counts too, right? And maybe I wasn't so much honoring his memory as rubbing his nose in the fact that he was all talk and no action, as he had been throughout the course of our marriage, but Maggie Miller was the kind of woman who got things done.

It may have taken thirty-nine years of living and a broken marriage. But if there was one thing Maggie Miller was going to do, it was get things done.

Today was a dry run. The grand opening was

tomorrow. I was polishing the front counter and admiring my tenacity and fortitude in having made it this far when a lanky forty-something male entered the shop. Rats, I'd forgotten to lock the door behind me on my way in this morning. I live in a small one-bedroom apartment three blocks over from the shop, so walking or cycling to work are my preferred modes of transportation. That and the fact that I didn't have a car.

I once had a car – a pretty neat 2001 flame red Plymouth Neon – but I sold it to help set up this café. I hated seeing her go. It so happened that 2001 was the last year of the Neon – the last year for Plymouth, too, as it turned out. But every dollar counted and I didn't have many dollars left to count. At this point, I could probably count them all on two hands and a foot.

This morning I'd biked in and, pulling the old Schwinn in behind me, I'd forgotten to turn the key in the lock afterward as I was too busy hauling packages to the back to worry about petty things like locks and doors.

And look what the proverbial cat drags in.

This being Table Rock, I'd been thinking of hanging a No Shirts, No Shoes, No Aliens sign on the door. Not that it would have necessarily helped in this instance.

He reached out a long-fingered hand the color of sandstone. 'Hi, I'm Clive Rothschild.' We shook. He aimed a finger stage right. 'My husband and I own The Hitching Post next door.'

I nodded. I'd passed the place a hundred times since coming to town. I'd been meaning to drop in and introduce myself but getting the café up and running had taken all my time.

This being the Old West, of sorts, you'd think The Hitching Post would be selling lassos, lariats, spurs and saddles. But this was Table Rock. This was the New West. Heck, this was the New Age West. This Hitching Post sold bridal gowns and accessories – items of the 'I do and forever after' variety. It was that kind of hitching that Clive Rothschild was promoting. Clive had red hair and freckles. I liked him already. What can I say? We redheads have to stick together, even if his mane was prettier and more luxuriant than my own.

I was going to have to ask Clive what shampoos and conditioners he was using once I got to know him better. I didn't want to scare the man off by getting too personal too quick. I'd made that mistake enough times to know better. Clive was dressed casually, but expensively, in designer jeans and a T-shirt.

'Maggie Miller,' I replied. 'Welcome to Maggie's Beignet Café.'

He did a turn. 'Nice place you have here.'

'Thanks.'

'Is there a Mister Maggie Miller?'

'He's dead,' I replied, without mincing my words, looking him straight in his green eyes. I told you I tell everybody he's dead. See? I meant it.

His hands came up to his face. 'Oh, I am so sorry,' he cooed.

'Don't be,' I said. 'I'm not.' He blanched and I immediately felt bad for the man. OK, maybe

4

I should have minced my words just a little. Shame on me, as Mom would say. And often did.

'Hey,' I said, trying to lighten the mood and bring a little color back into Clive's face, 'how would you like to be my first customer?'

That seemed to do the trick. Clive's face brightened immensely and his hands fell to his sides. 'Could I? That would be wonderful. I love beignets!' He rubbed his flat belly through the shiny material of his shirt. I expected a genie to pop out of his belly button and offer us a few wishes apiece. Unfortunately, no such luck, as none appeared.

'Sure,' I said. 'Today is a dry run. I was just going to prepare a batch of dough and give all the equipment one last test.'

OK, so it was a *first* test. I know – this was something I should have done before the day before the grand opening. If this second- and third-hand but seemingly working equipment didn't work, it wasn't going to be so much a grand opening as a grand failure.

'Why don't you have a seat at that table by the window—' I stopped. 'Oh.' I'd set out the eight tables that filled my small café to capacity but hadn't gotten around to setting up the chairs. I'd ordered three dozen from a big box store down in Phoenix. The whole lot of them were still stacked in the backroom.

I knew I'd forgotten something. I just hoped the chairs were the only thing. I placed a hand on either side of my head. Yep, it was still there. That was a good sign. Hopefully my brain had come along for the ride.

'Tell you what, Clive, let me get the fryer started.' The fryer was right there at the counter so the customers could watch all the beignet magic as it happened. I turned the dial up to three hundred and seventy degrees. That's the temperature you want if you're gonna make beignets. Anything less and they wouldn't rise properly. Anything more and, well, you'd end up with beignet chips. 'While the fryer heats up, I'll go get a couple of chairs.' And try to find my rolling pin. It seemed like every time I turned around, it went missing.

'Can I help?'

Aww, wasn't he sweet? But even though he was a fellow shop owner, I barely knew the man. I didn't want to be inviting some strange man into my storeroom this early in our relationship. Besides, I was Maggie Miller. I could handle yanking a couple of laminated wood chairs out of cardboard boxes. 'Thanks, but I can manage. You hang in there for a minute. I'll be right back.'

I pushed through the swinging doors to the windowless back storage room. It was small but adequate for my needs. Rows of shelving reached to the low ceiling. A small refrigerator and separate freezer stood in the corner near the back door.

It was a tad musty, due mostly to age, I supposed, and there was a pungent smell that seemed to have gotten worse over the course of the past day or two – like somebody was ripening Pont L'Eveque cheese rather than deep frying pastry dough.

Maybe I needed one of those dangly air

fresheners they sell next to the cash register at the convenience store. But I figured once I got the business up and running in earnest, the provocative and mouth-watering smells of sweet-fried dough and fresh coffee would soon take over. Besides, those air fresheners cost two to three bucks apiece.

Or maybe the skanky odor was all due to me, running around like the proverbial hen with her head cut off, spending too much time prepping to open the café and too little time showering.

Eighteen boxes, each containing two chairs, took up the bulk of the space. I couldn't wait to get them unpacked and out of my way.

Why hadn't I done it earlier? Are you kidding? Did you hear me? Eighteen boxes? Thirty-six chairs?

Sheesh, I had enough to do around here. I had more things on my plate than I had plates. And not being open for business, who cares if you have chairs?

I grabbed the box cutter off the shelf above the microwave, fought my way past a pallet of pastry dough, flour and coffee and grabbed the nearest box. Each one was about three and a half feet tall. I'm about a box and a half tall, give or take, at five foot seven. The box didn't stand a chance. There was a slight moon-shaped stain along the bottom edge of the one I'd grabbed. I hoped its contents were OK and that I wouldn't have to contact the shipper or the store about it. I had enough to do as things stood.

And tomorrow – hopefully – there'd be customers to deal with to boot. Fingers crossed.

I slid open the razor and sliced the top of the box right down the middle, listening to the satisfying zip sound. Nothing like the smell of freshly cut boxes in the morning.

I pushed the box cutter down in the back pocket of my jeans, frowning a little at how snug it felt – note to self: more biking, less beigneting – then pulled back the cardboard flaps.

I lifted a layer of translucent green bubble wrap and set it aside. My nephews could have all kinds of fun with it later making popping noises. *If* I turned it over to them. I loved making popping noises with bubble wrap, squeezing it between my fingers, jumping up and down when no one was looking . . . Ah, it's always the simple things, isn't it? Of course, Brian always chided that it was simple-minded of me. But Brian was dead now. I could do whatever I wanted.

The next thing I knew, somebody was yelling at the top of her lungs.

Then I realized it was me.

TWO

Beneath a second layer of bubble wrap, the blurred but striking image of a crushed scalp of curly black hair confronted me. A dark stain of something – I didn't want to know what – seemed to be trapped between two layers of the wrap. Hard to tell what it was from my vantage point. More bubble wrap was swathed clumsily around the body that was folded up inside the box, knees to chest, like an oversized marionette. I wasn't sure what the corpse was doing here, but I was pretty certain I hadn't ordered it.

I was having trouble thinking straight because that obnoxious big-lunged woman would not stop screaming.

Clive came crashing through the door, thrashing through the dry goods, and laid a hand on my shoulder. The screaming mercifully stopped.

'C-c-c—' My finger pointed. My tongue lolled.

'Dead guy,' finished Clive.

I was going to say corpse – I'm much more alliterative than Clive – but dead guy would do. Summed it up pretty darn good.

I leaned into Clive. Big strong arms and all that. But I was forgetting this guy owned a bridal shop. He didn't lift wrenches, chop down trees or wrestle bulls to the ground for a living. This was a guy who lifted gowns off hangers, hefted angel weight bridal veils and only wrestled the occasional eight-foot tulle wedding gown train when a bride-to-be was tripping over her feet while practicing her walk down the aisle.

Sure enough, Clive collapsed to the ground, and my attempts to keep him up proved futile.

His big feet banged against the box containing the dead guy. The dead guy wasn't complaining. My shoulders were, though, as I grabbed hold of Clive by his armpits and dragged him back out front.

I pulled him up against the counter and left him there, his head lolling slightly to the left. I put a finger against his chin and straightened him out. Maybe that was a little OCD of me but I hated seeing him sitting there unconscious and crooked like that. I mean, somebody walking by might look in the window and see him that way. We couldn't have that, could we? Imagine how embarrassing that would be for Clive.

I took a step back. He looked so much better now. Almost peaceful.

Then I remembered the dead man in the box. I whipped out my cell phone and punched in the three digits that everybody knows.

'Hello, this is Information, can I help you?'

'Dead man! Storeroom!'

'Can you spell that, please? Is this a business you are seeking?'

I pushed the phone out at arm's length. Huh? I reeled it back in.

'Hello?' the tinny voice said again. 'Ma'am, can I assist you with something today?'

OK. I took a deep breath. Wrong three digits. 'Sorry, wrong number.' I pushed the button for ending the call and tried again. More slowly. 9-1-1.

I had to hand it to the cops, they were quick. I don't think if I'd yelled 'Free beer!' at an Arizona State University frat that a bunch of guys could have moved any quicker. Maybe it was a slow day. Maybe all the loonies were out worshipping the sun gods or aligning their chakras while listening to some self-help program on the local NPR station.

Whatever it was, they were lightning quick – Zeus quick.

The big detective in the lead burst through my front door, his right hand laid atop the gun snuggled up in his holster. He was quite dashing, actually.

At least, I expected he was a detective, decked out in that cheap brown cotton suit and milk-stained tie. In the movies, these guys were always the detectives. Unless they were from Miami, then they dressed like David Caruso and Jonathan Togo, or so I'd been told. I've never been to Miami.

Those guys on *CSI: Miami* knew how to dress. Well, at least their wardrobe person knew how to dress them. I wouldn't have minded dressing either of them myself.

Two men in blue followed close behind. Hmmm, either they were with my detective friend or I had misread the situation completely. Maybe this was all a big coincidence. He was a baddie and these two delightful and hardworking officers of the law were in pursuit.

'Please, step aside,' ordered the big guy. Before I could move a muscle, he'd placed a hand on each of my trembling shoulders and moved me toward the window.

He pointed at Clive. 'Check him out!'

Since the boys in blue responded by approaching Clive, who still lay peacefully against my counter, I figured I'd been right in the first place. They were definitely a party of three.

While the stern-faced blond cop focused his weapon on Clive, the second one moved in and felt the side of Clive's neck. He turned to the big guy in the rumpled suit.

Didn't he know how badly cotton wrinkles? Sheesh, he'd have been better off, in his line of work, with polyester. Or how about gabardine or wool? No, too hot in summer for wool. This was Arizona, after all. Land of the heat wave. But, hey, it's a dry heat. Which, if you ask me, is about as pleasant as the dry heaves, but that's just my opinion—

'He's alive,' said the cop hovering over Clive.

The big man's well-formed forehead formed ripples. 'Are you sure?'

The cop nodded. 'Here come the EMTs. You can ask them if you don't believe me.'

He sighed. Not a bad sound. 'I believe you.' He turned his gaze on me. Those were yummy brown eyes, sort of the color of brown M&Ms. I like M&Ms. He wasn't exactly looking at me with affection, though.

I squirmed and took a step closer to the window. I'd have gone through it but it was solid glass and I wasn't good at transmutation. I've heard there are several folks wandering around Table Rock who are. I'm just not one of them.

I discovered I was shaking my head. 'That's not him.'

The big guy crossed his arms over his chest like he was going in for the kill. Hmmm, this was not the way I wanted or expected this to go. I pushed down the hem of my shorts and swiped at my black T-shirt. That smudge of powdered sugar down the front wasn't helping my look.

Two EMTs reached for my new neighbor, Clive, while a third ran back from the ambulance with a stretcher.

'I'm going to need to get your statement,' said the brown-suited man. He reached into the inside pocket of his suit, pulled out an overstretched sad black leather wallet and extracted a business card, which he handed to me. 'Detective Mark Highsmith.'

I chewed my lower lip and fiddled with his card.

'You are?'

I watched poor Clive being carted out the door. 'That's not the dead guy.' I pointed at the stretcher.

Detective Highsmith followed my finger. 'I know that's not a dead guy.' He didn't sound happy. 'What made you think he was dead? Didn't you check his pulse?'

'Well, no.' I was beginning to feel a little nervous and defensive. 'I did adjust his neck.' He was close enough for me to catch a whiff of Old Spice. So, the guy was old school. And he looked so young.

His left eyebrow twitched.

'He was leaning a little to the left. I straightened him out.' I rotated my hands to demonstrate. I

13

could feel the sweat pooling up on the bottoms of my synthetic rubber flip-flops.

He pulled a yellow pencil, with impressive sleight of hand, from inside his coat pocket – what was the man, part magician? Did he keep a white rabbit in there, too? Maybe a string of multi-colored scarves knotted together? OK, so now you know, I love magic.

Not that there'd been any magic in my love life of late.

Highsmith scratched behind his right ear with the eraser end. The tip was all smudgy black. Looked like the guy made a lot of mistakes.

Like he was making now.

'I'm telling you, Officer—'

'Detective.'

I gulped. 'Detective.' My eyes followed the EMTs as Clive was shoved into the rear of the ambulance and whisked away, lights flashing. 'If you'll just let me explain—'

'Clive! What's happening?' A white-fleshed fellow no wider at the shoulders than he was at the hips had burst through the door. His hands were thrust out at his sides, fingers spread. 'What's happened to Clive?'

He wore a black button-down short-sleeved shirt that looked like real silk and tight black jeans. Man, I'd never have dared wear a pair of jeans that tight. Well, if I had as little body fat as this guy, sure, but not in my current condition.

His eyes bounced off Highsmith and me, then zeroed back in on me. Just my luck. 'What's happened to Clive?' he demanded. There was a feminine quality to his voice and I didn't think it was merely the heightened emotion of the moment.

'Nothing to worry about,' I said, thrusting out my hand. 'I'm Maggie Miller. Clive came in to introduce himself and then when I screamed and he saw the dead guy—' I shrugged. 'Well, he just fainted.'

The stranger gasped and his hands flew to his cheeks. Up close, I could see that his wavy hair was blacker than nature had ever intended. His eyes were a nice charcoal blue though. His affect, however, was all coxcomb. That's the kind of affect that affects me. And not in a good way.

'Who are you, anyway?' Seeing as how he wasn't going to shake my hand, I put it back where it belonged – masking the powdered sugar blotch on my T-shirt.

'Johnny Wolfe.' He turned to the detective. 'Who are you? Are you the police? Where have they taken Clive?'

Detective Highsmith took a deep breath, which seemed to pull all four walls of the bakery closer together. Man, this guy had some lungs. 'Relax, Mr Wolfe. The emergency team has taken your friend to the medical center for evaluation and treatment. Mesa Verde, I'd guess.'

'Hey,' I said, gears in my head turning and suddenly meshing. 'Johnny Wolfe.' I beamed. 'I know that name.' I pointed an accusing finger. 'You were the nineteen ninety-six Winter Olympics bronze medalist.'

'I should have won the gold,' he grumbled as he pirouetted out the door or whatever it is that

15

figure skaters do when they spin around on dry land instead of hard ice.

He stepped out into the sun and, I swear, I almost went blind. The glossy hair gel he drenched his *au* not *naturel* hair with must've had a reflectance factor that was off the charts. His follicles lit up like Fourth of July sparklers. They'd probably catch fire just as easily too, given how flammable I'd read some of those hair products currently on the market can be.

Where did Johnny think he was? At the XIX Olympic Games? I had news for him. This wasn't Salt Lake City, home of the Salt Lake City Ice Center, nor BYU, home of the MRS degree. This was Table Rock, Arizona. Home of the University of Metaphysical Theology where you could get your degree in something with real world application, like paranormal studies and crystal skull communications and analysis.

Hmmm, well, I guess I had to give Johnny that one. He fit right in here in Table Rock.

I watched him disappear into a black BMW convertible and wondered what his relationship to Clive was all about. Was this the husband he'd mentioned? Was this Mr Clive? Heaven help him if it was.

I caught sight of the two men in blue idling beside their squad car parked at the edge of the sidewalk, stiff paper coffee cups in hand. I recognized the logo and the branding. Karma Koffee occupied one of the storefronts across the street from me. I'm not sure that they were keen on me opening directly opposite them – we did both sell coffee, after all. But I was mainly pushing the beignet and chicory coffee experience. They were more the organic, exotic, home ground, high-end place that people like me couldn't afford.

I could tolerate them if they could tolerate me. Live and let live, I always say. Well, except for the dead guy in my storeroom.

'You wanna tell me about this dead body you keep telling everybody about?'

Detective Highsmith was way too close for comfort. A girl could overdose on Old Spice if she wasn't careful. I gulped and nodded, tugging the hem of my shorts down again. Darn things kept riding up. 'Follow me,' I said. 'He's through here.'

I took a step toward the space between the genuine Formica counter and the wall that led to the storeroom, then paused. 'Better yet,' I said, pushing the cop forward, 'you first.'

The long countertop bisecting the shop to maintain the shopkeeper/customer relationship was a hideous lime green and flecking away at the corners. Its color pretty much summed up how I was feeling. If I had my way, I'd take a sledgehammer to it. But it sort of goes with the theme, so I'm making it work by working around it. Besides, it came with the place and replacing it would cost money I didn't have for such frivolities.

There was a hinged section of the counter that I could drop down to keep the customers at bay. So far, I hadn't seen any reason to use it. I hadn't had any customers. Except for dead guy and I didn't think he'd paid for anything – *customer* wasn't technically the word I'd use to describe him.

He certainly hadn't left a tip in the jam jar from the local Safeway supermarket that had been reincarnated into my tip jar. I'd check the till later to double check. Maybe he'd helped me out by putting the money directly in the register. Crazier things had been known to happen. Like the way he'd stuffed himself into a carton in my backroom when I wasn't watching.

Maybe if I'd used my piano-hinged countertop earlier it would have kept the dead guy out of my storeroom.

Then again, he may have come shipped from the factory direct. And that big box store down in Phoenix had tacked on shipping charges based on the weight of my order. Dead guy must've weighed one hundred and sixty pounds, maybe more!

I pulled a face. No way was I going to pay the shipping charges for that carton!

Before stepping behind the counter, the detective gave me a wary look like he suspected I was going to trick him – maybe clobber him when he wasn't looking and steal his gun – but after only the briefest moment of hesitation he stepped ahead of me. I guess he figured he was so tough that even if I did try to clobber him, he wouldn't be fazed one bit.

Sadly, I thought, inspecting my bare arms and under-toned biceps, he was probably right.

I guided him to the box in question with its questionable contents. I mean, all I'd wanted was a couple of chairs for my dining room. He inched toward the box and pulled back the flap, then extracted a handful of bubble wrap. He spoke calmly in clipped tones into the radio he'd somehow dug out of his pocket without anyone seeing. Magic, see?

'Chip, Webster. You guys better get back in here.'

He shot a picture with his cell phone then drew a knife from his pocket. His pants pocket this time. I guess the magic was gone, dissipated like the effects of a fine glass of zinfandel the morning after. 'You wanna step back?'

Gladly, I thought, taking two giant steps to the rear. I watched as he sliced the box down the side seam. A man's body came into view. His head was slightly turned. I fought the urge to barge in and straighten him out to get a better look. As it turns out, that wasn't necessary. As the bubble wrap fell away, his face became clear.

'Rick!'

Big Easy Beignets

The beignet is the Louisiana state doughnut. Personally, eating a plateful always puts me in sugary heaven . . . Here's what you'll need to create your own little bites of heaven:

1/2 cup water

1 tablespoon yeast (active dry yeast – none of that lazy inactive yeast – but not too active. I don't know what hyperactive yeast will do to a beignet but I'd rather not find out. You don't want your beignets flying around the kitchen, just into your mouth)

7 1/2 cups flour

1/4 cup shortening

1/2 cup sugar

1 cup give or take confectioner's sugar for dusting

1 teaspoon salt

1 cup boiling water

1 quart vegetable oil (I recommend cottonseed, but you can substitute your own)

1 cup evaporated milk

2 large eggs, lightly beaten (you may not know what they did wrong but they do)

Combine active dry yeast and half a cup of warm water in a bowl; let stand for five minutes. Then, combine the shortening, sugar and salt in a second bowl. Pour the boiling water over the shortening mixture and then stir in the evaporated milk. When the mixture cools to lukewarm, add the yeast/water mixture and beaten eggs. Mix in the flour until the dough forms a ball. The dough should be relatively soft, not firm like a pie crust. Cover the dough with plastic wrap and refrigerate for thirty minutes to one hour. Longer is OK, too. Personally, I just can't wait any longer!

Spread a generous layer of flour on your countertop or prep surface, then roll out the dough a quarter-inch thick. Cut the rolled out dough into two- to three-inch squares. You can use your pizza cutter for this, if you have one. It works perfectly.

If you do not have a fryer, heat your oil for frying in a deep and wide skillet or pot. You want a vessel deep enough for them to float in. And remember, the temperature to shoot for is 370°F. Carefully slide your cut dough into the deep fryer and cook until puffy golden brown. This could take three to five minutes. Remove finished beignets and place them on a paper towel to drain and cool for a moment. Next, sprinkle powder sugar to taste and . . . enjoy!

THREE

The next urge I found myself fighting was the urge to barf. Have you ever seen a dead guy? *Twice?*

OK, then, twice within the span of several minutes in the back of your *own* shop? Your own *beignet* shop?

I didn't think so. Well, I just had. Though his face was puffy and gray and his eyes looked like miniature billiard balls had been callously lodged in his eye sockets, I recognized this dead guy. This was my landlord, Rick Wilbur.

My mouth snapped shut when Detective Highsmith's neck turned around and I found those M&Ms of his staring down at me. I straightened my back but I wasn't getting any taller.

I tried not to look at Rick but the battle was lost. It's hard to look at a dead guy. It's even harder *not* to look. I pushed Detective Highsmith to the right, hoping to block Mr Wilbur from my view.

Unfortunately, it was at that time that I lost the fight I was having with my acid-filled stomach. I barfed all over Detective Highsmith's lace-up brown shoes. They must have cost a pretty penny, too, because boy did he howl. You'd have thought I'd stepped on his toes or ran over his precious puppy with my bicycle or something. Did he even own a dog?

'Hey!' he cried, leaping back and swatting at his pants. I'm not sure why. My barf hadn't come anywhere near his trousers. Highsmith lost his balance, slipped on something wet on the floor and went careening into the box containing my landlord. 'What the—'

There were a couple of snickers from the boys in blue. And, well, there might have been one or two from me as well, but I attributed that to the state of shock I was falling into. That wet slick on the floor I attributed to the vomit I'd just scattered over my storeroom floor. I'd just had, and passed, my county health inspection, too. I sure hoped this didn't cost me any points on my health certificate.

The young man named Chip Kurkov, according to his very handsome badge, stuck his hand out. Highsmith latched on and together they heaved him off the box and out of Rick Wilbur's lap.

After dusting himself off, Detective Highsmith slowly turned and approached. I'd flopped down on a wooden stool at the work counter along the wall between the storeroom and the storefront. I was having a hard time seeing straight and felt like my body was trying to turn itself inside out.

As his shadow fell over me, I said, 'Is it crazy cold in here, or is it just me?' I attempted a disarming smile. A failed attempt, as it turns out.

His scowl didn't exactly signal compassion. Neither had he been disarmed – both arms were present and accounted for. In fact, he was heavily armed judging by the girth of the textured grip of the gun at his side. At least it was still in its holster. Always a good sign when talking to an officer of the law.

Still, he grabbed a ratty old navy blue parka I kept on a stickup hook beside the walk-in cooler and held it out to me. 'Put this on.'

'Thanks,' I mumbled. My mouth tasted like the inside of a garbage disposal and I was pretty sure that my tongue had swelled to the size of a boiled liverwurst. I draped the parka over my shoulders. I was shaking so badly I started making plans for a dental appointment to order some new teeth. These were definitely at their breaking point.

A woman in a crisp white shirt and loose black slacks moved Highsmith gently to the side. She pushed a strand of way-too-healthy-looking blonde hair behind her ear, then strapped a blood pressure cuff over my upper arm. 'She's in shock.'

'Tell me something I don't know.' That was me.

'Tell me about Rick.' That was Detective Highsmith.

My eyes fluttered toward the carton o'Wilbur. When had the storeroom filled with people?

Wow, if I could get this many paying customers tomorrow, the business would be off to a flying start. I forced myself to meet the detective's gaze. The blood pressure cuff hurt like the dickens and I hoped this woman would finish up. Instead, she stuck a thermometer in my mouth. 'Heshmylanard.' The thermometer moved like a Radio City Music Hall Rockette.

He snatched it from my lips and handed it back to the medic. 'She's fine.'

'She's in shock.' The blonde's blue eyes flashed warning signals.

'She's a witness to a murder. Heck, she might *be* a murderer,' he said, lowering his face to mine and searching my eyes as if a written confession might be rolled up in my cornea somewhere.

'I didn't kill anybody. I found him like that. Then I called Information.'

'You called Information?' The medic looked confused. I guess it was because she was a blonde.

'Not on purpose. I got confused. Then I called you guys.' I waved at Highsmith and the million-odd other men and women sucking all the air out of my storeroom. 'The cops.'

'Do you want to explain about this Clive person I found on the ground when I got here? What's Clive's relationship to you? How did he get hurt? Was there a struggle?'

I swallowed a couple of mouthfuls of air. I figured I'd better get a couple in before all these people used it all up. 'In the first place, Clive was not on the ground. He was leaning carefully, *neatly*, *against* the counter.' I was getting a bit hot under the collar from all this negativity. The infrared light that was supposed to be used to keep beignets warm but I was using for a work light at the back counter could also have been part of the problem. I was mad, though. And tired. And just a wee bit queasy.

Dead guy, remember?

'In the second place, there was no struggle. Unless you want to count the struggle I had lugging Clive's unconscious butt out of the storeroom.' I glared at Highsmith. 'After he fainted.'

The medic unwound the blood pressure cuff. 'A little high,' she said brightly. 'But considering the circumstances,' she glanced at the crime scene behind us, 'not unexpected.'

I nodded.

'What's your name?' she asked.

'Maggie,' I replied. 'Maggie Miller.'

The medic turned to Detective Highsmith. 'Miss Miller here has had quite a shock. She needs to be evaluated more fully. Shock can be dangerous if not treated.'

'Dangerous?' I squeaked. What was the worst that could happen?

She nodded sagely. 'Hypoxemia, cardiac arrest, diaphoresis, poor end-organ perfusion.' She paused, then added, 'Confusion.'

Confusion was right. I didn't know what most of that gibberish was she'd just spouted but fear of them was only serving to make my shock, well, more shocking.

'I suppose . . .' Highsmith said, somewhat reluctantly. Gee, what a sweetheart.

'Detective?'

It was Chip again. Good old Chip. Help a man when he's down, Chip.

'What is it, Kurkov?'

Chip held out his hand. Rather girlish fingers, if you ask me. 'We found this in the box between the victim's legs. There's blood on it. Probably the victim's . . .'

Huh, so that's where my rolling pin had gone.

Detective Highsmith's fingers latched over my wrist. 'Let's go down to the station,' he said.

Somehow, I didn't think he was asking me out on a date.

As we swung through the front, I tossed the parka over the counter, then grabbed my purse from the table where I'd dropped it when I came into the shop. I hitched the strap over my shoulder.

'What about my shop?'

'Closed for business.'

Ouch. I hadn't even officially opened yet.

FOUR

'Is there a Mr Miller?' Highsmith asked.

'Is there another detective I can talk to?' I countered. I was still mad that he'd kept me waiting while he changed into a clean pair of trousers he kept stashed in his locker. It wasn't my fault he'd fallen in barf. Not completely, anyway.

He smiled. I didn't like it. It was the first time I'd seen him smile since I'd met him. 'Nope.' He flattened his hands against the table.

I turned up the corner of my mouth. 'Why not? The rest of the bunch out raiding yoga studios for serving up non-organic chai tea? Or scouring kiddie daycare centers looking for underage toddlers?'

I had a bit of a smart mouth and I was on a roll. Sometimes it could get me into trouble so I tried to watch myself. Apparently, I wasn't watching myself too closely this afternoon. And after finding a dead guy in my shop and my rolling pin between said dead guy's legs, you'd think I'd be at the top of my game.

Highsmith's reply cut into my self-analysis. 'Because I'm the only detective the department's got.' The smile never left his face. 'Table Rock's got as many dog catchers as it's got detectives. Animal control officers, if you want to be politically correct.'

Wow. One detective in the whole Table Rock Police Department? Who'd have thought? Not me.

And one dog catcher? Now I knew who not to call if I ever had a wild animal like a coyote to deal with or even a hyperactive poodle. I pulled myself up. The slouch was never a good look. Mom always chided me about my tendency to curl into myself.

'Sit up straight, Maggie, dear,' she'd always say. 'A man doesn't want to marry a jellyfish.' Those words had always annoyed me. Still did. But I made an effort to heed Mom's advice now because I really needed to be a little nicer to this guy. Table Rock's only detective, remember?

He repeated his last question. 'So, Ms Miller, is there a Mr Miller?' He was holding his magic pencil. It hovered over a top-hinged spiral notepad.

'He's dead.'

Highsmith's eyebrows shot up so fast I thought the inertia would lift him right out of his chair.

'Don't get all flustered,' I added quickly. 'I didn't kill him.'

'You didn't?'

I sensed a certain dubiousness. 'Hey, if you don't believe me,' I said, my impatience showing, 'just ask him.'

The detective leaned back in his chair and huffed out a breath. The chair balanced precariously on its back two legs. I wondered how long that would last. I'd seen lesser legs break under the strain.

'OK,' I said, letting out a woof of air myself.

29

Unfortunately, I'd let it out through my nose and the accompanying whistle was definitely unladylike. Sounded a bit like Yankee Doodle – and I'm a Georgia girl. I've never even been to Connecticut.

'He lives in Phoenix and he's driving a truck.' I paused and glanced out the window. Maybe I was hoping to catch a glimpse of a happier time. Maybe I just needed to look at something besides Detective Highsmith. 'We're divorced,' I added, still looking out the window.

'I see.'

I doubted if he did. Heck, I didn't really see it myself.

I blotted back a tear before turning around to face Detective Highsmith. The last thing I wanted was for this guy to see me crying.

After running through the basics: name, address, *ad nauseam*, Highsmith got down to business. He leaned in for the kill. That freshly sharpened pencil looked terribly weapon-like. I promised myself not to say or do anything that might provoke a pencil attack.

'You said you randomly opened the box with your box cutter. Did you notice any sign that the box had been tampered with?'

I thought hard. 'Yes?'

'Is that a question or an answer?' he scowled.

I really wasn't sure. I wasn't sure of anything right now except that my nerves were frayed. I answered as definitely as I could. 'Yes?'

Highsmith squeezed his eyes shut. 'How well did you know Richard Wilbur?'

My shoulders bounced up and down. 'Not well.'

I ran the back of my hand across my forehead. It came back damper than it had been when it started its journey. 'Is it hot in here?' I fanned myself.

'Define "not well."'

I resisted the urge to shrug once again. 'I've only been in town about six weeks.' I thought back to those, in hindsight, simpler times. With the divorce finalized but my feelings for my now ex still fresh in my mind, I'd made the trip from Phoenix to Table Rock.

Time for a new start and all that. Besides, I had a support system here. Like I said, a sister, her kids and our mother. The fact that my new start was a hundred-plus miles from my dead husband was a bonus. A Big Bonus.

Barely divorced six months, Brian had already found and made an honest woman out of a divorcee with two kids of her own. Funny, when we were married, he'd never wanted children.

I couldn't get far enough away from Brian and his new family for comfort. And I'd have gone further, too, but Table Rock was far enough for the old Plymouth Neon. Maybe Old Red, as I liked to call her, had been drawn to the red rocks this part of the world was known for. I got that.

'I met Mr Wilbur – Rick – a week or so after I got here. I was shopping for a location for my business. Wilbur Realty owns a number of properties in the area.'

He nodded, so I continued. 'I signed the lease about a month ago.'

'When was the last time you saw the victim?'

I gave it some thought. 'Two, three days ago?'

To tell the truth, I had no idea. The detective had me so worked up I couldn't think straight.

'Is it two or is it three?' His pencil went up and down.

I thought harder. 'Two.' He started writing. 'No. Three.'

He stopped writing. He glared.

'I'm not sure,' I growled. 'Let's call it two and a half.' I smiled prettily.

Highsmith cleared his throat and squeezed his eyes shut. 'So, you saw Mr Wilbur two or three days ago.' He sounded a bit rattled. He rubbed his cheek. 'How did he end up in a box in your storeroom?'

'Parcel post?'

Highsmith responded with a stone-faced silence. It had been a lame joke and I knew it. Here I was poking fun at the dead. Shame on me.

'Look, Detective, Rick was kind enough to give me thirty days free rent to give me time to get Maggie's Beignet Café up and running. He was nice to me,' I said. 'Why would I want to kill him?'

The knock on the small conference room door kept the detective from replying. A tall, skinny young man who could only be described as a hippie entered the room. He had long, dirty blond hair pulled into a stiff ponytail that hung over his left shoulder. His tie-dye shirt was so bright pilots of small planes could use it to guide them-selves safely in on night landings. His denim shorts were too big on him, but then anything was probably too big on this rail-thin specimen with legs like volleyball net poles.

Come to think of it, this young man was just about tall enough to pass the test to become a flagpole. Hoist up the shirt and presto! No need for air traffic controllers.

'Detective Highsmith?' he inquired, one hand reaching forward. A tattered, spiral-patterned hemp bracelet flopped around his slender wrist.

Highsmith rose. By the look on his face, I could see the detective was obviously struggling with the sight before him. 'That's me.' Highsmith shot a look down the hall, as if wondering how on earth this guy had made it this deep into the police station. 'Can I help you?'

'I'm here to assist Ms Miller.' The two men shook and sized each other up, the way men and apes always seemed to do. I noticed that though Highsmith was easily over six foot, he came up short in comparison to the man who'd just entered the room, all six foot five of him.

Highsmith's surprise couldn't have been more apparent. Maybe he thought the guy was here to sell me some incense or mind-altering drugs. That would be pretty gutsy of him, wouldn't it?

'Hi, Andy.' I sighed. 'How did you find out?' So soon, too.

Andy allowed himself a smile. 'Get used to it, Mag. You aren't in Phoenix anymore. Table Rock's a small town.' He eased up behind my chair and rubbed my shoulders affectionately. 'Jean over at the Enlightenment Art Gallery noticed all the commotion. She phoned Donna.'

'And Donna phoned you.'

He nodded.

Donna is my kid sister. Andy Singer is her

33

husband, my brother-in-law. A sweet kid. He could also be a pretty sharp attorney – when he wanted to be, which he mostly did not these days. He and Donna ran the Mother Earth/Father Sun Grocers a couple of blocks over from my fledgling beignet business. They're all New Agey. I'm more middle agey.

Andy had given up one of those high-powered attorney jobs you only read about to become an organic farmer and shopkeeper.

Though I'd never gotten the whole organic thing, I was beginning to build a case for nepotism.

'You're a lawyer?' From the incredulity in Highsmith's voice, you'd think Andy had just confessed to being Kris Kringle.

'Yep. Funny, huh?' Andy was beaming. He loved throwing people off guard. He said it made them easier to manipulate. It was like judo but without having to get your knees dirty. 'Are we done here? Is Ms Miller free to go?'

Detective Highsmith nodded but he didn't look happy about it. He stood over the desk, his pencil tapping against the notebook. 'We will be able to reach you at this address, won't we, Ms Miller?'

'Absolutely,' I promised. 'I'm not going anywhere.'

'Right now, you're coming home with me,' said Andy. 'We need to talk.'

'We?'

'Donna's at the house. She left one of the girls in charge. Truck's outside.'

I nodded. Donna normally spent a pretty full

day in the food store. I didn't know what we'd have to talk about though. I didn't feel much like talking about Rick Wilbur.

Still, I was glad to be away from Highsmith and his M&Ms. And his questions. I was also glad I wasn't going to have to walk back to my store. That was a long walk and there was a hot sun up there in the blue sky just waiting to burn me to a crisp – a dehydrated crisp.

As we passed the desk sergeant on our way out the door, I whispered, 'Have you even got a license?'

'I've been driving since I was fifteen.'

'You know what I mean.'

He held the station door open, his eyes looking deep into mine. 'I gave up practicing law. I didn't give up my license.'

He hustled me away from the building and out to the parking lot where his cherry condition mid-1955 Chevy pickup sat in one of the slots farthest from the entrance. Andy boasted that the Yukon yellow paint job was factory original. I had to take his word for that. I doubted the original 1955 factory was around to corroborate his claim.

'You do know I can't afford to pay you anything.' The full weight of the sun hit me across the back and I thought I'd melt down. 'I don't have any money.'

He waved a hand through the air, then rested it back on the edge of my shoulder. 'Heck, Maggie, everybody knows that,' he replied, playfully pushing me toward the Chevy. 'Besides, you're family. Won't cost you a nickel. You may have to put up with hearing my and Donna's two cents' worth, though,' he said from the other side of the truck bed.

I smiled. 'I think even I can afford that much.' But I could have been wrong about that.

This pickup was Andy's baby and he loved it almost like his own flesh and blood. Not as much as he loved his wife and boys, but still . . .

He'd purchased it from a man down in Tucson and started restoring the truck at home out in the extra bay of their three-car garage. Donna and Andy had resided in one of Scottsdale's tonier neighborhoods. About the time that the restoration was nearing completion, so were Andy and Donna. He quit his job. Donna resigned from her elementary school position as well and off they went.

They left behind a lot of worldly possessions. Some very high-end worldly possessions. Donna sold off a Lexus that I'd have given a couple quarts of blood for at the time. But he'd held onto the Chevy. I couldn't blame him.

I stroked the side panel before opening the solidly built door and sliding onto the bench seat. The interior was small but comfortable. There was one obdurate spring, however, that seemed to have an affinity for my coccyx every time I sat down inside. I wiggled around a bit in an effort to reach a compromise with the stubborn thing.

The truck was very bare bones by today's standards. That was the way Andy liked it. He was pretty bare bones himself.

Though it might not have seemed a very

ecofriendly vehicle for someone operating an organic farm and food store, Andy had pulled out the original V8 engine and refitted it with a motor running on biodiesel.

This baby didn't have a lot of oomph, but she sure did smell good. He twisted the key in the ignition. I could smell the French fries already. Maybe he'd agree to stop at Bell Rock Burgers on the way home if I promised not to squeal on him. Since arriving in Table Rock, I'd discovered they had the best fries. They didn't skimp on the portion sizes either. I liked that in my fry purveyor of choice.

'You OK?' He turned to look at me, one foot on the clutch, the other on the brake pedal. 'You know you can count on me and Donna. Your mom, too.' He locked his index and middle fingers around one another. 'Family, right?'

I shifted in my seat. Suddenly I was feeling a bit more comfortable on this old stiff-springed bench. Yep, nepotism – that's the way to go. I nodded. 'Yeah, I'm OK.' This was my chance. 'I am a little hungry, though.'

He smiled and eased the truck out of the small parking lot and onto the main road. 'Don't worry. I'm sure Donna will have lunch waiting for us when we get home.'

So much for Bell Rock Burgers. It looked like it was going to be okra burgers and steamed broccoli stalks or something equally as menacing for me.

'OK,' I said, keeping my true thoughts to myself. 'After that, I need to get back to the shop. I'm opening tomorrow, you know.' Plus, I'd left the police rummaging around the place this morning. Who knew what sort of mess they might have left for me to clean up?

Andy kept his mouth shut and his eyes on the road.

Did he know something I didn't?

There was no way I was putting off opening tomorrow. I was down to my last dollar. I needed to open the doors and see some greenbacks float back in my direction for a change. Besides, I'd spent hundreds of dollars on flyers and an advertisement in the local newspaper, the *Table Rock Reader*. I couldn't afford not to open. Customers were counting on me.

Who was I kidding? I was counting on them!

FIVE

Thank goodness there were no okra burgers. I hadn't skipped breakfast, but I had barfed it up in the café, so despite the disquieting morning, I was famished. 'What have you got, Sis?' Whatever it was boiling away there on the stove behind Donna's back, it didn't smell too bad.

She poured the concoction into a glass baking dish and popped it in the oven. Twenty minutes later, Donna slid a deep-rimmed plateful in front of me at the kitchen table. I looked down at it, then back up at her. 'Dare I ask what this is?' I scrunched up my nose, took a closer sniff and then instantly wished I hadn't. 'What on earth!'

Donna chuckled, wiping her hands on the #1 Mom apron hooked over her neck and around her waist.

A gelatinous mess of browns, greens and reds lay like, well, this morning's barf, on my plate. I clutched my spoon, wondering if I dare.

The boys, fourteen-year-old Connor and twelve-year-old Hunter, chortled. Yeah, I was one funny aunt.

'What is this?' I looked at Andy but he maintained a lawyerly silence.

'Go ahead, try it,' my sister insisted, pulling up a chair at the small kitchen table. The kitchen was quite cozy itself with a fifties atmosphere to it, discounting the microwave and blender and other modern appurtenances. The stove was definitely out of a page from the fifties.

My spoon dangled over the plate.

'It's intestines!' cried Connor.

'Yeah,' echoed Hunter. 'It's intestines, Aunt Maggie!' He bounced, his pine chair scraping against the oak floor.

'Easy there, Hunter,' Andy said.

I blanched. 'In-intestines?' But they were strictly vegetarian! Weren't they? Had I missed something?

Donna scolded her boys. 'Now, now, don't go freaking poor Aunt Maggie out.' She looked pointedly across the table at Andy. 'She's had a very difficult morning.'

I knew from my brief discussion with Andy and Donna before lunch that they hadn't broken the news of my discovery of a dead body in the beignet shop to my nephews yet.

Donna turned to me. She held up a spoonful of muck and stuck it in her mouth. She followed this with some *mmm-mmm-good* noises. 'See?' She smacked her lips, then went back for more.

'It's veggie haggis,' explained Andy, breaking his silence. 'I suppose,' he said, looking at his sons, 'you could think of it as vegetarian intestines.'

I squirmed, looking for the exit. 'I wish everybody would quit saying intestines,' I squeaked. My stomach had done one hundred and thirty-two flip-flops since Connor had first blurted the word out. I know, I'd counted.

Donna gave the boys one of those mother-type

looks that seem to be genetically encoded and both boys quickly sobered.

'Sorry, Aunt Maggie,' Connor said.

'Yeah, I'm sorry, too,' Hunter said with an accompanying shoulder shrug.

Believe you me, nobody was sorrier than I was, but I kept my thoughts to myself. I knew what haggis was – stuff like sheep's heart, liver and lungs. What I didn't know was what my sister's vegetarian version was. I recognized some bits, like onion, carrots, red lentils and oats, maybe some mushroom and peppers. But there was no telling for sure.

And there was nothing to do but eat.

I had to set a good example for the nephews, didn't I?

Especially now, because soon enough they might be hearing how a dead guy had been found in my new café with my missing rolling pin between his legs. My role modeling record would go right out the window. Which was where I wished I could go right then. Head first.

I judged the distance from where I sat to the kitchen sink and the window that framed it. Yep, I could definitely manage the leap.

My spoon somehow found its way to my lips. 'Mmmm,' I said. 'You're right. This isn't bad at all.' I'd rinse my mouth with kerosene later. 'You'll have to give me the recipe, Sis.' So I can burn it.

She promised she would. I could only hope she'd forget that promise. If Donna did write it down for me, the next thing you'd know she'd be expecting me to brew up a deadly batch for the next family gathering hosted at my apartment. Please, don't let that happen. My apartment's foul enough as it is.

After lunch, if you could call it that, Connor and Hunter went back to their bedrooms to study. Donna was homeschooling my nephews. They had a place to study at the store downtown as well because Donna spends so much of her time there running Mother Earth/Father Sun Grocers, too.

Donna and Andy lived in a ramshackle 1870s-era house plopped down on a rare one-acre lot a few blocks from the Historic Old Town, as the locals liked to think of it. I liked to think of it as just plain old and desperately in need of a DIY Network makeover, preferably by the guy from *House Crashers*. That man could crash my house anytime. Table Rock Crashers, anyone?

Andy's phone chirped and he fished it out of his shorts. Hey, they're hippies, not Luddites. His brows shot up as he listened intently. Donna and I waited and wondered.

'I see,' he said finally. He rang off and laid the phone on the table.

I raised an eyebrow in question.

'That was the Table Rock Police Department.' Andy had told me he had a friend there. 'It's definitely blood on your rolling pin, Mag.'

Ouch.

He continued relaying what he'd been told. 'Rick Wilbur was definitely struck on the back of the head with a blunt weapon. You know what that means . . .'

As his voice trailed off in one direction, my

thoughts trailed off in another. And it wasn't a good one. Something told me this was going to make me Suspect Number One. I could see the line-up now. Turn to the left, turn to the right. Step forward.

Face the firing squad . . .

I shook myself. This trail was leading no place good, way too fast for comfort.

'Of course, they don't have official autopsy results yet. Nothing conclusive to say that's what killed him. Nothing to even say that's his blood on the rolling pin.' He gave me his best lawyerly face. The one that said, *Don't worry, everything's going to be just fine.*

But all three of us knew that was a load of, well, veggie haggis.

Donna's Vegetarian Haggis

(for those with intestinal fortitude)

Here's the recipe I got from Sis:

1 large carrot, finely chopped
6 medium mushrooms, chopped
1 large turnip
2 cups red lentils
1 cup kidney beans
1 cup of rolled oats
1 cup buckwheat
1 cup of nuts (mix peanuts, almonds, walnuts)
1 cup vegetarian suet
1 tsp black pepper
1 1/2 cups vegetable stock
2 tbsps oil
1 tbsp lemon juice
Salt to taste
Dash of soy sauce
Dash of gravy browning

Fry the onion, carrot, turnip and mushrooms in a large frying pan or wok. Cook the lentils in stock and reduce. Add the cooked lentils, kidney beans and nuts to the onion mixture. Stir-fry the rolled oats and buckwheat for several minutes, then add to the other mixture with the soy sauce, lemon juice, suet, gravy browning and black pepper and simmer for a few minutes until the liquid begins to thicken. Pour into an ovenproof dish and allow to stand for approximately twenty minutes, then cook in a medium oven for thirty minutes and . . . enjoy?

SIX

'Are you sure you're going to be all right?'

I nodded as firmly as I could. Frankly, I was feeling a bit jellyfishy – it was almost as if Mom was watching covertly over my shoulder.

But the answer was no, I was not going to be all right. 'Hey,' I said aloud, sitting in Donna's Mini Cooper on the street outside my fledgling beignet business, 'I'm Maggie Miller.' I smiled. 'Of course I'm all right. I get things done. And I'm going to get through this,' I insisted, looking directly at my sister. 'You'll see.' I waved up the street. While the shops were open, it was that time of the day when things got hot and quiet. 'Trust me – tomorrow morning there's going to be a line out the door – people clamoring for a plate of hot beignets!'

Or my head on a platter when the newspaper comes out with my mugshot on the front page. Not a pretty thought. I sort of liked my head where it was.

Donna's nod looked as false as my own. 'You want me to come in with you?'

I popped open the passenger-side door and checked for traffic. It was mid-afternoon and the Arizona sun was letting us know it. One hundred degree heat baked the already baked bricks that lined Laredo Street. Laredo is just a couple of blocks over from and runs perpendicular to Main Street – Table Rock's main thoroughfare.

Main and Laredo make up two sides of Table Rock Town Square. There's a bronze statue there of our fair town's founder, Arthur B. Honicker. I can see it if I stand on the sidewalk outside my café and squint. They say he founded Table Rock as a haven from religious and political persecution. The religion he founded, still operating out of an abandoned feed store just up the road, is something called The Universal Guiding Light. Sounds more like a soap opera to me. They say the middle initial B in Honicker's name stands for Brigham. I say it stands for Bonkers.

But back to the heat. A few more degrees and I swear the blacktop in the alley was going to turn into black goo. I'd seen it happen before and the footprints I had left in the alley behind the shop proved it. I'd lost a good pair of flip-flops that day. I wondered if this heat wave would ever end and if we'd get back to that fabulous Mediterranean climate that this part of Arizona boasted about.

'No,' I said finally. 'You've got plenty enough to do of your own.' I dusted my hands on my shorts. 'I've got to handle this alone.' We both looked through the plate glass window of Maggie's Beignet Café. I could see several men and one lone woman chatting inside.

It seemed the long arm of the law had taken up residence. This was one thing I was going to have to handle immediately. After all, I had a business to open. I couldn't open my doors tomorrow with a shop full of cops in the place. Unless they were paying customers, of course.

I had a nearly insurmountable amount of work

to get done. I hadn't even been able to complete my dry run with Clive.

Clive. I hoped the poor man was OK. But it was only a fainting spell. I mean, sure, it was a fainting spell brought on by the sight of a dead guy in a box. But still, a faint is just a faint. Happens all the time, right?

'See you, Sis.' I tapped on the car roof and crossed the street as the Mini disappeared up the road. It was warm inside the shop.

Highsmith was speaking in low tones to a tony young woman in a black power suit. She looked like she'd look more at home in the Scottsdale Neiman Marcus than she did the streets of downtown Table Rock. That tailored pleated peplum jacket and those matching black pleated peplum cigarette pants she was rocking were surely Alexander McQueen originals.

And if I didn't know better – and I admit I often didn't – I'd swear she and Highsmith were flirting. Every time she swung her hips, the jacket's teasing red lining flashed and his eyes followed. If this kept up, the ape would be drooling all over my clean floor. Well, mostly clean. For the second time today, I thought I might barf.

Then I wondered if anybody had bothered to clean up that barf I'd left earlier or if I was going to have to do the deed myself. But I'd worry about that later. Right now, I had another deed to do. I strode between luster and lustee. 'Detective Highsmith,' I said loudly. 'You're back.' I crossed my arms over my chest. 'Come to plant some more evidence?'

There was a smirk on his mug. 'I don't have to,' he said rather smugly. 'Judging by what we found this morning, I'd say you'd done a good enough job of that yourself.'

Oh, right. The rolling pin. *My* rolling pin. The one I hadn't been able to find yesterday. 'Yeah, well,' I blustered. 'It's all circumstantial.'

He looked like he didn't know what I meant. To tell the truth, I didn't know what I meant. Circumstantial is one of those words you hear tossed around on cop shows, though, so it had to mean something important. 'You know what I mean,' I said.

Tailored lady finally broke her silence. 'So you work here.'

'I'm the owner,' I replied, pushing my hand out. 'Maggie Miller.'

She ignored me and turned back to Highsmith. 'She's the one who reported the murder.'

He nodded.

I held my hand out an embarrassing second longer, then drew it back. Sheesh, this was the second time in one day that someone had refused to shake my hand. I looked it over carefully.

My nails could use a coat of polish and I had gnawed a little at my right thumb back at the station. But I had a right to be nervous. She couldn't possibly be holding that against me, could she?

I looked at those manicured fingernails and the tips of those pedicured toes of hers as they peeked out of those Kors Collection peep-toe pumps. Yep, she could.

'Her prints were on the murder weapon?' She

looked Latin but her English was *muy bueno*. Not a trace of an accent. I was betting she probably bought her grammar the same place she bought everything else she wore – some snooty high-end place that beignet shop owners could never afford but always dream about.

'Yep.' He looked at her brunette locks, then at me.

'The rolling pin? Of course my prints are on it. It's *my* rolling pin.' Highsmith had instructed an officer to collect my prints as soon as we'd gotten to the station.

It had taken me a solid twenty minutes in Donna's hall bathroom scrubbing away with a bottle of Mrs Meyers and a hand towel to get all the ink off my fingertips. I was going to owe Sis a new pump bottle. I'd pretty much polished hers off. I ran a finger past my nose. I could still smell the lemon verbena. Come to think of it, I probably was going to owe her a new hand towel, too. That fingerprint ink might prove difficult to get out of unbleached organic Egyptian cotton.

'Have you spoken to Judge Wiggins yet?' Highsmith asked.

She shook those lustrous tresses of hers and I swear every cop in the place stopped to watch. Even the woman. 'Not yet. He's down in Flagstaff.' She pulled back her sleeve and checked a slender, diamond-encrusted watch. 'I'm meeting with him later this afternoon.' She touched his cuff. 'Let's catch up after.'

Highsmith nodded. 'I'll call you.'

''Bye, Veronica,' waved a middle-aged officer

with a buzz cut who stood framed in the doorway leading to the storeroom.

She tossed a languid hand in the air as she fluttered out my front door. Quite a majestic gesture really. She'd probably practiced it in her bathroom mirror.

'So that's the famous Veronica, eh?' I quipped. I had no idea who she was or why she was being treated so regally. We watched as a man in blue held open the door to a dark blue Mercedes. She slid behind the wheel and melted into traffic with barely a lookout for oncoming cars.

Sure, I thought, drivers probably sense her impending royal presence and stop just to let her go by. OK, I might have been a little bit jealous. It's not that I wanted to be her. It's not that I wanted Highsmith to want me. Though for a moment there earlier I'd thought . . .

I gave myself a mental slap. No, I was not going there.

I didn't know what it was. But it was none of those things. Maybe I'd take up that haughty wave of hers. That looked pretty cool. Ice-woman cool.

'You know her?' Detective Highsmith asked, turning back to face me. Finally.

'No,' I replied with a shrug. 'But I feel like I should.' I looked around the shop. 'Everybody else around here' – at least those afflicted with the Y chromosome – 'seems to treat her with a certain . . .' I paused, couching my words, '. . . deference, shall we say?'

I could have said 'lecherous yearning' but I was talking to Table Rock's only detective. I was trying my best to stay on his good side. He could be the one person keeping me this side of the slammer doors.

He chuckled. 'Veronica Vargas.'

'OK,' I said. 'The name means nothing to me.'

'Table Rock's attorney. Prosecuting attorney.'

Why was he looking at me like that? 'Prosecuting attorney? Why would a town the size of Table Rock even have a prosecuting attorney?'

'Because VV's papa is the mayor. Besides, it's only part-time.'

I hated her already. I could think of several things VV stood for besides Veronica Vargas. Venomous vixen, for one. 'So,' I said, going into fake nonchalance mode, 'find anything new?' Like vain viper for two.

He leaned his elbows back against the countertop. 'No. You still claim you have no idea what Rick Wilbur was doing in your backroom?'

'I told you,' I said sharply, 'he was nice to me. Gave me a break on the rent. Maybe he thought he'd be nice again and help me unpack the chairs. He's not still here, is he?' I asked, shivering as I peered through the doorway to the storeroom.

Detective Highsmith shook his head. 'The coroner removed him some time ago.'

Thank goodness for that. A dead guy in a box was a hard thing to work around.

'You know, Ms Miller, the Wilburs have lived in Table Rock for generations. Rick Wilbur and his family have been nice to a lot of people in this town. He was well liked.'

'Not by everybody,' I shot back.

'What's that supposed to mean? You and he not getting along?'

I made as sour a face as I could muster. 'Of course not. I mean, of course we weren't not getting along.'

I took a mental step back. What the heck had I just said? 'I mean, that's not what I meant at all. What I meant,' I said, gathering my wits back up, 'was that there was at least one person in Table Rock who did not like Rick Wilbur.' I pointed through the doorway to the storeroom. 'In fact, I'd be willing to go out on a limb and say that somebody around here took a strong disliking to the man.'

That's when I noticed my counter held three empty Karma Koffee cups and a rumpled Karma Koffee brown sack from which spilled several scones. Right there where anybody looking in the window could see them, too.

Good grief. Now I was advertising the competition. I swept the cups up and tossed them in the trash can beside the register. Next, I balled up the bag of scones and thrust it at Highsmith. 'Here. Please leave now and take your posse with you. I have a lot to do to get ready for tomorrow.' I nodded toward the door. 'The grand opening is tomorrow at seven a.m. So . . .' I gestured toward the door again. 'If you plan on coming, leave your badge at home and bring your wallet.' I then mentally urged him to leave through said door.

Highsmith didn't budge. Well, he budged just a little. He removed his elbows from my counter and relieved me of the Karma Koffee bag. 'Sorry,' he said.

I couldn't tell if he meant it or not.

'We're not done here.'

'Well, try not to get in the way. I've got baking, frying and grinding to do.'

'Sorry,' he said again, laying a hand on my arm as I moved toward the fryer. 'I can't let you do that.'

'Why not? Watching your weight?' It hadn't stopped them from eating all those fattening scones bought from my competitor across the street.

'I'm afraid you'll have to leave, Ms Miller.'

Was he crazy? 'Are you crazy? Did you hear me? I'm opening in less than twenty-four hours. I can't leave now.'

'We're waiting for county to get here. Table Rock's a small town. County's got resources we haven't.'

'So,' I said, my face an angry knot, 'when will they get here?' I suppose I could afford to lose an hour or two. But this was cutting things close.

'Tomorrow. First thing. I promise.'

'Tomorrow!' I practically leapt out of my flip-flops, which isn't really all that hard to do, but still. 'You can't do that!' Could they? 'I'll call Andy.' OK, I should have said 'my attorney.' That sounds so much better. The word Andy conjured up images of a lanky, pony-tailed, anachronistic hippie.

'Your attorney is fully aware of the situation. We have a warrant.' Detective Highsmith handed me my purse. 'I suggest you take the rest of the day off. Try to relax.'

Relax? Who was this guy kidding?

'I'll let you know the minute that we can release the café to you.'

I blubbered, I blustered and I begged. I almost cried. None of it mattered. I'd been bounced from my own shop. Me and my bicycle.

This couldn't be happening. But it was. I wondered what the town philosophers would make of that. If I had time to audit a class down at the University of Metaphysical Theology, I no doubt would have gotten my answer. But I didn't have time for such mind- and soul-searching questions.

I had a bank loan to repay. I had suppliers I owed money to. Heck, I even owed Mom several thousand dollars. If I couldn't open Maggie's Beignet Café . . .

I started to pedal as fast as I could.

In hindsight, I should have been looking where I was going. If I had, I wouldn't have crashed straight into Johnny Wolfe.

Fortunately, I was able to get my feet down in time to stop myself from falling over. Unfortunately, that hadn't helped Johnny Wolfe. He went down like a sack of potatoes. Skinny fries might be more apt a descriptor. The man needed some carbs. A trip to Bell Rock Burgers would do him wonders – get his body-fat index right up there.

I leapt from my Schwinn, rested it against the side of the window of the nearest shop and rushed to help him up. 'Are you OK, Mr Wolfe?' I lifted the back of his neck from the sidewalk. He looked at me, a little crazy-eyed at first, then seemed to gather his senses.

'You!' he cried. He pulled himself up to his knees. 'Why don't you watch where you're going?'

'I know,' I said, helping him to his feet. 'I'm sorry. I am so sorry.' But still, it wasn't like he'd permanently lost the use of his legs. He was strutting around just fine. And it wasn't like he was competing at skating any longer. He was way too old for that now. So what was he so upset about?

Sure, his designer slacks now had openings for the knees. But it was too hot for long pants anyway. The man should have known better. A guy could get heatstroke walking around in one hundred degree weather in black pants. Did he have a death wish?

And he was alive and breathing. More than alive and breathing. He was alive and cursing. 'You could have killed me!' He tugged at the holes in his black jeans. I could see he was not letting go of this. Some people have a hard time letting go of things. Johnny was obviously one of them.

'Don't be upset,' I said. 'I'll buy you a new pair.' I crossed my fingers behind my back. There was no way I could afford to buy Johnny Wolfe a new pair of jeans. 'Where's Clive?'

Johnny frowned at the handlebar of my bicycle. I hadn't exactly been gentle in getting off my bike in my haste to assist him. The edge of the handlebar seemed to have wiped out the lower halves of two letters of the storefront's hand-painted sign, The Hitching Post.

I cracked a smile, gently edged my Schwinn

away from the window and put down the kick-stand. I ran a finger along the scuffed-up lettering. 'A little paint and she'll be good as new. I can do it myself.'

He slapped my hand away from the window. 'I'll have my own man do it.'

I nodded. Heck, I was just trying to do the guy a favor. But some people are like that, not good at accepting help. 'So,' I began again, 'where's Clive? Is he going to be OK?'

Johnny's lips seemed to be permanently down-turned. 'Clive is still in the hospital.'

'He is?' That surprised me. One little faint ought not put a man in the hospital, let alone keep him there. I attributed this to an apparently weak constitution.

'What's he got? Shock?' I remembered all those gruesome symptoms the nice lady with the blood pressure cuff had described to me, which only made me start feeling queasy all over again myself.

Johnny stepped aside to let a couple pushing a baby stroller pass. 'Clive suffers from low blood pressure. The doctor simply wants to keep an eye on him a little longer. I had to get back here to run the shop.'

I nodded, looking at the beautiful display in the front window. Two exquisite gowns stood side by side. One was a cream-colored fit and flare, the other a snow-white mermaid gown.

I'd gone the traditional ball gown route myself. Yeah, I'd thought I was a princess, Cinderella come to life off the silver screen. What can I say? I'd had dreams.

Now I had new dreams. Bigger dreams, better dreams.

That wedding dress was now hanging in my bedroom closet. All that beautiful silk organza just hanging there, doing nothing. Maybe I'd turn all that expensive fabric into a pair of curtains for Maggie's Beignet Café. That just might class the place up a bit. Did organza work for curtains? I'd have to ask Mom.

He turned and faced the beignet café. 'I see the police are still in your shop.'

'Yeah. They seem to be searching the place molecule by molecule. Detective Highsmith just told me that some team from the county is coming over tomorrow to dig around some more.'

'What exactly are they looking for? I heard they already found the murder weapon. A rolling pin.'

I shrugged. 'I have no idea. Fingerprints, DNA, loose change. Wait,' I stopped. 'How do you know about the rolling pin?' It seemed word travelled fast. Andy was right. Table Rock is a small town. Everybody seemed to know my business almost before I did.

It was his turn to shrug. 'Clive must have told me.' He peered into my eyes, squinting against the sun. 'So it's true?'

I nodded. 'I don't know how the rolling pin got there, though. I don't know how Mr Wilbur got in a box in my storeroom either, for that matter. I only know that I didn't put him there.'

Johnny made several *tsk-tsk*ing noises. 'Such a shame. Rick was a gentle man. He deserved a better end than to be stuffed in a cardboard box.'

I agreed, and said so. 'So you knew Rick Wilbur?' I stood up against the plate glass window, under the awning, enjoying what little shade there was.

'Of course.' Johnny ran a finger through the air. 'He is – was – our landlord. Wilbur Realty owns this entire row of storefronts.'

That made sense.

'I sure hope the police finish up in there soon.' Johnny pressed his face to the glass of my store.

'Thanks. Me, too.'

He turned to me. 'All this unsavory activity will be quite disquieting to my clientele.'

What a peach of a guy, I thought, as the door to The Hitching Post swung shut behind him.

A peach of a guy.

SEVEN

I decided it was time to check on Clive at the hospital. I dropped my purse in the basket attached to my front handlebars and climbed back aboard my bike. I dropped my foot over the pedal and went nowhere. The gears spun wildly, but the tires stayed where they were. I stayed where I was.

I felt like somebody was looking at me. You know that prickly feeling you sometimes get? Well, I was getting it now. I glanced between the wedding dresses in The Hitching Post window. There was Johnny Wolfe, arms folded, brow a knot of thunder, glaring at me. He probably thought I was creating an uncomely scene outside his bridal salon.

I smiled, waved, wiped the sweat under my nose with the back of my finger and hopped off my seat. A quick look down showed me that the chain had jumped the gears. Great. I looked at the chain. I looked at Johnny. No way was I asking him for help.

Should I ask Detective Highsmith or one of the other boys in blue? I decided no. I'd had enough of him and his posse for one day. Besides, they probably wouldn't want to be seen assisting a possible murder suspect make her getaway, anyway.

I decided to push the Schwinn to Laura's

Lightly Used. That was the thrift shop where I'd purchased the Schwinn on moving to town and selling the Plymouth. The store was only a couple of blocks east so it wouldn't be too much trouble. Laura would know what to do.

She'd explained to me that she was always having to perform repairs, refurbish and restore the goods she took in for resale in her shop.

Despite the heat, the front door was open wide with a big fan blowing down from overhead. I stood there a moment, using my bike for support. The strong, cool breeze blew down relentlessly. I closed my eyes. This was heaven.

'Maggie?'

I opened my eyes. Laura Duval was straightening frocks on a round rack at the far end of the store. I waved and rolled the bike her way.

'It's good to see you again. Is there something wrong with the Schwinn?' Laura asked.

'No, not really.' I patted the saddle. 'I love this bike. Best forty-five bucks I ever spent.' And it was. She was a bright pink beauty with white-wall tires and matching pink rims. The price had been a bargain. And I was being ecofriendly, I'd retorted, when Donna snickered at the sight of me the first time I drove up to her house on it. That shut her up.

It wasn't that the bike was pink. She just wasn't used to seeing me ride a bicycle. I'd tried it once as a kid. My father had insisted I learn to ride. Funny, I'd despised it then, but I was loving it now.

So, I suppose his little girl was finally all grown up. I fought back a tear. If only he was around to see it . . .

'Popped your chain, huh?' She bent at the knees and, before I could explain, had the chain back on its track.

'How did you do that?' I stared at the magically restored chain.

Laura shrugged and glanced at her fingers. 'I'd better wipe up.'

I followed Laura to the counter along the rear of her shop. It was a large place, probably four times the size of my own dinky café. Maybe more. She carried clothes, bikes, kayaks. You name it, Laura's Lightly Used probably has it in stock. She grabbed a small towel from under the counter and rubbed her fingers clean.

Laura is a very attractive ash blonde with soft features and inquisitive blue eyes. Today, like the day we'd met, she was sporting a classic A-line bob and wearing a flowery yellow cami top and denim shorts. Her leather sandals looked a thousand times nicer and more comfortable than my own flimsy flip-flops.

Though I always felt inferior around her, she never made me feel that way. She was as friendly as she was unassuming. I could only blame myself for seeing how much I paled in comparison to her.

I'd been to the shop on several occasions now. It was hard to beat these prices. Besides the Schwinn, I'd managed to equip my apartment kitchen with stuff I'd found here and even got a few things for the beignet shop.

Including the marble rolling pin. I turned my head around the store. Come to think of it, I was going to be needing a new one. Even if the police gave me back the original, I wasn't touching it. They could send it to the bottom of the Grand Canyon for all I cared.

'How's the store coming along? You're opening tomorrow, right?'

My face must have given away my answer faster than my lips could.

'You're not?' Laura reached across the counter for my hand. 'Why not? I don't understand. I even saw the advertisement in today's *Table Rock Reader*.'

Of course, the ad had been running for a week.

'What's wrong, Maggie?'

I don't know what it was – her compassion, her selflessness, the way this woman who was practically a stranger took my hand and held it to lend me comfort and support. Whatever it was, all or none of the above, it was working some sort of mojo on me. A fat, embarrassing tear splattered against the glass-topped counter. 'Sorry,' I choked, rubbing the damp smear with my palm.

'Oh, dear.' Laura grabbed a box of tissues and swung around to my side of the counter. 'Have a seat.' She grabbed one of a matching pair of chairs that sat on either side of a small table that held a crystal candy dish and lowered me into it.

I heaved a sigh, giggled with embarrassment and swiped away the tears. 'I don't know,' I snuffled. 'There's been an accident.' I thrummed the bottom of the seat. The chair looked new, the candy fresh. I popped a lemon drop in my mouth, partly to choke down the tears I feared might flow again.

Her brow dug furrows. 'An accident?'

'Well, more of a murder . . .'

Laura looked confused.

What was it about people that they looked so confused so often? Was it something in the water around here? I looked up at Laura with big, moist, red eyes. 'Oh, and I'm going to need another rolling pin.'

Laura's confusion turned to befuddlement. She dropped into the opposite chair. 'Maybe you should start at the beginning, Maggie,' she said softly.

She was right. So I did.

I told her how I'd arrived at my shop in the morning, how my neighboring shopkeeper had come by to introduce himself and how that had ended up with me finding a dead guy in a box in my storeroom and Clive in the hospital.

'Wow,' she said, her voice a mere whisper. She ran her hands along her thighs. 'That's incredible. How do you suppose Mr Wilbur ended up in your storeroom like that?'

I could only shrug. 'That's just it. I don't have a clue.'

We were both silent a moment. Laura offered me a glass of iced tea. I gladly accepted.

'Great. I've got a fresh pitcher in the break-room. It's in the fridge. I'll be right back. Don't leave.'

I nodded and ruminated on the wonderful day I was having so far. I wondered if the University of Metaphysical Theology might offer a class in omphaloskepsis. That's the contemplation of one's navel as part of a mystical exercise. It's what I was doing at the moment. Hey, I have my Zen moments too.

I was great at contemplating my navel. Especially after two glasses of cabernet. Then I was *really* great at contemplating my navel, more so since the divorce. If this beignet business didn't pan out maybe I could get a job at the university – Adjutant Professor of Omphaloskepsis.

It had a nice ring to it, I thought, contemplating my navel.

Laura returned a couple minutes later with two tall ice-filled glasses of something that tasted like ginger with hints of lemongrass and mint. 'Not bad,' I said, taking my first sip and maneuvering my lips around the lemon wedge clutching the rim for dear life. It was no Lipton's, but it wasn't terrible.

I took another sip.

'So the grand opening has been postponed?'

I nodded morosely. 'At least for another day. I'm hoping the police let me have the place back after tomorrow.'

'I'm sure they will.' She set her glass upon a sandstone coaster on the table between us.

'I know that will make Johnny Wolfe happy.'

'Johnny Wolfe? The figure skater?'

'Yeah. He's not real thrilled with the riot squad squatting outside his hoity-toity bridal shop.' I polished off my tea. 'You know him?'

'Not personally. But I've seen him on TV. I heard he was living in town.' She beamed. 'I haven't had a reason to visit a bridal salon.' She held up a ringless finger.

'Join the club,' I said.

'You know . . .' Laura hesitated.

'What?'

'Well, I don't want to say anything that could get anyone in trouble.'

I straightened. 'What? What is it, Laura?' My heart started racing. 'If there's something you know that could help me out of a jam, please, you've got to do it! This is my livelihood at stake.' I clasped her hand. 'I've got my lifesavings tied up in this business.'

Laura's lower lip turned down. Finally, she said, 'Well, it's just that when you mentioned Johnny Wolfe, I remembered something.'

I waited. Sheesh, it was like pulling teeth with this girl. My eyes practically bulged out of their sockets.

'I saw Johnny Wolfe arguing with Mr Wilbur.'

'You did?' This was news indeed. 'When? Where?'

She tapped her front teeth with the nail of her right index finger. 'A day or two ago?' She wagged her head. 'I know it was fairly early. Before nine, I'm sure. I was walking to work and passed them on the street.'

'Where was this?' Ha! Wait until I threw this in Detective Highsmith's face. I had a brand-new suspect for him!

'On Main, right outside Wilbur Realty.'

'Did you hear what they were arguing about?'

Laura shook her head. 'No. They clammed up as I went by. And I don't know either of them on a personal level so we didn't so much as say hi. I nodded, they nodded back and on I went.

They both looked angry, though.' She lifted a shoulder. 'Sorry I can't be more specific.'

I leaned back in my chair. So the two men had been arguing on the street. That was something. I'd need to look into this further. 'Thanks, Laura,' I said. 'You've helped. A lot. And I don't mean just fixing my bike chain.'

She rose and gave me a body wrapping hug. 'You hang in there, Maggie. I'm sure everything will work out.'

She tapped the space over my heart. 'Maintain positive energy; let the power of the universe speak.'

I promised I would, though I wasn't sure I'd understand what the universe said. I'd studied French in school, not Universe 101.

I rolled my bike out the door and waved. It was time to check on Clive.

A Quick Fix

If your bicycle chain comes off while on the go, continue pedaling slowly and move the front derailleur up as if you are going up to the larger chain ring. Don't move the derailleur all the way as if you're making a true gear change, just move it enough to cause the chain to slip back onto the smaller ring. Continue to pedal slowly for a few turns to ensure the chain is firmly set. You can now continue riding – just watch out for Johnny!

To fix your chain manually on a multi-speed bicycle like mine, first park the bike someplace stable. Next, press the rear derailleur, located near the rear sprocket, forward to release some tension from the chain. Hopefully, you've got a rag or a shirt of your ex-husband's around you can use to keep your hands clean.

With your other hand, lift the chain and place it on top the small chain ring. Release the rear derailleur, lift the back wheel off the ground and manually turn the pedals until the chain is set. If this doesn't work, walk it over to Laura's Lightly Used. If she's around, and she usually is, she'll get you fixed up in a jiff.

EIGHT

Mesa Verde Medical Center is small as hospitals go – a simple, yet elegantly designed, adobe-styled one-story butterscotch-brown building on the edge of town, a couple of miles from my café. I left my Schwinn in a slot at the bike rack and rushed through the automatic doors.

'Maggie Miller,' I said, sagging against the counter. It had been a long, hot ride. My eyes cast around for a drinking fountain. There was one off to the left between the men's and ladies' rooms. 'One sec.' I raised a finger. I raced over, grabbed my fill of cool water then hurried back.

'Can I help you with something? Is there some sort of emergency?' The brunette was perched on a tall cushioned stool behind the reception counter. She was wearing a teal pantsuit so I guessed she wasn't a nurse. Her features were a bit on the mousy side and I noticed a small diamond or at least a reasonable-looking fake piercing her left nostril. Ouch, that had to hurt. I'd practically fainted when my mom had me get my ears pierced at age five.

Speaking of fainting, 'I'm here to see Clive,' I said.

'Clive who?'

She had me there. What was Clive's last name? I scratched my head trying to remember. Had he

69

even told me? 'I'm not sure,' I admitted finally. 'He's tall, has red hair and freckles. Like me,' I said pointing to my face. 'He saw a dead body and fainted.'

Recognition lit the receptionist's face. 'Oh, of course. Mr Rothschild.'

'That's it!' Now I remembered. Clive had told me his last name. My head bobbed up and down. 'Can I see him?'

The receptionist, whose name tag identified her as Halley, glanced at the clock on the wall behind her. A green and blue stooped-over image of Kokopelli occupied the center of the clock – flute glued to his lips. Kokopelli's image was as ubiquitous around Arizona as tumbleweed. Kokopelli is a Hopi word. Andy told me it means hump-backed flute player or some such thing. He is supposed to be a prankster, storyteller and, most of all, fertility god. Maybe Mesa Verde was trying to build up its maternity department.

'I'm sorry,' Halley said. 'You've just missed visiting hours for the afternoon. If you could come back between seven and nine tonight?'

I leaned over the counter. Halley took a step back. 'Please.' I locked my hands together. 'I rode all the way out here. I don't even have a car. I drive a Schwinn.'

'I'm sorry, miss, but—'

I cut her off before she could dismiss me completely. 'You don't understand. Clive is my dearest friend and I feel responsible for what happened to him today. I mean, if I hadn't screamed when I saw the dead guy in the box—'

Halley raised both hands in the air. Her head

70

turned side to side. 'Would you excuse me a moment?'

'Of course,' I said. Anything to make Halley happy. The receptionist disappeared through a door between two low filing cabinets.

I drummed my hands on the counter and waited. Several minutes later, Halley returned with a man in a white coat and matching trousers. He had short-cropped black hair and a day's worth of stubble along his strong chin. I pegged him at my age, give or take, with a deep olive complexion.

'This is the woman I was telling you about, Doctor.'

I smiled at the two of them.

The doctor nodded and came around the counter toward me. He gazed into my eyes but something told me this wasn't love at first sight. He pulled out some odd-looking device from his front pocket and aimed it at my pupils. 'I'm Doctor Vargas,' he said, his voice as calm and deep as a Rocky Mountain stream. 'How are you?'

'Uh, fine,' I replied. I glanced at the receptionist, who continued to watch us closely. 'Can I see Clive now?' That Rocky Mountain stream of his sounded a bit like Antonio Banderas as it trickled in my direction.

He laid a cool hand against my forehead. 'Any dizzy spells, blurred vision? Palpitations?'

I bit the inside of my cheek. 'No, I mean, not really. I was a bit on edge there this morning what with the dead guy and all. And the medic, or whoever that woman was, did think I might be in shock and having some sort of . . .' I snapped my fingers as I thought. 'What did she

71

call them?' I scrunched up my brow. 'Poor oral confusion?'

His brow shot up to match mine. 'Do you mean poor end-organ perfusion?'

'Yes, that was it!' His hand reached for my wrist and he felt for my pulse, which, of course, I had – a pulse, that is.

'Can I see Clive now?' I asked as he let go of my arm.

'What did you say your name was?'

'Maggie Miller. I own Maggie's Beignet Café on Laredo.' I fluttered my drooping lashes. 'The grand opening's tomorrow. You two should come.'

Halley got busy with some paperwork. Dr Vargas guided me to a chair in the visitors' lounge near the front. We sat. I could see my Schwinn through the window.

'What is your relationship to Mr Rothschild?'

I fidgeted. What was with all the questions? Were the staff of Mesa Verde like this with all the visitors? 'We sort of discovered a dead body together.'

He nodded as if that made sense, which it didn't, so I explained. After I'd finished my spiel, he rose, took a deep breath and let it out again. 'Do you have some identification?'

I quickly pulled out my driver's license and held it out, very discreetly placing my thumb over the spot that gave my date of birth. That was nobody's business but my own.

He laid a gentle hand on my shoulder and led me back to the counter. 'Halley, would you give me a visitor's pass, please? I think it will be all right for Ms Miller to check in on Mr Rothschild.'

'Thanks, Doc,' I said.

'Room twenty-two, East Wing.' Halley pointed over her shoulder.

Dr Vargas shook a finger at me. 'Keep it short. Technically, I shouldn't be allowing this at all.' He laid his hand on my shoulder and looked deep into my eyes. 'And if you feel any disorientation, confusion, any unusual symptoms of any kind,' his fingers pressed into my flesh, 'do not hesitate to call me.' He handed me his card.

I shook his hand up and down, clipped the visitor's pass to my blouse and took off down the hall.

Room twenty-two was at the end of the corridor. Mesa Verde was laid out in a U-shape, with reception and emergency services at the bottom of the U and rooms running up the sides. 'Hi, Clive!'

Clive looked up. He was clutching a fork at the end of which was something that looked like brownish-pink chicken. 'How are you feeling?'

'Maggie!' Clive's red hair was a mess and his green eyes looked like nervous insects looking for some safe place to escape to.

Clive had a nice bed by the window. There was obviously a second bed in the room but it was half-hidden by cream-colored curtains that hung from a track built into the ceiling. 'Nice place,' I said. I dropped into the chair at his bedside. A vase of flowers sat on a small table under the window. I glanced at the card. The roses were from Johnny Wolfe. Very sweet. Maybe he wasn't such a jerk after all.

Up close, Clive's face looked like something

73

that had come out of a Silly Putty egg. 'You look great, Clive.' I patted the covers. Well, certainly much better than he had passed out against my counter this morning. 'When are you getting out?'

I pushed an errant strand of hair from his forehead so it wouldn't bug him. Unfortunately, my thumb got caught in his eye socket.

'Ouch!' he squealed.

I said I was sorry.

'They're releasing me tomorrow morning,' he replied, setting aside his dinner tray. His left eye was looking a little red. I thought he might want to get that checked out while he was here. He tugged at some gadget on his arm. 'They've got me hooked up to some sort of heart monitor.'

'Is everything OK?'

'It's just a precaution, the doctor says.' He waved a wan hand through the air. 'It's nothing, I'm sure.' He peered at me. 'How are you, Maggie?'

I shrugged. 'You know me – I'm great.' Of course, Clive didn't really know me at all. We'd just met.

But he nodded as if he understood.

I glanced over my shoulder at the vase of flowers. 'I see Johnny sent you flowers. He mentioned he'd be coming.'

'You saw Johnny?'

'I bumped into him earlier,' I answered. 'So he's the husband you were telling me about?'

Clive sipped from his water glass, spilling a drop on his hospital gown. 'Yes, three years next month.' He swiped at the material. 'We were married over the Fourth of July weekend.'

74

'That's great. How's the back of your head?' Clive had cracked it pretty good when he hit the floor.

He rubbed it and winced. 'Not bad. The doctor said there was no concussion.'

Thank goodness for that, because if Clive sued me my insurance would go through the roof.

A man's shouting voice from behind the curtain startled me. 'Trying to rest over here!'

'So stop shouting!' I shouted, putting my hands over my ears. 'Sheesh, you could burst somebody's ear drums like that.' I turned to Clive and mouthed, *Who is the big mouth?*

Clive motioned me closer with his finger. I sat beside him. 'My roommate. Though I'm not sure he's very happy that they moved me in here with him.'

'A bit of a sourpuss, if you ask me.' Not that anybody had. I kept my voice low.

Clive shrugged. 'I believe he's been here a couple of days. I've only spoken to him briefly. His name is Edwin something.' He was looking at the curtain. 'I heard one of the nurses talking. He had some sort of heart attack or stroke or something. I feel sorry for him.'

Suddenly I was feeling sorry for him too. I turned my eyes to the curtain. 'You think I should apologize?'

'No,' Clive answered quickly. 'Let's just let him rest.'

I nodded, rose and paced the small room twice before speaking again. What was the social etiquette for broaching the subject of a dead guy in a box? Was there a protocol? Especially when

75

you thought a guy's husband or even the guy himself might be responsible for the dead guy in that box?

'I don't know if you heard,' I said, glancing up at the TV mounted to the wall in the corner – the screen was dark – 'but that guy in my storeroom was Rick Wilbur of Wilbur Realty.'

Clive's head drooped to his chest. 'Yes, the police told me.'

'The police were here?'

He nodded. 'Yes, a Detective Highsmith, I believe he said was his name.'

I stifled a groan. Detective Highsmith. Great. He'd probably bad-mouthed me to my next-door neighbor. If Maggie's Beignet Café was forced to shut its doors before it had even opened them, I was pretty certain I wasn't going to be able to rely on Mark Highsmith as a personal reference for my next job.

'I can't imagine anyone killing Mr Wilbur,' Clive said, his voice just above a whisper. 'Especially like that.' He shook himself. 'I still can't get that image of him out of my brain. That was simply gruesome. I'd never seen anything like it before.'

I agreed. You just don't see a dead guy in a box every day. 'I did hear that your husband, Johnny, was seen having an argument with him yesterday morning.' I watched Clive for signs of prevarication or surprise. But as I barely recognize big red stop signs in the road, such subtleties as subterfuge were outside my limited powers of observation.

'Wherever did you hear that?' He sat up

76

straighter, straining several tubes attached to his right arm.

'Oh,' I waved a dismissive hand through the air, 'you know, around.' No way was I going to give my source away. If Johnny Wolfe or Clive Rothschild, or both, were killers, I didn't want to put Laura Duval in their line of fire.

'Well,' said Clive, pulling up the covers, 'whoever told you that is just plain wrong.'

'Oh?'

Clive huffed. 'I'm not saying Johnny didn't have a word with Mr Wilbur. But it was certainly no argument.'

'So what did Johnny have a word with Rick Wilbur about?'

Clive tossed his shoulders. 'The air conditioning, if you must know. Ours has been on the fritz – blowing hot and cold – for nearly a week. Mr Wilbur's been promising to fix it. He said he'd send somebody around. Johnny was quite upset about the matter. You can't imagine how unhappy our brides-to-be are trying on wedding gowns in such conditions.'

I nodded to show my commiseration. We were having the same problem. We probably shared the same ductwork.

Clive waved a hand in front of his face. 'The heat, the sweat. You have no idea the damage all that perspiration can do to our inventory.'

I could well imagine. Wedding dresses can hold a lot of heat. But I could not imagine it being enough reason to knock Rick Wilbur on the head with a rolling pin and stuff him in a box in my beignet café. What I needed was to learn more about Rick himself. Maybe it was time I visited Wilbur Realty.

A white-haired nurse entered the room. She wasn't old, just white-haired. Either she was part albino or she liked playing around with peroxide. 'I'm sorry, ma'am, but you'll have to leave.'

'But Doctor Vargas said—'

She shook her head. 'I am sorry, but some of our patients are trying to rest.' She glanced at the curtain.

Now I understood. Clive's roomie must have buzzed the nursing station and complained about me. 'I'm leaving now!' I said, a little too loudly.

'About time!' came a gravelly reply.

I threw a scowl toward the curtain, said a more civilized goodbye to Clive and followed the nurse out to my bike. 'Sorry about that,' she said once again. 'Mr Teller is still quite weak though. He does need his rest.'

I pulled my bike out of its slot. 'What's wrong with him anyway?'

'He suffered a stroke. The poor man lives all alone too.' With that, the nurse retreated to the hospital.

I hesitated a moment, then hopped on the Schwinn. Maybe I'd send the guy some flowers. Not that I could afford to buy any, but Sis did have some pretty nice flowerbeds around her house. Surely she wouldn't miss a few petunias?

NINE

Not surprisingly, Wilbur Realty occupied a prime piece of Main Street real estate next to Table Rock Bank, which had the big spot on the corner of Main Street and Cocopah Avenue.

Their offices took up about a quarter of the block with big plate glass windows advertising properties for sale and to rent in Table Rock and throughout the greater north-central Arizona region. Glancing at the asking prices, there weren't any that I could afford to buy.

I scratched my head. It looked like I'd be renting for a very long time. Unfortunately, a tug on the door told me the real estate office was closed for the day. I peered through the glass. There didn't seem to be anybody around. Either they kept short business hours – it was barely after six – or they had shut down as a sign of mourning for their boss, Rick Wilbur.

I pedaled home, dragged the bike in with me and leaned it against the wall near the door. I cranked up the boxy room air conditioner that dangled precariously from the window beside the dinette set that I'd picked up at Laura's Lightly Used.

I kicked off my shoes as I yanked open the refrigerator door. I was famished. Vegetarian haggis isn't as filling as you might expect. I nuked a couple of frozen enchiladas and quaffed a frozen margarita.

Arizonans love their margaritas. I'd added a bit of prickly pear cactus juice to the mix for taste. Donna claimed prickly pear cactus was medicinal and sold it in her food store. According to her, it was good for diabetes, high cholesterol, obesity, hangover, colitis, diarrhea and benign prostatic hypertrophy – you name it. Heck, maybe it even fended off zombies. I didn't know about any of that, but as I slid back onto the sofa, I sure thought it tasted sweet.

I took a second sip and pulled the plastic back from my tray of supermarket enchiladas. Of course, the doorbell rang.

I sighed as I rose from the comfy old sofa – it had come with the apartment because the last tenant had left it behind and my landlord had not wanted to bother to remove the clunky green beast – and approached the front door.

'Who's there?' I called. I didn't have a peephole and wasn't about to answer the door to just anybody. I mean, it could have been a door-to-door poncho salesman, or somebody wanting to proselytize me and tell me the wonders of Alpha Centauri's new religious order or something. It was too bloody hot for a poncho and I wasn't in the mood for any take-out alien theosophy.

'It's me, Maggie.'

I froze colder than the prickly pear margarita in my glass. It was Mom. I paused a little too long because she rang the bell again. 'Open the door.'

I pasted on a smile and yanked open the door, letting in a rush of hot dry air. 'Mom, what a pleasant surprise!'

It's not that I don't love my mom. It's just that Mom's a little, well, crazy. When she and I were both younger – as in when I was a teenager – I simply thought she was weird. But then, I was a teenager, so the feeling was probably mutual.

It wasn't until after Dad died after almost thirty years of marriage that Mom seemed to, well, flip out, shall we say? Six months after Dad's passing, Mom had sold the house in Phoenix, packed her things – what she hadn't given to friends and family or sold off at yard sales – and moved to Table Rock.

She got all mystical and starry-eyed and dove headfirst into yoga, practicing moves like downward drooping dog doodles, or at least that's what it sounded like to me.

And watching her do it? Well, that was just plain mortifying! No child should have to see her mother in those positions! I mean, really, what were the folks who thought up yoga thinking?

Couldn't they have come up with something more ladylike for the over-fifty crowd? Mom was pushing sixty.

Anyway, Mom's moving up here is what got the old seed of moving planted in Donna's and Andy's heads, I suppose. And now I'd ended up here myself. Donna and Andy had their kids, their farm and their food store. Mom had gotten so skilled with her yoga that she now taught a class part-time at a green-certified spa retreat. Me? I was just trying to make sweet beignet treats in between finding dead landlords in my storeroom.

81

Mom squeezed me until it hurt. This could only mean one thing – Donna had filled her in on my day. 'How are you holding up, Maggie?' She pulled me back to the sofa and pushed me down beside her. One disapproving eye took in my cooling store-bought enchiladas.

I set my margarita glass beside them atop an old copy of *People* magazine. Better it should leave a ring on Brad and Angelina than my wood coffee table.

'Maybe you'd like to change into something more comfortable? We could meditate out on the patio.' She patted my leg.

'This is as comfortable as it gets, Mom,' I replied, tugging self-consciously at my stained black T-shirt. 'And if we go out on the patio in this heat, the only contemplating I'm going to be doing is to wonder how long before I can escape back to the air conditioning.' I rolled my eyes. 'Such as it is.' The noisy old machine made lots of racket but blew tepid and weak at best. Margarita beckoned. I pulled my drink to my lips.

'Nonsense,' said Mom, ignoring my words. Nothing unusual about that. Mom always knows what's best for me – even when she doesn't. 'You've got a murder to solve.'

To say I looked at her rather dubiously would be an understatement. To say I spat margarita all over the lumpy sofa would be more honest. 'A murder to solve?' I blubbered skeptically, wiping uselessly at the microfiber pillow cushions.

'Of course. You aren't going to simply sit here and do nothing while the universe smothers you with negative energy, are you?'

I twisted my jaw to the side. That was sort of what I'd been planning, at least for the evening. What else was a girl supposed to do on a Thursday night?

I pushed the enchilada tray Mom's way. 'Care for an enchilada?'

She looked down her nose at my dinner. 'No, thank you. And you know how unhealthy all those frozen prepared foods are for you.'

I slid the tray back my way and bit into an enchilada. Rich and not too spicy. Just the way I liked it. 'Well, I like them.'

'Suit yourself, dear.'

Sure, I thought, she says that. But she *never* means it.

'And as far as solving a murder goes, I'll leave that to the Monks of the world.'

Mom's forehead creased. 'The monks?'

'Like on TV.' I dropped my enchilada, licked my fingertips, then stuck my hands out and waved them around the room as if my palms were picking up unseen magnetic vibrations. 'Like that detective on TV. Monk?'

Mom harrumphed. She was a world-class harrumpher, too. 'TV never solved anything, Maggie. You should know better.'

'They sure seem to solve a lot of crimes on TV.' I chomped down the remainder of the first enchilada and washed it down with the dregs of my margarita. Mom was making me nervous and nerves always made me eat.

I stared forlornly at the glass, wishing I'd made more. If I'd known Mom was dropping by, I would have. Heck, I'd have had a pitcher chilling in the freezer.

My mother rubbed the long quartz crystal that hung from a gold chain around her neck. 'As I said, what you need is a good meditation session.'

'How about a good medication instead?' I suggested.

She wagged her head. 'Always with the jokes.' She eyed me sternly. 'Tell me, Maggie, just what are you planning to do if your beignet café is forced to remain closed? Or,' she added, leaning in for the kill, 'if the police should decide to charge you with murdering Rick Wilbur? What will you do? How will you earn a living? How will you pay your rent? Your bills?'

My stomach jolted. Suddenly, I wasn't feeling so hungry. In fact, I was feeling rather clammy. I ran a hand over my forehead. Mom had brought me to my figurative knees and she hadn't even mentioned the big one – how would I pay her back the money she'd lent me?

'No, what you need, young lady' – I liked it when she called me that because I was way past young – 'is to meditate. Let the universe open to you and reveal Rick Wilbur's killer.'

Don't get me wrong. I worship the New Age as much as anybody. And if I could pick a new age, it would be twenty-five – no, make that twenty-seven, still pre-dead husband meeting . . . My fingers drummed the coffee table nervously. Maybe it was the margarita talking, but I could see that Mom had a point. 'OK,' I answered, pushing my hands off my knees. 'Let's do this.'

Mom beamed serenely and stroked her crystal.

'Do you have the crystal necklace I bought you?' She stared accusingly at my bare neck. I scurried to my bedroom, pulled the necklace from the dresser drawer and hooked it around my neck in the bathroom.

What I saw in the mirror was scary. I really needed a shower and a change of clothes.

'Ready, Maggie?' called my mother.

I joined her on the small patio off the kitchen. It wasn't much and there was no view, what with it being a stuccoed concrete block wall that stood six feet tall. At least it was private. Nobody had to see me sitting cross-legged on the concrete communing with Quetzalcoatl or Aunt Jemima or whoever it was that Mom was intending on contacting tonight.

She patted the hard ground. 'Have a seat, Maggie.' Her fuchsia summer caftan was pulled up to her richly tanned knees and she had removed her roman sandals.

My knees protested as I settled onto the rough patio floor. My butt protested even more. The patio was warm. I really should get some plants to keep out here, add a splash of color. Maybe a cactus in the corner.

'Let's close our eyes,' Mom said, taking my hands in hers. 'First, we must clear our thoughts of all negativity. Let all the bad energy escape, like stale air from a leaky balloon.'

I was feeling rather leaky. I nodded and complied, or at least attempted to. But thinking about my mother and my sister – it's like I'm the only sane person in the entire family.

I could only hope she didn't try to bring my

father into this. I felt like, ever since Dad died, Mom has been trying to communicate with Dad's spirit. Up there in the sky somewhere, floating around in the cosmos. I wasn't sure what freaked me out more – the fact that she's always trying or the thought that she might succeed.

I wasn't at all certain how I'd react if the ghost of Dad suddenly appeared before my eyes, here in the apartment or over at the café, but I was reasonably certain my reactions would involve things like dropping, breaking, shouting, panic, tears, fainting . . . and calls to the *National Enquirer*!

I tugged at my hunk of quartz. Quartz crystals are as ubiquitous around this part of Arizona as red dirt. Believers use the rocks in their quests to expand their minds and to touch the spirit world. According to my mom, crystals also enhance the beneficial life force. Donna even sells crystal water (water that a quartz crystal has been soaking in) at Mother Earth/Father Sun Grocers because of its purported health benefits.

I wasn't sure I believed, but I sure wanted to.

'Now,' my mother said softly, 'we must follow Rick Wilbur's energy.' She squeezed my hands tighter. 'Can you feel it?'

I could feel the circulation in my fingers being cut off. I raised an eyelid, sneaking a look at Mom. She wasn't cheating at all; her green eyes were firmly shut. Mom's a green-eyed redhead, like me, though she tends to keep hers trimmed shorter than I do. Dad had been a sandy-haired blonde in his youth. When I was a teenager, I'd have killed for hair like his. 'This is weird,' I grumbled.

'So is murder,' my mother answered softly. 'Now, let's listen to what the universe tells us.'

I pricked up my ears, hearing nothing more than the sounds of crickets cricketing, barking frogs barking and my own heart beating.

I sighed loudly. I didn't want Mom to miss it.

Mom shushed me. She jerked my hands. My eyes popped open. Mom's popped open next.

I waited, my foot tapping in expectation. 'Well, anything?' I looked around the small, cramped patio. At least there was no sign of Dad's ghost. I sure hoped he wouldn't be waiting for me in my bedroom and pop out of the closet sometime late in the night.

'Rick Wilbur's energy is . . .' Mom paused, then added, '. . . unsettled. You must help uncover his killer and bring them to justice. Only then will Mr Wilbur's union with the universe be complete.'

I rose, dusted off my butt and stuck out my hand to help Mom up. Not that she needed it; what with the daily yoga practice, she was in way better shape than me and twice as agile.

'I have faith in you, Maggie,' Mom said, wrapping her arms around me at the front door.

I wished I could say the same for myself. I downed the last cold enchilada and drank a cool glass of water from the tap. I was exhausted mentally, physically and psychically.

I went to bed. But not before opening the closet and checking it first. 'Dad?' I whispered. 'Are you in here?' I clutched the inch-long hunk of crystal around my neck and tugged at the slim gold chain. No point bothering to take it off tonight.

Besides, from what Mom said, these chunks of rock are guaranteed to keep evil spirits at bay. I had a feeling there was one or more hovering nearby, just waiting for the chance to jump me.

It's a Stretch

According to Mom, the Downward-Facing Dog (*adho mukha svanasana*) is a handstand, forward bend and inversion pose. She performs this pose as part of her sun salutation series but says you can also do it alone. Here are the steps she follows:

Standing with your feet about hip distance apart (on a yoga mat if you've got one) with your arms at your sides, spread your toes, making sure your balance is evenly distributed between both feet.

Now, keeping your back straight, lean slowly forward from the waist and plant your palms flat on the floor, fingers pointing ahead and spread apart. If necessary, bend your knees (I always do). Once steady, step each foot back until you are in the top part of a push-up. Your hands should be beneath your shoulders and your palms flat on the mat.

Slowly lift your hips toward the ceiling, sort of like turning your body into an inverted V. Slowly again, press your chest toward your knees, keeping your eyes on your toes, then press your heels toward the floor.

Take slow deep breaths and move deeper into the pose each time you exhale. If you are flexible enough, Mom says you might be able to touch the floor with your heels like she can. Mom can be quite the show-off.

TEN

It had been a long, fitful night. I'd tossed, turned
and awakened to find my legs twisted up in the
sheets. The coffee machine beckoned like a life
support system. With a poorly working air conditioner in the bedroom, I'd had no choice but to
keep the bedroom door open and pray a little
cool air came my way.

I took my coffee out on the patio. The cool
cement under my toes was a pleasant surprise. It
seemed the heat wave had finally ended. I pulled
in a breath of cool, dry air. My toes wiggled with
delight.

Now this was the weather Donna and Mom
had promised me. I flipped on the TV. Sure
enough, the weather girl was predicting a high
of eighty-two degrees and a low of sixty-four.
Perfect. Good going, weather girl!

And there was nothing on the news about Rick
Wilbur. No banner running across the bottom of
the screen letting the world know that he'd been
found in a carton in the back of Maggie's Beignet
Café. As much as I wanted and needed publicity,
banners like that I could do without. So far, I
was batting two for two.

I threw on a pair of lightweight LL Bean khaki
shorts and a saffron-colored empire-waisted cami
and rolled out the Schwinn.

I locked the front door and hopped on the

saddle. As I pushed off, I noticed that something didn't feel quite right. I looked down. Sure enough, I had a flat tire. The rear one.

That was going to be a pain, because that's where all the gear and sprocket doohickeys are located. My batting average had just gone down.

I threw the bike back in the apartment and traded my flip-flops for a pair of sturdy sneakers. Fortunately, Maggie's Beignet Café was a mere couple of blocks away. I'd take the bike to Laura's Lightly Used later or maybe try the bike shop on Main.

I draped my purse over my left shoulder and headed toward town. I hadn't gotten far when a white Prius slowed down alongside me.

'Need a lift or simply enjoying the weather?'

I turned. 'Oh, hi, Laura.' She stopped and I stepped off the curb and stuck my head in the open window. 'I'm enjoying the weather, all right. I'd rather be riding than walking though, but my rear tire's flat.'

'What a shame,' Laura replied. 'I can fix it for you, if you like.'

I nodded. 'I was thinking of bringing it by your store later. I have some errands to run first, though.'

'Heading to the café?' She motioned for me to open the car door. 'Come on, hop in. I'll drive you over.'

'Well, since you're offering,' I said, 'would you mind dropping me off at Mesa Verde instead?'

'The hospital? What for? Is everything all right?'

As I climbed in the Prius, I explained how my

fellow shopkeeper, Clive Rothschild, was still there for observation. 'I feel like it's all my fault.' I felt it my duty to go check on him. After that, I'd walk to the shop and see if Highsmith and his out-of-town goons were done with searching the place.

Laura agreed and within minutes I was standing outside Mesa Verde Medical Center. Before driving off, Laura said, 'If you like, I can pick up the bike, take it to the store and repair the tire for you.' She pointed a thumb toward the back. 'I've got a bike rack.'

'Wow, that would be great!' I had to admit, people around here might be a little flaky, but they sure were sweet, kind of like frosted flakes, when you thought about it. I explained how the bike was inside the apartment. 'There's a spare key under the dog dish on the patio, though.'

Her brow went up and I thought I saw a flash of concern. 'I didn't know you had a dog. What breed is it? I hope he doesn't bite.'

'I don't actually have a dog,' I answered. 'The dog dish was there when I moved in.' I never got around to throwing it out. 'It's a little icky, but it won't bite you.'

Laura laughed and putted away.

There was a new face at reception, which I found refreshing. I hadn't liked the looks that Halley woman had been shooting me with the day before. I wouldn't have minded seeing that nice Dr Vargas again, though. He was easy on the eyes. And the ears. This young man was locked in conversation with an equally young couple. The woman held a fuzzy-headed baby

92

who she bounced up and down in her arms, while the man with her seemed to be doing all the talking – for the moment, anyway.

This time, with the receptionist busy, I had no trouble getting permission to visit Clive. I didn't even have to ask. The man at reception looked my way; I waved and kept on walking. I tensed as I rounded the corner, waiting for him to bark at me. But since he didn't, I just kept on going.

Sometimes a little self-confidence is all it takes to get things to go your way.

Clive's door was open and I marched right in. But Clive was gone.

A doughy faced man with a thick, dark beard sat glaring out at me. It was the infamous man from behind the curtain. The curtains were now pulled to the sides, exposing the man in the mystery bed.

Clive's bed, on the other hand, had been stripped of its bedclothes.

I stood in the doorway. Heavens, he hadn't died, had he? 'Where's Clive?' I blurted.

'Gone.' The man had a basso voice and you could barely see his lips for all the hair surrounding them like a mangy Mongol horde of follicles. There was a matching tangle atop his skull. His broad nose was mottled red and his eyes were a muddy brown.

He snatched a black-rimmed pair of glasses from the bedside table and slipped them over his nose. 'You're the woman from yesterday. I recognize your voice.'

He seemed quite sure of himself so I supposed there was no sense in lying – though that had been my first instinct. 'Yes.' I stared at the empty bed. 'Do you know where they took him?'

'Doctor sent him home this morning. I wish I could be so lucky.'

I nodded. 'Don't worry,' I replied. 'I'm sure you'll be going home soon.'

'Doctor says I need to rest,' came the gruff reply. 'Are we done here?'

I bit my tongue. What a nasty old coot. Well, he wasn't exactly a centenarian but he was certainly in his fifties. I left without saying goodbye. I only hoped the nasty man didn't have a taste for beignets.

Back at Maggie's Beignet Café, I found Detective Highsmith and several men from the county busily conferring behind my counter. Once again, I was infuriated to discover a bag and several paper cups from my nearest competitor, Karma Koffee, cluttering my countertop. I was going to have to have a talk with those people across the street. I mean, let's respect each other's turf, for crying out loud.

'Must you?' I howled, grabbing everything up and tossing it in the trash bin near the cash register.

'Hey, what are you doing?' snapped an angry older gentleman in a navy suit. 'Who is this person?' he demanded of Detective Highsmith.

'I'm Maggie Miller,' I answered. I pulled myself up to my full height, dusting my hands together. 'I own this place. And I'd appreciate it if you wouldn't keep bringing in coffee and pastries from my competition!' I said, squaring off with Highsmith. I could feel my cheeks heating up.

'OK, OK,' Highsmith replied, putting his hands out. 'We're about done here, anyway.'

I flinched. 'You are?' My heart quickened. Could it really be true? Could I be getting back my store?

'For now,' he answered with some obvious reluctance. He studied his watch. 'We'll be out by early afternoon.'

'So, I can open for business then?' This wouldn't be so bad after all. One day lost. Not the end of the world.

'Suit yourself.'

I couldn't hide my relief. 'Tell you what, how about I make you men some coffee?'

'I don't know . . .' Highsmith hesitated.

'Oh, come on, Mark,' said the man who'd snapped at me. He stuck his hand in the trash bin and lifted a damp cup. 'I paid four bucks for that coffee and barely got a sip. I say let her make coffee.' He waved a hand at the equipment on the wall. 'We've got all we need from this stuff, anyway.'

Highsmith acceded and I set about brewing up a pot of fresh New Orleans-style coffee. Finally, I had some victims to practice on before the big day.

'So,' I said, making conversation as I pulled out a bag of whole coffee beans and poured them into the grinder, 'making any progress?' In my opinion, there's nothing on the market that compares to freshly ground beans. That's all I'd be using in my café.

'You mean on finding out how Rick Wilbur ended up dead in a carton in your backroom?'

'No,' I replied rather snottily, 'I was enquiring whether you'd gotten past second base with Veronica Vargas. You know, VV?'

The man in the navy suit laughed.

'Don't encourage her, Larry.' Highsmith shot daggers at me but I didn't mind. I'd rather he shot daggers at me than bullets out of that handgun that I could see poking from the shoulder holster under his jacket.

I grabbed the French press and measured out portions of coffee and chicory, using a mix of two parts coffee to one part chicory root. Chicory is grown and harvested similar to the sugar beet and is common in parts of France and Africa. I buy mine from a supplier in France.

I prefer the French press method of making coffee because, unlike regular automatic drip coffee makers, with a French press you can more easily regulate the water temperature that you want. The water in a French press is heated up separately then added to the grounds once you've reached the temperature you're looking for. You can also control how quickly or how slowly the water takes going through the grounds. Plus, because there is no filter, just a screen at the bottom, all those yummy oils in the coffee bean are extracted and end up in your cup where they belong.

I laid half-a-dozen mugs out and invited the men to help themselves to sugar and milk from the small built-in fridge under the counter. 'You can leave the cups on the counter when you're finished,' I said. 'I'll clean up when I get back.' No point standing around watching these guys sip my coffee and tear up my café. I had other beignets to fry.

Like finding out who else might have had a reason to want Rick Wilbur dead. So far, my only suspects were Johnny Wolfe and Clive. I'd hate to learn that Clive was guilty of anything other than having Johnny for a husband.

As for Johnny, I shook my head as I jogged up the street and crossed at the corner. As much as I'd like to find him guilty of something, I wasn't sure he had what it took to be a cold-blooded killer.

Now, if the police told me later that Mr Wilbur had been done in by a steel ice skate blade, I'd be changing my tune.

But for now, the tune remained the same.

So, who else around Table Rock had a motive for Rick Wilbur's death? So far, I didn't have a clue. I'd barely known the man. But Mom was right: if you want something done, you've got to do it yourself. I needed to learn as much as I could about Rick Wilbur, who he was, what he did, who he hung out with, who his friends were . . . and, most of all, who his enemies were. Because, despite what Detective Highsmith said, nobody was that likable to everybody. Rick Wilbur had rubbed somebody up the wrong way.

After all, somebody had taken a very strong disliking to the realtor. I just had to figure out who that someone was.

That meant another trip to Wilbur Realty on Main.

ELEVEN

It was quarter past nine and several workers sat at the half-dozen desks scattered throughout the large office space. Everything was neat and nicely done, not ostentatious like some real estate offices I'd seen. The decor had a decidedly Arizona flair with western art on the walls and what might have been a genuine Frederic Remington sculpture on a long table near the window depicting a bronco rider on a bucking horse.

If that bronze sculpture was an original, it could be worth some big bucks. Nearly two feet tall, it was an impressive piece and, with the morning sun hitting it the way it was, rider and horse practically sprang to life before my eyes.

It had been weeks since I'd been here. Nothing had changed, except that the lights were off in Rick Wilbur's office in the far right-hand corner. His was the only office with walls though he had a big plate glass window, through which I supposed he kept an eye on his employees.

My eyes settled on the nearest occupied desk. I remembered Moonflower from an earlier visit. She was a recent young associate of the firm. She'd handled the actual typing up of my lease with Wilbur Realty.

I smiled and sauntered over, laying my hands on the mahogany desktop. 'Hi, I'm Maggie Miller. Remember me?' I flashed white teeth and extended my hand. I noticed I'd left two sweaty palm prints on the mahogany surface. I hoped the woman seated behind the desk in a chair that looked built out of giant rubber bands hadn't.

She had. She opened a drawer to her left, slowly removed a roll of paper towels, ripped one from the roll and wiped off the desktop.

'Sorry about that.'

'No problem,' Moonflower replied, tossing the soiled paper towel quickly into a trash can beside the desk. 'Have a seat.' Her voice was as soft as gentle rain falling and her smile made me feel even worse than any rebuke would have. She pushed her long black ponytail over her right shoulder.

Moonflower Eagleheart was Hopi. I had always found her to be friendly and open. She'd told me previously that she'd grown up on the nearby Hopi Indian Reservation. Her dress, with its Hopi influences, spoke to how proudly she held and displayed her Native American heritage. Today's pleated purple skirt and beaded top were no exception. A turquoise necklace dangled from her bare neck.

I swiped my hands against my shorts and dropped into the proffered chair. It was made of rubber bands, like hers. Though I'd sat in these chairs here before, I still wasn't quite used to them. Sitting there, I felt like I was back in third grade. I didn't know whether to sit or play bounce house.

'How can I help you today, Miss Miller?' She folded her hands across the desk.

I noticed now that her eyes were rimmed in

red. Tears for Mr Wilbur? 'Actually,' I replied, 'I came to pay my respects.'

A half-smile passed Moonflower's face and she leaned back in her chair. 'I still can't believe it.' She shook her head.

'Me, too.'

'And I heard that you found the body.'

'Yes, but I want you to know I had nothing to do with Mr Wilbur's murder,' I added quickly.

Her smile set me at ease. 'Of course not.' She waved a hand through the air. 'You are a kind-spirited woman. You could never do such a thing.'

'Thank you,' I said, genuinely touched. 'But, tell me,' I said, glancing around the office – the two other men and one woman at their desks seemed to be paying us no attention – 'can you think of anyone who might have wanted to harm your boss?'

Moonflower leaned even further back and stared at the ceiling a moment. She pushed forward again and shook her head. 'Not really. I mean—' Her benign expression suddenly hardened and her eyes turned to steel.

I heard the door open behind me.

'Hey, Moonflower.'

I turned. A tall young man in jeans, a short-sleeved Western-style button-down shirt and bolo tie moved quickly toward us.

He towered over the desk. 'I came as soon as I heard.' He shook his head a little too much. 'Poor Uncle Rick.'

'What do you want, Tommy?'

'I came to help. With Unc gone—'

'With your uncle gone,' Moonflower said

sternly, 'we may all be looking for work soon. Like your uncle told you before, there is no job for you here, Tommy.'

His face clouded over. 'Listen, Moonflower. You're not the boss of me or this office.' He waved his arms through the air like windmill blades. 'We'll just see what Aunt Patti has to say about this.'

'Please go,' Moonflower said. All the others were openly watching the altercation.

Tommy looked down at her and then glanced down at me. The mole under his left eye twitched like a tick. 'I'm going,' he said. He pointed a finger at Moonflower. 'But I'll be back. You wait and see.'

With that, the young man stormed out the door, his cowboy boots thumping loudly as he went.

I raised a questioning eyebrow. 'What was that all about?'

Moonflower pulled a sour face. 'Mr Wilbur's nephew, Tommy, has been pestering him for a job.'

'And there were no openings?'

Moonflower's hands toyed with the yellow and green sun-faced coffee mug on her desk. 'I suppose Mr Wilbur could have made room for him.' She paused. 'If he had wanted to.'

'Which he didn't?'

'Tommy is a difficult boy.'

'So I noticed.' I punctuated my comment with a laugh. 'Who's Aunt Patti?'

'Mr Wilbur's widow.'

I hadn't realized the guy had been married. Was she a grieving widow or a celebrating one? I was going to have to look into that. 'Was what you told Tommy true? Could Rick Wilbur's death mean the end of Wilbur Realty?' If so, was there somebody around Table Rock that would benefit from that? A competing realtor, for instance?

'Everything is such a shambles,' sighed Moonflower. 'First, Ed ends up in the hospital. Now Mr Wilbur's sudden murder.'

'But surely his wife will keep the business up and running.'

Moonflower shook her head in the negative. 'Mrs Wilbur never had any interest in the business. She preferred her gardening and her birding. Mr Wilbur was the heart and soul of this place. Real estate was his life.'

And his death, I thought.

She set her mug down on the edge of the desk. 'Who knows? Perhaps she'll sell the business – find a buyer who will be keen to continue it as is.' She managed a smile. 'Maybe I'll be able to keep my job.'

'Is that really a possibility? I mean, that you could lose your job?'

She leaned forward conspiratorially. 'Business has been difficult lately.' Moonflower glanced left and right at her coworkers. 'The rumor around the office is that there's cash-flow trouble.'

I knew what that was like but was surprised to hear that a successful-appearing business like Wilbur Realty might be having financial problems. 'I'm sure everything will work out.' I patted her hand encouragingly. Who was I kidding? I wasn't sure of anything. 'Wait a minute.'

'Yes?'

'You said Ed was in the hospital?'

'Yes.' She looked puzzled. 'Why?'

'Ed? Edwin Teller?'

'Yes,' she answered again. 'Ed handles all those things such as repairs, maintenance and the like. He's a sort of jack-of-all-trades.' She tapped her upper lip. 'And with Ed out of commission . . . Do you know him?'

'I thought he looked familiar,' I mumbled. 'I ran into him at the hospital. He was sharing a room with my friend, Clive? That Ed?'

'Yes.'

'I almost didn't recognize him.' I'd seen him around once or twice but never been introduced. He'd let his beard grow out since the last time I'd seen him. It did not suit him. Besides, the dark beard clashed with his hospital pallor.

A tear came to the corner of Moonflower's eye. 'Poor Ed. He suffered a stroke, you know.'

'I didn't,' I admitted, 'at least not for sure. He was sharing a room with an acquaintance of mine. To tell you the truth, he seemed quite, how shall I put this, gruff?'

Moonflower laughed loudly. 'Ed's a sweetheart. I'm sure it's just the circumstances that have got him down. He was one of Rick's oldest and dearest friends. This whole thing has hit him pretty hard.'

'And he's had a stroke.'

Moonflower nodded. 'I've heard it said that irritability can be a consequence of heart attacks and strokes – any extreme, life-threatening illness, I suppose . . .'

I shifted in my chair. 'I guess I shouldn't be

103

so hard on the man.' If and when I saw the guy again, I promised myself I'd play nice. 'Is there a Mrs Teller?'

'No, he's a widower.'

'Children?' I asked, hopefully.

'One son.'

My spirits lifted. 'That's nice.'

'Died at childbirth.'

My spirits fell. Oh, great. So now I'd been thinking ill of a man who'd lost his wife, his only child and his best friend, *and* suffered a stroke, just to put icing on that cake of misery. I looked up at the ceiling. Thankfully, I didn't see any lightning bolts heading my way.

'So,' Moonflower said, 'you'll be opening Maggie's Beignet Café soon? I saw the ad in the *Table Rock Reader*.'

'Tomorrow,' I replied, rising from my chair. 'If all goes well.' Of course, all rarely did. The stars were not exactly aligning right for me these days, more like aligning me right behind the proverbial eight ball. 'Do you think it would be all right if I pay Mrs Wilbur my respects?'

'Of course.' Moonflower reached for a pen and wrote out Patti Wilbur's address on the back of a Wilbur Realty business card. 'I'm sure Mrs Wilbur will appreciate the gesture.'

I thanked her for it and left. I had a few questions for the widow.

TWELVE

The Wilbur house was located in the Historic Old Town and was one of those picture perfect, white picket fence places you only dream about. No *House Crashers* needed here. Today, most people lived in the small suburbs of Table Rock, in modern adobe-style ranch houses. The Wilburs obviously preferred the old ways. Maybe Rick just liked to be able to walk to work every morning.

I stopped at the gate, smelling the freshly mown lawn. Taking it all in, I could see that Moonflower's depiction of Patti Wilbur had been spot on. The yard was immaculate, from the lawn, to the flower beds, to the plants spilling out of tall pots on each side of the richly oiled wood of the front door.

Most folks around these parts stick to desert motif landscape. You know, some red rocks, some gravel and dirt, maybe a few strategically placed cacti.

But not the Wilburs. They had actual patches of green grass. Keeping up with the watering must cost a pretty penny.

There were a half-dozen or more bird feeders and two bird baths, one on each side of the path leading to the front porch. Two cardinals, one male, one female, pecked away at a clear acrylic tube filled with sunflower seeds, while a sparrow fluttered its wings in the deep end of one of the birdbaths. Maize yellow curtains fluttered from an upstairs window. A late-model Chrysler sedan sat in the drive.

Like I said, picture perfect – except that the man of the house was now residing in the morgue.

I stepped up onto the veranda and knocked. A dog barked somewhere in the distance and I suddenly felt very lonely. Listening to the soft sound of steps approaching, I frowned, looking down at my clothes. I wasn't exactly dressed to pay my respects to a grieving widow.

The front door opened quietly and a slim woman in a black frock looked out at me expectantly. Her brows knit together. 'Can I help you?' She had straw-blonde hair cut shoulder length and was deeply tanned, probably from all that time spent working in her yard. I estimated her age to be approximately that of her late husband's, somewhere in the early sixties.

A wirehaired fox terrier yipped from between her legs. The little guy, or gal, was mostly white with a patch of light brown atop the head and back. The short, twisted brown hairs reminded me of the stuff that grows on a coconut shell. I used to have a carved coconut shell with a monkey's face that Dad bought for me on a trip over to Myrtle Beach one summer. I wondered whatever happened to it . . .

'Quiet, Milky,' she said, though with more affection than conviction.

'My name is Maggie Miller,' I said. 'Your husband was my landlord.'

The name didn't seem to ring a bell or set off

106

any alarms, at least none that showed up as I watched for signs in her eyes. 'I own Maggie's Beignet Café on Laredo.'

Recognition came quickly. She pulled her chin up and her hand clutched the doorknob. Her eyes shot up and down the street. 'What are you doing here?' Her voice had turned hard. 'I know all about you. The police have been here, you know.'

Oh, great. Probably Detective Highsmith himself coming to spread or rather smear my name all across town. I could only imagine the unkind things he might have had to say about me. 'I wanted to tell you how sorry I am for your loss.'

A tall, white pickup that proudly labeled itself a four-by-four pulled up at the curb and stopped, honking once. A big guy in a tan cowboy hat jumped down from the cab. He looked rather uncomfortable in a charcoal suit, white shirt and black tie, which he tugged once or twice as if checking to see if it was still there. A small woman came around the other side.

He stomped up the front walk in polished black cowboy boots. The small woman in a simple elbow-length A-line black dress followed at his side, taking two steps to his every one. She balanced an aluminum foil-covered casserole dish in her hands.

He pushed out his chest. 'Good morning, Patti.' Dang, he was big. Did this guy keep a wine barrel behind all those buttons? He looked down at me. 'Everything OK here?' He removed his hat and held it against his chest.

107

I stepped away from the door. This guy was big as a brontosaurus. I did not want him accidently stepping on me. I'd be reduced to a smudge on the sidewalk.

'Yes,' answered Mrs Wilbur. She waved a hand in my direction. 'This is a client of Rick's. She came to express her sympathy.' She looked pointedly at me. 'She was just leaving.'

I held out my hand to the quiet Asian woman. Her brown hair fell to her waist. Those long locks had to be murder in this climate, not to mention the potential for neck and spinal injury due to the weight of all that hair trying to tip her over. 'I'm Maggie Miller. I'm so sorry.'

'Thank you,' the woman replied quietly. She passed the casserole dish to Patti Wilbur and lightly pressed my hand, then dropped it as she looked up at the giant beside her. 'This is my husband, Bill. I'm Suki.' She looked like she'd been crying, which was more than I could say for Mrs Wilbur.

'Family?'

'Bill is Patti's brother.'

Did that mean these were Tommy's parents? I certainly didn't see any family resemblance.

'That's enough,' growled Bill with a voice like gravel bouncing around in one of those cement mixer thingies. 'We're here to pay our respects.'

And chow down on what smelled like chicken and pasta casserole judging by the smells wafting my way. If I were either of these two ladies, I'd grab a plateful before Big Bill laid his meaty hands on that casserole and laid it to waste.

I was left standing on the veranda as Patti

moved aside and Bill and Suki entered. Bill closed the door behind them after giving me one last look that very clearly said, *What are you still doing here?*

I asked myself the same question and left. Time for a cup of joe.

I hoofed it over to Karma Koffee for my midmorning coffee fix. Not to mention I wanted to have a chat with these guys. Plus, I could keep an eye on my own place across the street, see if Highsmith and his henchmen were done rooting around so I could get back to business.

Karma Koffee was bustling so I got in line and waited. By the time my turn had come, I'd pretty much memorized every detail of the place. The store was a beauty, too. I'll bet they paid some hotshot interior designer to do the layout and decorating. Me, I'd taken over an empty deli, shoved a few things around, had new signage painted on the window and called it a day.

Karma Koffee had shiny glass cases filled with fat-inducing yummy-looking pastries, cookies and muffins. And whatever it was they were brewing up smelled fantastic. These guys were going to be tough competition. Suddenly I was wondering if I should have checked them out a little more closely before signing the lease on the place right across the street.

I'd been in such a hurry though, so eager to sign on the dotted line. And Mr Wilbur had told me several other parties were interested in the space. I'd had to act quickly. I'd agreed to the terms right then and there.

As I drooled over the offerings handwritten on

the chalkboard behind the young lady at the counter, I got the feeling I may have acted a bit impetuously.

'How can I help you this morning, ma'am?'

First off, she could stop calling me ma'am. I couldn't have been ten, well, OK, fifteen years older than the strawberry blonde behind the counter. She wore a fern-green logoed Karma Koffee polo shirt, matching visor and light brown khaki shorts. All the employees were dressed the same, the two out front and the three I caught a glimpse of in the back.

Karma Koffee had really pulled out all the stops when it came to branding. I counted shirts, visors, T-shirts, coffee mugs, travel mugs and coffee blends for sale. I even spotted *A History of Karma Koffee and the Koffee Experience* book for sale alongside some fancy-dancy fair trade chocolate bars.

More food for thought. Speaking of food, I figured it couldn't hurt to sample the competition. Plus, I was famished. I ordered a large coffee that had some exotic African name. I couldn't pronounce it; at least, I was afraid to try for fear of sounding silly, so I'd simply pointed to it on the menu board. I mean, how were customers supposed to pronounce something like Karma Irgachefe?

The barista smiled and called out the order. 'Will there be anything else?'

'What flavor are those muffins there?' I pointed toward a stack of something labeled Heaven's Building Blocks.

'Oooh, those are totally my favorite,' she

bubbled. 'Maple glaze, raisins, walnut and cinnamon in a pumpkin flour base.'

'I'll take one,' I said. I may have smacked my lips, too, as I watched the young woman remove a piece of wax paper from a small tissue box and use this to pick up my muffin.

'Will this be for here or to go?'

'Let's make it for here,' I answered. There was an empty table right at the window. I could scope out my café perfectly from there – after I spoke to whoever it was that owned this place, assuming they were even on the premises. It could be this young woman. Then again, it could be some multinational conglomerate or absentee owner. There was only one way to find out. I broke off a corner of the muffin and tasted. OMG. These guys were good. I wondered if they did the baking themselves or had these things made for them. Or were they actually shipped down daily from heaven?

'Actually,' I said, 'I was hoping to have a word with the owner.' I made a show of looking around as if I'd know them if I saw them, which, of course, I wouldn't. I arched an eyebrow. 'Is that you?'

'Oh, no,' the strawberry blonde answered quickly. 'You want Rob and Trish. They own Karma Koffee.' She gave me my total.

I winced as I paid the exorbitant sum the girl named. The inside of my wallet was looking rather thin. 'Are they around?' I lifted my Karma Koffee to my lips and took a tentative sip. Rats, this was great too!

She nodded. 'Let me check.' She asked some

guy named Lee to man the cash register and disappeared in the back.

I retreated to the table at the window with my late-morning snack and sat down. I could see a few of the boys in blue in my shop across the street and thought wistfully how this was supposed to be the big Maggie's Beignet Café grand opening celebration. Here I was, instead, sipping coffee and munching on a muffin at the café across the street – my 'sort of' competition.

I kept reminding myself, as I savored the brew and munched on my own little piece of heaven, that we weren't really in competition. I was selling New Orleans-style coffee and beignets. No competition at all.

This was a mantra I decided I'd better repeat over and over. After all, if you say it enough times, it has to be true. I'm pretty sure that's in the Constitution somewhere. I think Thomas Jefferson slipped it in.

'Hi, we're the Gregorys.' The thirtysomething man extended a strong brown hand. It was warm to the touch. 'I'm Rob. This is Trish, my wife.' His fingernails were clipped short and neat and looked twice as polished as my own. They were a handsome couple as far as competitors go, I had to admit grudgingly to myself. If they stood any closer to each other, they'd be conjoined twins. Talk about lovey-dovey.

Neither of them seemed to be carrying around any extra pounds and I wondered how they managed that feat with all the goodies around here. He had short, wavy brown hair with sun-bleached streaks at the temples that fell casually around his rectangular face. His hairline appeared to be receding, slowly though, not like it was the Bay of Fundy of hair or anything extreme like that.

Trish's hair was two shades darker than his and about shoulder length, though it was pushed back now behind her unadorned ears, held in place by her own Karma Koffee visor. A few light freckles dusted the bridge of her nose. Like the girl behind the counter, the Gregorys sported green Karma Koffee polo shirts and khakis as well.

They both displayed healthy, glowing tans and looked like they spent a lot of time outdoors. Red Rock Country is a hotspot for nature-loving outdoor types, and they were apparently no exception. Owning a coffee and pastry shop didn't seem to keep them stuck indoors all that much.

Some come to Table Rock for the weather, some for the natural beauty, others for the aliens. Some for all three, I imagine. I pictured perky couples in matching, tight-fitting nylon bike shorts, pedaling through the red rock wonders surrounding Table Rock in blissful search of alien vortices and the great Mother Ship.

Please, somebody beam me up.

Trish looked to be about my age, with light wrinkles at the corners of her eyes. She stretched her arms over her head with a cat-like grace. The edge of her shirt rose and I caught the flash of a silver navel ring. In my opinion, nobody over the age of thirty-five ought to be sporting one of those. Then again, I'm not all that comfortable flashing my belly button, period.

'Peace,' said Trish, flashing a waist-high peace sign. She wore purple fingernail polish with tiny, intricate sunflowers painted on the centers of her thumbnails. I smelled patchouli. She probably kept a drawer full of love beads in her dresser at home.

Oh, brother.

'Thank you for coming to Karma Koffee.' Rob inhaled deeply. 'I see you're trying the Karma Irgachefe. Good choice.'

I smothered a frown. Of course, *he* could pronounce it, it was his coffee. Still, everybody hates a show-off, me included.

He laid his hands across the arched back of the empty chair across from mine and glanced toward the register where the line was now four deep. 'Aubrey tells us you wanted to have a word?'

Some of those customers might have been mine if I'd been able to open today as advertised. It was just my luck that all that advertising I'd paid so dearly for prior to opening might have had an unintended consequence – bringing people to Karma Koffee when they had come up Laredo Street for my grand opening only to be turned away by the police. Not a pleasant thought. I smothered that, too.

I took another sip of my coffee. Not bad, slightly acidic but full-bodied, with earthy and spicy undertones. Next time, I'd try the Karma Kameleon. *That* I could pronounce. Wait a minute. What was I saying? There would be no next time! 'Yes, I'm Maggie Miller.' I pointed, paper cup in hand. 'I own Maggie's Beignet Café across the street.'

Dark clouds passed over both their faces. I had a feeling they weren't all that happy about my moving into the neighborhood. 'Great coffee, by the way,' I said, holding my cup out toward them. I watched their faces. A reddish-brown crumb spilled from my chin to the table. 'And muffins!'

Nothing. Except for some weird look that passed between them. What? Were they plotting which of them was going to hold me down and which was going to slit my throat? I cleared my throat. 'You did hear what happened, I suppose?'

Now Rob smiled. Sure, nothing like a guy in a box to break the ice, get the smiles started.

'You mean about the police finding Rick Wilbur's dead body in your walk-in cooler?' He pushed a hand through his hair and seemed to bristle.

Trish tugged her husband's sleeve. 'Now, Rob . . .'

'What?' he said by way of reply. 'The man was a jerk – a thief and a liar!'

'It wasn't my walk-in cooler,' I replied, suddenly getting a little hot under the collar. 'He was in a box in my storeroom.' I wasn't sure why that fact and that setting this clown straight was important to me but suddenly it was. 'And the police didn't find him, *I* did. Then I called the police. Well, after I called Information, that is.'

'Now, now, Rob,' replied Trish. 'We must maintain our inner chi.' She centered a fist in front of her chest.

He scowled, nodded and took a breath.

'Yeah, you don't want to knock your chakras out of alignment.' I had no idea what I was saying but it sounded good at the time. Besides, even if I didn't know what I meant, I was betting that Rob did.

Trish said, 'Remember what you tell your students.'

'Students?' I inquired, my mouth filled with pumpkin muffin. Dang, this thing was good. I couldn't keep it away from my lips. Had somebody implanted some sort of pumpkin spice magnet in my lips while I slept? If so, it sure beat Botox.

Maybe Trish and Rob would be willing to trade recipes sometime. I had some great beignet recipes they might like. If not, there was always Donna's veggie haggis recipe I could swap them for.

'In addition to owning this shop, Rob teaches yoga part-time. We have a classroom upstairs.'

'Oh, yeah? Yoga, huh?' I snatched a bit of muffin crumb off my lip using the tip of my tongue. 'Hey, you should talk to my mom, Miriam Malarkey, sometime. I'll bet the two of you have a lot in common. She teaches yoga, too.'

There, I'd said it. My factory original surname was Malarkey. I'd considered going back to my maiden name after the divorce, but for obvious reasons stuck with Miller. Not that I was thrilled that there was a newer, younger Mrs Miller running around down there in Phoenix. But it seemed to beat the alternative.

The name Malarkey is Irish, I'm told. I'd taken enough ribbing as a kid not to want to go back down that path. 'Margaret Malarkey full of malarkey, walks like a turkey.' Ugh, I could hear

116

the singsong taunts of the boys in my elementary school running around in my skull even now – them and Gillian Goodeve.

She'd been a real thorn in my side all through my school years and such a tomboy. She'd chided me almost as much as the boys had. I'd heard she'd joined the army after high school and I pictured her as a master sergeant hounding and ridiculing new recruits, year after year; bringing them to their knees in agony and humility. Yeah, she'd be perfect at that.

And can I help it if I had a funny walk when I was a kid? I blame it on Mom always buying whatever shoe was the cheapest rather than what fit best. That often meant living with a pair of shoes two sizes too small or three sizes too big. I'm a grown woman now. I buy my own shoes. OK, I still walk a little funny. If I can't blame my mother, I'll blame it on shoe manufacturers everywhere. Why can't they build a decent pair of flats for under fifty bucks?

'What kind of yoga does your mother teach?' Rob asked.

Huh? I squished up my face. 'The bendy kind?' I said, pushing my elbow out like a chicken.

Rick rolled his eyes. Either he was trying to make some sort of point or it was one of his yoga moves. '*Vinyasa, ashtanga, kali ray tri?*'

I was dumbfounded. What was this? Some secret language he and Trish shared? Was he speaking in tongues? 'I beg your pardon?'

Trish ran a hand along her husband's arm. 'If you'll excuse me, I'd better lend Aubrey and Lee a hand.' Trish left to help out with the customers

117

who continued to pile up at the counter, leaving a patchouli, coffee and pastry cloud in her wake.

I rubbed my nose. 'So, I'm guessing you and Rick Wilbur weren't golf buddies.'

Rob's face betrayed confusion.

Sheesh, how dense was this guy? 'I mean, I get the feeling the two of you weren't friends.'

'No, we weren't friends. He was my landlord.' Rob Gregory crossed his arms over his chest. 'And a lousy one at that.'

'Well, I don't know about that. I wasn't acquainted with Mr Wilbur long, but he always seemed very nice to me.'

Rob smiled wickedly. 'That's because he was trying to get you to sign a new lease. That was his job. He knew how to turn on the charm then. Oh, he was a great salesman. But after . . .' He let his words fall away.

'After what?'

Rick hesitated, then started speaking in a sudden flurry of words and emotion. 'After he gets you to sign a long-term lease, he gets real hard to find. In the beginning, it's if there's anything you need, just call Wilbur Realty. If something breaks, call Wilbur Realty. If you've got a problem—'

'Call Wilbur Realty,' I finished. Got a dead body in a box in your storeroom? Don't call Wilbur Realty.

Rob nodded. 'Yeah, but when he's got your money and you want the man, he's never anywhere to be found. Nothing gets fixed, nothing gets cleaned like he says and then, even though you've signed a lease promising you exclusivity,

promising that he won't lease one of his properties within two blocks of yours selling the same
product, he goes and rents the store directly across
the road,' he pointed angrily, 'to you.'

His eyes flashed. 'Speaking of which, I see two
policemen heading this way. Either they'd like a
decent cup of coffee, or,' he said, scorching me
with those dark gray eyes, 'they're looking for
you.' Now he pointed even more angrily at me.

I turned and bit my lip. Rob wasn't kidding.
Two of Table Rock's finest were heading right
for me. They saw me looking at them and stopped
in the middle of the street. Didn't they know how
dangerous that could be? One of them beckoned
me with his finger. It didn't look like they were
on the prowl for a couple of cups of Karma
Koffee. That was both good news and bad.

I balled up the waxed paper and remnants of
my muffin, squished it into my coffee cup and
dropped the whole lot into the Karma Koffee-
branded trash receptacle near the door. A feeling
of dread shot from my toes to my eyes.

Suddenly, Heaven's Building Block wasn't
sitting so well in my stomach. What had I done?
I felt a line of sweat gather above my lip. Not
an easy thing to accomplish in this dry heat.

'Have a nice day!' Rob shouted as I pushed
out the door. Rather derisively, too, I thought,
given the circumstances. I mean, we were neighbors, after all.

THIRTEEN

'I hear you and Rick Wilbur had an argument a couple of days ago.' Detective Highsmith had his butt parked on one of my tabletops. Did he have any idea what a health inspector would have to say about that?

My eyes narrowed. 'Who told you that?'

'That's not important.'

It was important to me. I asked again but he refused to answer. Probably refused to share his ball on the playground as a kid, too.

My hands bunched up. It had to be that butinski next door, on the other side of my little café. The Hitching Post sat on one side of me and Salon de Belleza occupied the space on the other. I remembered now how the woman who ran the hair salon had slowed as she walked past my shop the other night when I'd been having words with Rick Wilbur. The whole episode had sort of slipped my mind, what with all the craziness going on. Who knows? Maybe I'd been trying to block the episode for this very reason – that it might make me look guilty in the eyes of the law.

'All right,' I said finally. 'You might call it arguing,' I conceded, 'but we weren't,' I said with unbridled annoyance. 'We were having a heated discussion about air conditioning. Get it?' I said, wigging my eyebrow. 'Heated?'

Highsmith's chiseled jaw worked side to side.

We were alone in the café. The place looked a bit filthier than it had before this whole mess had started but nothing that a dozen hours of elbow grease couldn't rectify. 'Look,' I said as I went to the sink and soaked a rag in water, 'Mr Wilbur had told me that this store had air conditioning.'

I began wiping down the steel prep tables. I scratched my neck with my free hand. 'At least, I think he did. Anyway,' I sprinkled some Bon Ami and went back to scrubbing, 'when the heat shot up and I tried to get it running, pffft!'

I waved the rag in the air. 'Nothing. No air. No nothing.' I was beginning to wonder if there wasn't some truth to what Rob Gregory had said about Rick Wilbur's character, *modus operandi* and the way he was letting his properties fall into disrepair.

'So you demanded that Mr Wilbur show up and, when he did, you lured him into your storeroom—'

'What? That's absurd, I—'

Highsmith zeroed in on me. 'At some point, he turned his back and you clobbered him with your rolling pin.'

I slitted my eyes at him. If he wasn't an officer of the law, and twice as big as me, and carrying a weapon, I'd do some clobbering all right. I took a chi-centering breath before speaking. 'I called him on his cell phone and explained the situation. He came by and we discussed it like rational adults.'

Highsmith snorted and slid off the table.

'What's so funny?'

The detective shook his head. 'Nothing.'

I looked at him darkly.

'So the two of you had words.' He grabbed his jacket from the coat tree near the door and pulled that notebook of his from his coat pocket. 'Then what?'

'He promised me a fan.'

Detective Highsmith was silent a minute. 'When was the last time you saw Rick Wilbur?'

'Come on,' I said, throwing the towel over my shoulder and pressing my hands against the counter. 'I've told you all this before.'

He came toward me and it was all I could do to hold my ground, his pencil tapping against the notebook. 'No. For instance, you never told me about your argument with him.'

I took a step back. So much for self-control. 'I-I forgot,' I stammered. 'I've got a lot on my mind. Besides, I didn't think it was important. I didn't kill the man!'

'So you say.'

'Goodbye, Detective!'

I turned and got busy emptying the French press. I had to do something with my hands to stop myself from running after the man and strangling him. I carefully poured the damp grounds into a plastic container and shut the lid. I'd promised Donna all my used coffee grounds. She said coffee grounds make great fertilizer. Maybe I should wrap a container of grounds up with some ribbon and a bow and present it to Mrs Wilbur as a small gesture of condolence. She'd probably love it. I hit the spigot and rinsed the glass in the sink.

Suddenly Detective Highsmith was standing next to me. 'Are you still here?' I snapped. 'I thought you told me I could have my store back?' Dang, those M&M eyes of his were looking sweet. Too bad he was such a sour, obnoxious twit.

He grinned at me. 'Good luck with the grand opening tomorrow.'

My mouth fell open. I'm pretty sure it was still open as I watched him exit.

'If you keep your mouth open like that, you'll attract flies.'

'Huh?' I spun around. 'Laura!'

'It's something my mother used to say when I was little. "Laura, if you keep your slack jaw hanging open like that, you're going to attract flies."'

I laughed. 'I'll try to remember that. Flies are definitely not on my diet. Where did you come from, anyway? Were you here this whole time?' The whole time Table Rock's lone detective was accusing me of murder.

She shook her head. 'No, I just got here. The backdoor was open. I came in that way.'

I cocked my head in puzzlement. That explained how but not why.

She pointed a thumb over her left shoulder. 'Remember?'

'Umm . . .'

'Your bike?'

Memories fluttered back. I might be dense but with a good machete the thicket wasn't impassable. 'Oh, right!'

'I brought the Schwinn back. Flat's all fixed. I brought it in through the rear. The door was unlocked.'

'Thanks. Wait, the door was unlocked?' I shook my head. 'Darn those police. Don't they know better than to leave an unlocked door like that? Anybody could get in.' I held out my hands. 'No offense.'

Laura laughed. 'None taken.'

'Can I make you a cup of coffee? It's on the house.'

She shook her head. 'Sorry, I'd love to but I can't stay. I've left the store with only one new clerk on the floor. That's a recipe for disaster. I've really got to get back.'

'I understand.' I grabbed my purse and pulled out my wallet, looking for a credit card with some room to spare. 'How much do I owe you?'

'Forget it,' she said. 'I'll take it out in trade.'

I laid my wallet atop my purse. 'What did you have in mind?'

She tapped the center of her lips with her index finger and said with a grin, 'How about a cup of coffee and a plate of beignets after you open?'

I grinned back. 'How about a to-go box of coffee and a bag full of beignets?'

Laura made a show of giving my counteroffer some consideration. 'Sold!' she said finally. 'You drive a hard bargain, Maggie Miller.' She held out her hand and we shook.

'Nobody messes with Maggie Miller,' I replied. Well, somebody was messing with me and messing with me good. But I'd catch up to them sooner or later.

I walked Laura out and was about to lock the front door to keep out the strays and any potential lookie-loos who might want to see where the dead body had been found when the strawberry blonde from across the way skipped across the street in my direction.

'Sorry,' I said quickly. 'We're not open yet. And there's nothing here to see.' I grabbed the bar that ran the length of the door and pulled it toward me.

'I'm not here to buy anything.'

'Come to gawk at the scene of the crime, then?' Or had Rob and Trish sent her to spy on me? Maybe the girl was upset because I hadn't left a tip in the Karma Koffee-branded tip jar. But the price of that whatchamacallit coffee and muffin had been outrageous. Who could afford a tip after that?

She shook her body. 'Ewww, no. Don't remind me.'

I stirred the air with my free hand, waiting to see what the girl was up to.

'I wanted to ask you for a job.' She looked at me with hopeful jade-green eyes. My own green eyes suddenly seemed so drab. I wish my eyes were that shade of green.

'Wait,' I said, still clutching the door handle. 'You're Aubrey from Karma Koffee, aren't you?' Was I delusional? Hallucinating? Was this Aubrey's doppelgänger?

She nodded sheepishly. 'Aubrey Ingridson.'

I squinted at her with not a little bit of suspicion. 'And you want to work here?' I really hadn't given a whole lot of thought to hiring. Donna had mentioned that a couple of her part-timers might be willing to put some hours in if I needed.

'Yes,' she said shyly.

'Why?' I'd already thought of several reasons, none of them good, and all involving the Gregorys trying to sabotage my fledgling business. I angled my eyes across the street toward Karma Koffee. I couldn't be sure because of the glare from the glass, but that might have been Trish staring at me from the window. 'Come on in.' I held the door open and locked it behind us.

'So,' I said, returning behind the counter so I could face out and keep an eye on the goings-on at Karma Koffee. If those two were trying to set me up, I wanted to see it coming.

Aubrey faced me across the counter. She shrugged, shifted the strap of her brown leather purse from one shoulder to the other, then glanced back across the street toward Karma Koffee, too. 'To be totally honest with you,' she began in a conspiratorial tone that was totally uncalled for seeing as we were alone in the café, 'I really don't enjoy my position there. To be totally, totally honest . . .' Bright red nails tapped the countertop. 'Rob and Trish creep me out.'

I couldn't help smiling. 'Do you know anything about beignets?'

'Well . . .' She moved her tongue around the inside of her cheek. 'To be totally, totally honest again . . .'

I tilted my head. So far, this young lady was making me totally, totally crazy. 'Yes?'

'I didn't even know how to pronounce the word until you just said it.' A red glow lit her cheeks

126

and flared across her nose. 'I'd only seen the sign on your window.'

I beamed. I totally, totally liked this girl. 'Don't worry,' I replied. 'Lots of people have that trouble. It's "ben-yeah" as in "yeah, we're having beignets!"' I waved both hands in the air and we both laughed.

'Listen, don't sweat it. I hadn't been able to pronounce that weird coffee you sold me at Karma Koffee, ummy-gummy-yer-the-cheffy—' My tongue and my brain twisted up in a knot.

'Irgachefe?' she said. She pushed a strand of hair behind her ear. She must have left her Karma Koffee-branded visor back in the shop.

'That's it!' I said, slapping my hands down on the countertop, rattling the cups and saucers I'd laid out there. I stuck out my hand. 'You're hired!'

The truth was I really couldn't afford to hire the girl. Heck, I couldn't afford to hire anyone. I couldn't even afford me. But I totally, totally couldn't afford not to stick it to Rob and Trish.

I welcomed Aubrey aboard with a hug. 'When can you start?'

'How about now?'

'Don't you need to give Rob and Trish notice?' Not that I cared all that much. It would take the two of us working till midnight to get this place in shape for tomorrow's opening.

'I already did.' She smiled and snatched the towel off my shoulder. 'Where are the cleaning supplies?'

'In the back.' I hesitated before going into the storeroom. The police had removed Wilbur's body, hadn't they? Highsmith had told me they had. And any other ickiness, I hoped. My stomach churned. I took a tentative step in.

'Everything OK?' Aubrey said. She was so close behind me that I could feel her breath on the back of my neck.

'Oh, yeah. Sure, everything's fine.' The overhead lights were on and the door leading to the alley was closed. I rushed over and locked it. I don't know why, but I was suddenly feeling really creeped out.

Turning back to Aubrey, I said, 'I'll tell you what. Instead of cleaning, how about unboxing the chairs and setting them out up front?'

Aubrey smiled and shot me a quick salute. 'Sure, boss.' Her eyes danced around the back counter. She spotted the box cutter and went to work.

I couldn't help smiling. This might work out after all. The thought of opening up any more of those boxes of chairs totally, totally freaked me out. What if there was another body inside another box?

I didn't know what I'd do. But I was pretty sure where I'd end up. In the hospital, alongside Clive and Ed.

I watched Aubrey work for a minute or two. Thankfully, all she removed from the first two boxes were chairs. She pulled each pair out and neatly stacked them near the doorway.

'Sure you don't mind working for a murderer?' I said, half-joking.

She looked up from her chore. 'It beats working for Rob and Trish.' She hesitated then added, 'They're so weird.'

That I could believe. I pulled a ten-pound bag of flour from a pallet and headed toward the front.

'Besides, I wouldn't be surprised to learn that Mr Gregory himself murdered Rick Wilbur.'

I held the sack of flour against my chest. 'Yeah, I got the impression they weren't exactly besties.'

'Definitely not,' Aubrey said, 'but it's more than that.'

'What do you mean?' I hollered as I carried the flour to the workstation then returned for more.

'The Gregorys were always arguing with the landlord. I saw Rob arguing with Mr Wilbur just the other day.' Aubrey started breaking down the first two boxes with the razor blade.

'You did?' My jaw fell open, then I remembered what Laura had said about flies and quickly closed it again. I laid a hand on her arm to stop her. 'Where? When exactly?'

'Right here.' She folded the box up and set it near the door. 'I could see them from behind the counter at Karma Koffee. I was working the late afternoon-evening shift.'

I nodded. I'd been out doing some last-minute shopping for supplies at that time.

'Are you sure it was them?'

Aubrey nodded. 'The lights were on and everything. I could see them as clear as day.'

A frisson of excitement sent goosebumps up my arms. I held onto her. This could be my salvation. Put Rob Gregory away for murder, clear my good name and, if I was lucky, put Karma Koffee out of business all in one fell swoop!

'But why here? Why not at Karma Koffee?'

Aubrey shrugged. 'I don't know. All I know is that Mr Gregory saw Mr Wilbur over here at your place, cursed, threw down his apron and marched over.'

So, Rob Gregory just might have been the last person to see Rick Wilbur alive . . . Because after that he'd killed him! 'What happened after that?'

Aubrey shrugged once more. Sheesh, this girl was exasperating. 'I don't know. Things got busy. I had customers. A little while later, Mr Gregory returned.'

'Was he behaving normally?'

Aubrey chuckled. 'Describe normal.'

I nodded. She had a point. Nothing about Rob Gregory spelled n-o-r-m-a-l.

'He was quiet for a while and I could still see he was totally, totally upset. Trish came and they went upstairs.'

'Think,' I said, grabbing Aubrey's arms above the wrists. 'This is important now.' I locked her eyes with my own. 'Did you see Rick Wilbur after that?'

Aubrey bit her lower lip and closed her eyes a moment. 'No, no, I don't think I did.' She shook her head. 'But I really wasn't looking, you know?'

I knew. It really didn't mean anything. It certainly wasn't proof that Rob Gregory had bashed Rick across the back of his skull and stuffed him in a box.

But it was a start.

'Did you tell this to the police?' My voice quivered.

She twisted her lips. 'Should I?'

'Yes!' I said quickly. I grabbed her shoulders.

130

'The sooner the better.' I snatched the box cutter from the girl's hand. 'In fact, you should go right now.' I gave her a push. 'Do you have a car?'

She nodded.

'Great. Go down to the police station. Ask for Detective Highsmith.' Suck on this, Detective Highsmith.

She scanned the storeroom. 'There's still so much to do, though. I have all these chairs left to unbox.'

'The chairs can wait,' I said. 'This is much more important.'

'Well, if you really think so?'

'I do. Trust me. Look,' I said, 'you go, take care of making your statement to the police now and come back to work tomorrow morning. Would six a.m. be too early for you? There's a lot to do.'

She shook her head. 'No, I'll be here. And thanks.'

'Thank you!' I gushed. As Aubrey headed for the door, I yelled out, 'And please wear some other shirt instead of that Karma Koffee polo tomorrow!'

She tugged at the logo on her shirt and chuckled. 'Don't worry,' she replied, waving, 'I will.' She stopped in the doorway. 'Hey, we should totally get us some uniforms.'

'Not a bad idea,' I replied. 'See you tomorrow.' Speaking of uniforms, I wondered how Rob Gregory would look in a bright orange prison jumpsuit. I'd even heard of a sheriff down in Maricopa County who forced the prisoners there to wear pink jumpsuits.

I smiled as I carried a couple of chairs out to the front and placed them around one of the tables. Rob Gregory was not going to look good in pink. He had the wrong skin tone for that.

Life had taken a turn for the better. I turned and faced the storeroom. Maybe I could even handle the thought of opening the rest of those boxes . . .

I stood there for a minute or two. Still, no rush. Aubrey seemed to have the chair-box opening under control. Plus, I'd already told her she could do it. I didn't want the girl getting an inferiority complex by coming in tomorrow and finding that I'd finished the job for her. She might think I didn't think she was capable of setting up something as simple as chairs.

Besides, there were plenty of other chores to do around here before we'd be ready to open in the morning.

That's when I saw the rolling pin.

Tips on Buying a Basic Rolling Pin

The two most common types of rolling pins are the traditional and the French. The traditional rolling pin has handles on each end and provides more leverage when rolling out dough.

French rolling pins are generally much longer, up to approximately twenty inches, compared to a standard ten- or twelve-inch traditional roller. French rollers come in three general shapes: tapered from the middle, tapered only at the ends, and straight. The French pins are mostly made of wood and are easy to clean.

Traditional rolling pins are also commonly made of wood, like birch or maple, with or without handles. They are fairly inexpensive and durable. Be sure to thoroughly coat the roller with flour before use to prevent the dough from sticking.

Marble rolling pins, like my beech wood-handled beauty, are heavier than wood and will, by their very nature, help prevent the dough from sticking. With the extra weight, they can also make it easier to roll out the dough. You can also chill them before use.

There are also other types of rollers made from glass, stainless steel or even nylon and nonstick silicone. Metal and glass rollers can also be chilled before use. Some even have cavities that you can fill with water to keep them cold for longer.

Some things to consider when buying an all-around rolling pin might be:

Weight: A heavier rolling pin can make it easier to work the dough, especially when rolling thin sheets.

Length of the barrel: A standard barrel length for wooden rolling pins is twelve inches, and marble is ten inches. Like I said, French rolling pins are normally twenty inches long. These are perfect for making large sheets of pasta dough.

Diameter of the barrel: Traditional rolling pins average around two to four inches in diameter. French rollers generally average around one to three inches at their widest points. The thicker barrel, the less likely that your hands and finger-nails will accidently gouge the dough while you are rolling. Of course, with the thinner French rolling pin, you are closer to the dough and some say it gives a better feel. I say it's a matter of personal preference.

Comfort: A pair of contoured handles might feel more comfortable to you and be easier to grip. Again, it's a question of personal preference. Pick up a few rolling pins and see how the handles feel in your hands, whether the weight feels comfortable as well as you lift and maneuver it. Which do you prefer?

Ease of cleaning: Not all rolling pins are dishwasher-safe. Avoid soaking rolling pins, especially those that are all wood or have wood grips, excessively. Contact with water can cause wooden rolling pins to warp or even crack.

Wipe your wooden roller with a clean damp cloth and allow to air dry. Some rolling pins made of nylon/silicone may be dishwasher-safe.

Lastly, always store your rolling pin safely out of the hands of potential killers. That's a lesson I learned the hard way.

FOURTEEN

It looked exactly like the murder weapon. That is to say, my rolling pin. It was resting in the center of the small island in the middle of the storeroom. The stainless-steel island top served as prep space. Below were drawer and shelf space for the sundry things I needed to run this place. There was also a deep stainless-steel sink in the middle of the island.

I studied the rolling pin carefully.

From a distance. No way I was going anywhere near that thing. Still, there was no blood, and no guts that I could see. That was a good sign.

And it was a beautiful thing, really. Hand-finished gray and white Carrera marble. As smooth and shiny as ice on a frozen winter's lake and just as cold to the touch, with hand-carved beech wooden handles, too. Yep, beautiful. If you didn't stop to think how it could be used to bash someone's brains in with.

What was it doing here? It couldn't be mine. The police had confiscated it. It was surely locked up in an evidence locker somewhere waiting to be pulled out as evidence in my impending murder trial.

My eyes fell on a small square of paper beneath the roller, near the center. I bit down on my lower lip and edged closer, just close enough to reach out and extract the paper. The rolling pin rolled a quarter-turn as I looked at the words that someone had scrawled in pen: *Maggie, this is for you. Take care.*

I shivered and a short scream escaped my lips. Was this a warning? Was somebody threatening to bash my head in next?

What had I done? What should I do?

I thrust the square of paper in my pocket. I was definitely showing this to the police.

Suddenly, being alone in the empty beignet café didn't seem like such a good idea. I grabbed the Schwinn, left the rolling pin where it was and walked the bike out the front door. I'd get some fresh air and come back later. Maybe I'd been a bit too hasty asking Aubrey to leave.

I banged tires with the postman in said haste. 'Oops! Sorry!' I cried. Our front spokes had somehow gotten entangled and I yanked on my handlebars to unstick them.

'Whoa! Hold on there, missy.' The postman scurried off his bike, a simple red cruiser, and reached down between our wheels. In a thrice, we were clear of each other.

'Sorry,' I said again. 'Guess I wasn't watching where I was going.' The postman that delivered in this area was a wiry rooster of a man with jet-black hair from what I could see of it under his red bike helmet. As he pulled his dark sunglasses down his nose, I saw that his eyes were medium brown. I put him as a child of the fifties or early sixties.

All that bike riding seemed to be keeping him in tiptop shape. From a distance, he could easily have passed for forty. Only the hard-etched lines

137

around his face showed his age and demonstrated the power of the sun on skin that looked tough as shoe leather.

He brushed his hands. 'No biggie. You can't imagine how many times I've been bumped, banged, jostled and just plain knocked on my keister by people not quite looking where they are going during my years on the job.' He was smiling, so I figured he meant his words.

'That's very forgiving of you,' I replied. 'And resilient.' After all, he seemed to have all his parts in working order, both human and bicycle. I looked over the front wheel. Nothing appeared to be broken, bent or out of place, thank goodness. I didn't want to haul it over to Laura again so soon. What would she think?

I leapt back on my bike and started to push off. 'Well, I'm glad you're OK.'

'Hold on,' he said. 'Don't you want your mail?'

'Can you throw it through the slot? I'm sort of in a hurry.'

He pulled a water bottle attached to a clip on his bike frame and took a deep swig, then slowly wiped his lips with the back of his bare arm and returned the bottle to the metal holder. 'No can do.' He fished around in his sack. 'One of them is special delivery.'

I planted my feet on either side of the bike. 'Special delivery?'

He nodded and handed me a letter-sized white envelope with all kinds of official-looking papers stuck to it. 'Yep. Requires your signature.' He plucked a well-worn pen from his shirt pocket and handed it to me.

I turned the envelope over and over in my hand. The return address indicated the letter was from Wilbur Realty. 'What on earth could they want?'

'I don't know,' said the postal carrier. He held out his hand and wiggled his fingers, indicating that he wanted his pen back. 'Here's a couple more for you as well.' He handed me two more envelopes and three catalogs, all from food and restaurant supply concerns.

'Thanks.' As he pedaled off, I glanced at the remaining envelopes – nothing important, just bills – and shoved them and the catalogs through the front door mail slot. I stood on the street and ripped off the edge of the letter from Wilbur Realty, my curiosity piqued. Maybe Rick Wilbur had had a premonition about his murder and had written me a letter identifying his future killer. He'd sent me this registered letter because he wanted to be sure that someone got the truth got out and his true killer was caught.

I tapped the side of the envelope until the folded letter inside spilled out. I unfolded the linen paper and read the formally typed letter.

It was all very lawyer, real estate-type language, which is to say my brain fogged over and I didn't really understand a word of it or where the letter was leading until I got to the part that said the check I had written for one month's rent and the security deposit had bounced.

The letter fell from my fingers. How could this happen? I looked down at the paper fluttering lightly in the minimal breeze that scooted along the sidewalk, then stabbed my toe down on it before it got pulled into the street by a passing station wagon's wake. The sign suction cupped to the rear window of the vehicle said *Caution, I Brake for Aliens.*

What was going on? How could my check bounce? What did they mean insufficient funds? Why hadn't somebody told me earlier? I'd just been to their offices – why hadn't Moonflower or somebody else at Wilbur Realty brought it up with me in person? Why hadn't the bank contacted me?

I pulled my cell phone from the pocket of my khakis and checked the time. The good news was that there was still time to get to the real estate office before they closed.

The bad news was they'd given me an ultimatum: pay up in twenty-four hours or they'd padlock my doors and shut me down.

FIFTEEN

'What's the meaning of this?' I waved the official letter wildly in the air. 'Why didn't somebody tell me?'

Three realtors gazed at me with interest. A tall cowboy one row over and two desks back slowly rose from his chair. 'I'm Jasper Parvik. Can I help you?'

'Yes,' I said, rushing toward him, waving the letter like a battle flag. 'I want to know why I'm suddenly getting this letter in the mail telling me that my check's bounced.'

He took the letter from my hand and motioned for me to sit. I sat, but it was all I could do to sit still. I twiddled my thumbs while he read it. I could tell he was reading, too, because his lips moved as he passed over each word. Slow as molasses poured on a marble slab in the Arctic, but they moved.

He pushed back his brown horn-rimmed reading glasses and looked down his hawk's nose at me. A ring of inch-long peppery hair circled his pate. There was a small bony bump in the middle of his skull just above where I expect his hair used to be. The protrusion reminded me of a hawk's promontory made to match the hawk's nose.

'It seems very clear,' he said slowly, fixing me with his gaze.

'No.' I shook my head adamantly. 'It's not clear. I mean, it's clear that somebody here has made a mistake. But my check did not bounce.' I folded my arms tightly across my chest. 'I promise you that.' I looked around the office. 'Where's Moonflower? She might know what's going on.'

He shot a look at her empty desk. 'Miss Eagleheart? In the back. Let me fetch her.' He rose slowly and, after seeming to struggle with his sense of direction for a moment, disappeared around a wall near Rick Wilbur's office.

A sudden question came to mind – just who was in charge of Wilbur Realty now with Rick Wilbur gone? His wife, Patti? According to Moonflower, his wife had wanted nothing to do with the place.

Except I now noticed a light was on in Mr Wilbur's office. I rose and circled around to get a look through the plate glass window and grabbed a paper cup of water from the cooler near the restrooms. Angling my eyes to the left, I saw that the light was coming from a Tiffany desk lamp on Mr Wilbur's desk. At the desk sat Patti Wilbur, her nose buried in some document atop the open manila folder facing her.

She seemed oblivious to my presence. Was the reading that interesting? She was definitely one step up the evolutionary ladder from Jasper Parvik – her lips weren't moving at all.

'Miss Miller?'

I swung around. 'Oh, hello, Moonflower.'

'Jasper showed me the letter.' She glanced toward Mrs Wilbur. Was that a disapproving look

I saw? 'Come,' she said, gently guiding me by the shoulder. 'Have a seat at my desk and let's talk about this.'

I followed Moonflower and sat in my familiar rubber-band chair. Her hair was loose now and hung in wavy folds. I leaned forward on the edge of my seat. She held the letter in her hand and I watched her eyes flutter up and down the page. 'Why didn't you tell me about this earlier?' I asked. 'We could have talked about it. I mean, it's obviously a mistake. But someone should have told me. Heck, why didn't Mr Wilbur himself tell me the other day?'

She shook her head slightly and set the paper down on the desktop. Moonflower looked at me curiously when I said I'd seen her boss recently. 'He probably was as unaware of this as I was.'

'How is that possible?'

She shrugged. 'I'm a realty assistant. I don't handle things like billing and collections.' She pushed the letter toward me. 'Or legal issues such as these.' The phone on her desk rang and she pressed a button sending it to voicemail.

'I do know that the amount of paperwork around here is quite staggering. You'd be amazed, Maggie. We're always behind with the paper-work. I know you submitted the check some time ago but it may have only recently been deposited. Or it could be that this fell through the cracks, so to speak. I'm not sure anybody here knows everything that's going on.'

'But it's Wilbur Realty,' I said, snatching a card from the carved wood business card holder on her desk and pointing to the name Wilbur Realty embossed in bold red letters. 'Surely Mr Wilbur does.' Did.

Moonflower smiled wanly. 'I'm afraid not. Selling was his forte. And the big picture.' She spread her hands wide. 'No.' She leaned back in her chair and steepled her fingers. 'This sounds like Natalie's doing.'

I edged even closer to the end of my chair. Any second now I'd be landing on the hardwood floor. 'Who's Natalie?'

'Natalie is in charge of bookkeeping.' She held the letter up toward me and moved her finger to the signature line. Mr Wilbur's name had been electronically typed. Below this were a couple of initials.

'NH,' Moonflower said. 'Natalie Henson. Natalie's a little . . .' she paused, '. . . headstrong. Likes to scare folks – not that I approve. I'm not sure Mr Wilbur did either. But she's harmless really.'

'Harmless?' I screeched. I'd almost had a heart attack when I read this letter. Not to mention she'd threatened to have the café padlocked!

I leaned back and blew out a breath.

'Natalie handles all our bookkeeping and banking. She is – was – Mr Wilbur's sister-in-law.'

'Oh, I see.' Did that mean she was related to that big bruiser I'd crossed paths with outside Patti's house? 'Has she got a brother?'

Moonflower nodded.

'Big guy?' I said, holding a hand over my head. 'Drives a big white four-by-four?'

144

'That's right, Bill. You know him?'

'I met Bill and his wife, Suki, earlier today when I stopped by to pay my respects. So, Tommy is their boy?'

Moonflower shook her head. 'No, Natalie's youngest.'

That explained the lack of family resemblance. I glanced meaningfully toward Mr Wilbur's office in the corner. 'I see Mrs Wilbur has decided to take some interest in her husband's business after all.'

Moonflower's lips formed a straight line as her gaze followed mine. 'Yes, it would appear so.'

'She's not wasting much time, is she?'

'That really isn't something I can comment on. You understand. I wish there was some way I could help you, but I do not have that power.' Moonflower pushed the letter closer to me.

I took it. 'I understand. So how can I talk to this Natalie? I'd really like to get this straightened out. I can't afford any more problems or delays.'

'I'm sure. Unfortunately,' Moonflower rose, 'Natalie is in Reno visiting her oldest son and his family. I believe she'll be back in a couple of days.'

'I can't wait a couple of days,' I replied. 'That could kill me and my business.'

'Why don't you go to the bank?' suggested Moonflower. 'It's just next door. Perhaps they can get this cleared up.'

I beamed. 'That's a wonderful idea. I should have thought of that.' I rose too. 'That's just what I'm going to do.' They'd clear this mess up and I could get back to more important matters, like getting Maggie's Beignet Café up and running.

I thanked Moonflower for her time and headed for the door. I saw Patti Wilbur eyeing me from behind her husband's desk. I waved a hello. She returned my gesture with an icy glare.

Sheesh, try to be nice to some people. Maybe she'd heard about the bounced check – *mistakenly* bounced check – and had gotten the wrong impression about me. Well, I was about to get that little matter cleared up. Maggie Miller not only gets things done, she pays her bills.

Half out the door, I turned back. 'Yes?' Moonflower asked.

I explained how my air conditioner was on the fritz and how Rick Wilbur had promised me a fan in the meantime. Moonflower came toward me. 'I'm very sorry,' she said, laying a hand on my arm. 'I'll see what I can do, but with Ed in the hospital . . .' She shrugged. 'I'll see what I can do for you.'

'Hey, I understand.' I could hardly complain about a guy not doing his job when he was laid up in the hospital. 'You do the best you can.' I waved the letter in the space between us. 'And I'll get this whole insufficient funds thing cleared up! My check's good. You'll see.'

'I'm sure I will,' said Moonflower.

I hurried up the sidewalk to the bank and pulled on the door. The door rattled and held. I pulled harder. Nothing. I took a step back and looked at the sign staring me in the face. CLOSED.

I peered through the window. I could see a couple of folks in the back. I banged on the glass and pressed the letter against it. They threw up their hands as if to say they were sorry.

Yeah, they were sorry. Today was Friday and I could see by the sign that the bank was closed on weekends. That meant I'd have to wait until Monday to get this whole mess with the check straightened out. I couldn't afford to wait until Monday – from the tone of Wilbur Realty's letter my café could be padlocked before then! Too bad Rick Wilbur was dead – he really had seemed to like me. I could try pleading my case with his widow, but I got the feeling she wasn't my biggest fan.

A loud car horn began hooting maniacally and I turned, fearing I was about to be run over by an out-of-control truck or maybe a stagecoach and a team of horses.

But it was only Mom in her metallic green Beetle. She waved with her left hand. Her right hand was still pressing down on the klaxon.

She'd had the Beetle a good ten years. This was the last car she and Dad had bought together. I knew she'd never part with it for that reason alone. She'd had a pair of eyelashes placed over the headlights but, other than that, it looked the same as it had when it had rolled off the show-room floor. The only thing that's changed on it is that since moving to Table Rock she added an *Aliens Onboard* bumper sticker. I guess she wanted to fit in.

'Mom!' I screamed. 'Stop blowing the horn!'

'What?' she screamed back. 'I can't hear you!'

I cursed and ran to the open window. I lifted

her hand from the horn and shook my head, hoping to make the ugly ringing stop. I stuck a pinkie in my ear like a dipstick checking for blood, because I was pretty sure my eardrums had been burst.

'Mom,' I said, 'what do you want? I'm kind of in the middle of something.' I waved the letter in her face, not that she knew what it contained.

'You've got to get to the café. Get in, Maggie!' She motioned to the passenger-side door.

'I've got my bike, Mom,' I pointed to my Schwinn, settled on its kickstand outside the realty. 'I can't just leave it here on the street.'

'Then meet me there,' she hollered, throwing the car in gear and lifting her foot from the brake. 'And make it quick!'

Holy cow! What on earth was going on? Mom was acting crazier than usual and it somehow involved my business! Had the place burned to the ground?

I stuffed the letter in my front pocket, grabbed my bike and hopped on, my knees shaking, my brain running a thousand miles per hour while I pedaled away at about five miles per hour in a mad rush to face my next crisis.

Though I was beginning to wonder, as I pedaled hard and fast, already nearly out of breath, why I was bothering to pedal so fast.

Did I want to know what was going on? Could I really handle another crisis?

Wouldn't it simply make more sense to turn around, pedal my bike off into the horizon and maybe go someplace where I could start over starting over? Someplace more simple, more remote? Someplace without aliens and mothers and dead bodies in boxes? Could the Schwinn make it to Alaska?

Could I?

Did Alaskans like beignets?

SIXTEEN

'What the devil is going on?' I leapt from the Schwinn and leaned it against the mailbox beside the streetlamp post that sat between my café and The Hitching Post. Mom, Donna and Andy stood huddled outside my door.

'We're here to help you get ready, dum-dum,' quipped Donna. 'What do you think?' She was in a ratty old pair of jeans and a baggy green scoop-neck T-shirt. She jiggled the door handle. 'So unlock the door already.'

'Yeah, check out the sign.' Andy pointed at the café window. A professional-looking paper banner announcing Grand Opening Tomorrow in foot-tall red and blue letters was draped along the top from side to side.

My mouth fell open and, flies or no flies, I was leaving it open this time. I leaned over, placing my hands on my knees and sucking in breath. I bent my neck upwards and looked at Mom.

'You mean to tell me,' I huffed, 'I raced all the way over here,' I huffed a couple more times, then straightened, 'just because you wanted me to come unlock the door?' A drop of sweat landed in my left eye and I blinked hard.

Mom nodded.

I huffed. 'So you could—'

'Help you clean up,' finished Andy.

150

Mom smiled and nodded. 'Yes. Help you get ready.'

I steadied myself. My legs felt rubbery. That's the fastest I'd biked in ages, if ever. I pulled Mom into my arms. 'Thanks, Mom.' I laid a kiss on her cheek.

Mom beamed. 'You're welcome, dear.' She held a small tray filled with cleaning supplies and brushes. 'Now, open up. We've got so much to do if you want to be ready to open tomorrow.'

I fished the café keys from my purse. Sometimes family wasn't so bad, after all. 'Where are the boys?'

'Baseball practice,' answered Donna. 'A friend's parents picked them up and are bringing them home.'

'I'm gonna grab the banner and rehang it on the inside glass so nothing happens to it overnight,' Andy said. 'We just wanted to surprise you first.'

'Good idea.' And boy did they surprise me. I flipped on the lights.

'And tomorrow,' Donna added, 'all you've got to do is cut off the word "tomorrow" and attach this.' She showed me a roll of paper she'd been clutching in her hand.

I pulled off the rubber band and unfurled the roll. More red and blue letters. 'Today!' I read. I smiled. 'Thanks, guys.'

'No problem,' Donna said. 'Now, tell us what to do.'

'Yes, where would you like us to start?' asked Mom.

I tapped a finger against my chin. 'Andy, how

about if you finish up unboxing all the chairs and get them set up out front? Aubrey started on it but had to go.' I'd been saving them for Aubrey, but couldn't pass up the offer of all this free help. Besides, there'd be plenty more for Aubrey and me to do tomorrow morning.

'Aubrey?' said Donna, her brows pinched together. 'Who's Aubrey?'

'I hired her today,' I said, my voice carrying a bit of pride. 'She's my first employee.'

'Good for you, Maggie.' Mom squeezed my shoulder.

'Yeah, good for you, Mag,' Andy said. 'I'll get busy on those chairs.'

'Once you break down the boxes, can you take them out back to the dumpster?'

'No problem,' he called, passing through the swinging shutter doors.

'How about me?' Donna asked, pushing back her hair and pulling it all into a lavender scrunchie.

'How about making sure all the supplies out here are filled and ready to go? You know, dry goods like paper cups, plates, napkins. And things like flour, sugar, coffee.'

Donna got to it.

'I guess that leaves me on cleanup patrol,' Mom said. She hoisted her little blue tray of cleaning supplies. 'Good thing I came prepared. I think I'll start out back and work my way to the front.'

'Sounds like a plan,' I replied. While Mom and the others got busy with their assigned chores, I checked out all the equipment. I still had time to practice my beignet-making skills. 'I'll whip us up a batch of beignets!' I called.

'Don't bother on our account,' replied Donna as she swept in with a pack of paper napkins. She'd locked the swinging louver doors to the storeroom in the open position for easier access back and forth.

'No bother at all,' I quipped. 'I could use the practice. You guys will make great guinea pigs!'

Andy stuck his head out, box cutter in hand. 'You *can* bother on my account,' he said. 'You know I've got a weakness for sweets.' He patted his stomach. 'Besides, I'm starved.'

'You got it.' I aimed my big wooden spoon at him.

Andy stood in the doorway looking like he wanted to say something more.

'What is it?'

Andy's eyes flew to his wife. Weird signals that only married couples could master passed like lightning between them. Mom disappeared. Donna flew in her wake.

'I repeat: what is it, Andy?' I struggled to keep my voice even. My nerves steady.

'Nothing, really. I mean, it's just a little thing. Standard procedure.' He rested a hand on the edge of my shoulder. 'I don't want you getting upset about this, Maggie.'

I quaked. 'Geez, Andy, you're already upsetting me. So spit it out!'

He took a deep breath and looked me in the eye. 'The Table Rock police got a warrant to search your apartment—'

'What?'

Andy held both my shoulders now like he was afraid I'd go ballistic and bust right through the ceiling. Truth be told, I probably would have. 'Relax, Maggie. Like I said, it's normal police procedure.'

'I won't let them do it. You're a lawyer – can't you stop them?'

He bit his lip. 'I'm afraid not. Besides, they're at the apartment right now.' He twisted his watch around and studied its face. 'They should be about done, assuming they don't find anything.'

'Of course they won't find anything!' I screamed. 'Why would they find anything?'

'Relax, relax,' said Andy, pulling at my hands. 'I didn't mean it like that.' He pulled me to a chair and urged me to sit. 'Listen, Maggie, as your attorney I would never let any legal harm come to you.' He forced me to look in his eyes. 'And as your brother-in-law, I've got your back. So let's all relax. Focus on the future.'

The way my heart was racing and my head was steaming I was beginning to think there'd be no future for me. I felt my mother's hands massaging my neck and shut my eyes. 'You OK, honey?'

I nodded. Focus on the future. That was precisely what I needed to be doing. Let the police look – they wouldn't find anything. Well, I wasn't the world's neatest housekeeper and I did have a pair or two of undies that I wasn't too proud of, but nothing that was going to link me to the murder of Rick Wilbur.

I forced a smile and stood. 'Fine, let them look. If they want to waste their time, let them.'

'That's the spirit,' Donna said.

'Besides, if they clean up when they're done, they'll be doing me a favor.' I clapped my hands.

'OK, back to work, everybody. We've got a business to run.'

I turned the fryer up to three hundred and seventy degrees, then warmed up a bowl of water to get the yeast going. Next, I started pouring ingredients into the mixer on the front counter: shortening, sugar, salt. One day, if business got good, I was going to buy one of those big Hobart floor mixers – those things hold a ton. They cost a fortune, too, but I figured once the volume of business grew sufficiently I could pick up a pre-owned one for a reasonable price. In fact, I had been drooling over several available reconditioned units I'd spotted at an online restaurant supply site.

I attached the bread hook and began mixing – all the while imagining a shrunken-down copy of Table Rock's lone detective scurrying madly around in circles inside the bowl, one step away from being creamed.

Next, I poured the warm water over the shortening mixture. I grabbed the evaporated milk and added that, then pulled a couple of eggs from the carton in the undercounter fridge and beat them. I stirred everything together, adding the additional water and yeast, till the consistency was just right.

'Hey, Mom!' I shouted. 'Can you bring me the wooden rolling pin?' Since my marble one was now evidence and I hadn't had time to shop for a new one, I'd have to go with my old standby – the old wood roller I'd had since my married days. 'I think it's in the drawer next to the sink!'

While I waited for Mom, I grabbed the dough

cutter. It's an adjustable five-wheel stainless steel pastry cutter and dough divider that I used to slice the dough a uniform size. I'd been hoping to buy a countertop model, but again, too pricey for the time being.

The salesman had shown me this stainless-steel puppy. It looked more like an instrument of torture that any Spanish Inquisitor would have been proud to own, but it worked great and cost me less than twenty bucks.

'Here you go, dear!' Mom held out the marble rolling pin. The one I'd discovered on my back counter with the note beneath it.

'Not that one!' I shouted.

Mom jumped and the rolling pin fell from her hand. I snatched it before it hit the floor.

'Why?' gasped Mom. 'What's wrong with it?' She ran her eyes up and down its length.

'This could be evidence,' I clucked. I held it in front of me, my hands no doubt smearing a possible killer's possible fingerprints.

Her brow creased. 'Evidence of what? I washed it. It's perfectly clean.'

'What's all the commotion?' Andy stuck his head out.

Donna's head stuck out from beneath his arm. 'Yeah, what is it, Sis?'

I groaned. 'The killer might have left finger-prints on this.' I stared at the marble roller. Was it my imagination or was the thing mocking me? 'I was going to take it to the police tomorrow and ask them to check it.' All three of them were looking at me like I was crazy.

'You do know that the police have got the

rolling pin that probably killed Mr Wilbur under lock and key at the police station, don't you?' Andy gave me a funny look.

I placed the rolling pin on the counter. 'Yes, I know that.' I dumped the dough out of the mixer and onto the prep counter and wiped my hands on my shorts. 'I found this rolling pin, the *very twin* of my own killer rolling pin, I might add, on my back counter this afternoon,' I pointed toward the storeroom.

I tossed some extra flour down on the counter and slapped the ball of dough down on top. 'With a note warning me that I could be next.'

'Oh, dear!' cried Mom.

'Oh, no!' wept Donna.

'Oh, brother,' said Andy, shaking his head. His eyes narrowed. 'Why would anybody be threatening you, Maggie?' He oozed skepticism like a maple oozes sap in February, slowly but surely.

I shrugged one shoulder and beat down on the ball of dough with my fist. 'Beats me.' I turned to face my brother-in-law. 'Why would Rick Wilbur's killer leave his body in my storeroom?'

'You really need to be careful,' said my mother. 'Maybe you'd better stay with me tonight. I'll make up the guest room.'

'That's not necessary, Mom.' I repressed a shiver.

She sidled up beside me. 'Maybe the police will offer you police protection.'

I twisted my lips in a lopsided grin. 'I doubt that, Mom. Table Rock's only got one detective on the whole force. I doubt they have the manpower for around-the-clock protection.' And I sure didn't want Highsmith watching over me twenty-four-seven. He got on my nerves enough already. What would be left of my sanity if he shadowed me day and night?

'Mom's right,' Donna said. 'I hadn't thought about it before, but you could be next. The killer could be after you.' Her face froze and her hands came to her cheeks. 'Oh, Maggie!' she said with horror in her voice. 'I just realized – the killer might have been after you in the first place!'

Mom took up the tale. 'You're right. The killer came looking for Maggie. Poor Mr Wilbur might have seen them from the street, came inside to confront them and—' She slammed her hands together, her attempt at mimicking the sound of rolling pin hitting bone, no doubt.

Gee, Mom, thanks for the horrid sound effects.

'What? Why?' I snatched the marble rolling pin and began rolling out the dough to a consistent quarter-inch thickness. Hey, she'd already scrubbed it clean. I figured I might as well get some use out of it before whoever this killer was turned around and used it on me. Besides, I needed to busy myself; Mom and Sis were beginning to freak me out.

It was my sister's turn to shrug. 'Who knows? Crazed serial killer?'

'In Table Rock?' I said rather skeptically. I mean, I got the crazy part but not the serial killer part.

'Your ex-husband, Brian?' She raised a meaningful eyebrow.

I shooed the idea away with a wave of my

158

hand. 'He's down in Phoenix.' I set the rolling pin down heavily. 'Besides, why would Brian want to kill me? He's got a new wife, new family, new dog.' Big as Mom's Volkswagen, too.

It couldn't be for money. I wasn't collecting any alimony. I had refused it. Apparently I could still go to court and Brian would have to shell out, but I'd rather starve first. Besides, Brian and I had an understanding. And unless I'd misread the small print, that agreement did not include murdering one another.

Andy stepped forward. 'Can I see this note?'

I reached into my pocket and handed the wad of paper over. It hadn't started out a wad but it sure was one now. Apparently paper jammed in pockets doesn't travel all that well. Perhaps I should have preserved the evidence between a couple of stiff pieces of cardboard and sealed it in a plastic baggie, like something the police might do.

Andy studied it carefully. 'I don't know,' he said finally.

'Don't know what?' I asked.

'That this is a threat.' He handed me back the paper.

'What does it say?' asked Donna.

Andy replied, 'It says "Maggie, this is for you. Take care."'

'That doesn't sound good,' said Mom.

'Do you recognize the handwriting?' my sister asked.

I shook my head no.

'How do you know Laura didn't leave you this note?' said Andy. 'You said she was here.'

I hadn't considered that. 'Why would she leave me a note? I was right here. If she was bringing me a rolling pin she could have handed it to me in person.'

'Maggie's got a point,' agreed Donna. 'I think you should show the note and the rolling pin to the police. Don't you, Andy?'

He nodded.

'That's right,' said my mother. 'Let them sort this out. Maggie, forget what I told you earlier about finding this killer.' Mom waved a finger at me. 'Let the police do their job and figure out who killed poor Mr Wilbur and why. You,' she said, gripping my arm, 'stick to making your beignets.'

'You could stay with us tonight,' offered Andy. 'You could bunk in Connor or Hunter's room. The boys won't mind sharing.'

I agreed to show the note and rolling pin to the Table Rock PD and to ask Laura about them as well. I did not agree to camping out at my sister's or Mom's. Andy had received a call earlier that the police had finished searching my home and that was where I was going.

'I can take care of myself. Don't worry, I'll make sure the doors and windows are locked up tight.' I also wanted to be sure the Table Rock PD hadn't trashed the apartment or made off with my flat-screen TV. Twelve more payments and that baby was all mine.

'Sounds like a plan,' said Andy. He patted his stomach. 'So, when are we going to see some of these famous beignets of yours?'

While Andy finished unpacking the chairs, I fried up a batch of beignets and Donna and Mom set some plates and cups at one of the tables in front of the window. Though Maggie's Beignet Café wasn't quite open for business yet, it wouldn't hurt for passers-by to see a few satisfied customers sitting in the window munching my product. I could use the word-of-mouth. Soon the small café was filled with the sweet scent of fried dough.

I grabbed a couple of bottles of iced tea for Mom and me. Donna and Andy stuck to water. They claimed my store-bought tea contained artificial sweeteners and flavorings. I told them that the water they were drinking had probably once been dinosaur sweat. We agreed to a truce.

While we ate, I explained my latest dilemma to my family. In between bites, Andy read the letter I'd received from Wilbur Realty. 'Wow,' he said. One hand stroked his ponytail. 'I wish we could help, Maggie.' He looked at his wife. 'But we don't have three thousand dollars right now.'

Donna shook her head in agreement. 'Sorry,' she said softly, placing her hand over mine.

Mom sighed. I knew she'd help if she could, but she and my sister and brother-in-law had already loaned me plenty to help me get this café started. I knew they were tapped out. Mom was on a tight budget. She received a small pension from my father and earned just enough to pay for the essentials like food and gas running her yoga classes.

'Hey,' I said, forcing a smile, 'don't sweat it. I'm not. Monday morning I'll go to the bank first thing.' I polished off my third powdered

161

sugar-coated beignet. 'I'll get this whole mess cleared up.'

I gave my tea a shake, twisted off the cap and took a swig. 'Speaking of the police, have there been any developments in the case yet, Andy? Any new suspects?' As my lawyer, and having a friend inside the police department, my brother-in-law should know what's going on.

'Nothing yet,' he said. 'Don't worry. If I hear anything at all you'll be the first to know it. I plan to go down to the department tomorrow and have a word with the officer in charge. I'd like a full report of the search. I still don't know if they took anything.'

'I'd appreciate that,' I replied. Personally, I hoped they took that hideous cactus green lamp with the brown striped shade in the living room. 'Say,' I tilted back in my chair, 'what do you know about Veronica Vargas? Anything?'

His right brow shot up. 'The mayor's daughter? Enough to know that you want to keep on her good side.' He leaned toward me. 'Why?'

I shrugged. 'She was here earlier, that's all. I barely said a word to her.' Or she to me.

Andy nodded. 'Good, keep it that way. Remember,' he said, aiming a calloused finger at me, 'like it or not, you are a suspect in a murder investigation. As your attorney, I advise you, *strongly* advise you, not to say a word to anyone without me present. In fact, I'd better come with you when you turn over that note and rolling pin.'

Andy was talking but I wasn't listening. I gripped the sides of my chair as I leaned on the back two legs, my brand-new out-of-the-box chair. It looked good too. Real wood veneer, with a cherry finish. But there was something about chairs . . .

Something tickled just out of reach in my brain. What was it about chairs? I thought madly. Then it came to me and I slammed back down to earth, the front two legs banging the floor and vibrating our table.

Donna gaped at me. 'Are you OK, Sis?'

Mom shook her head. 'I'd say we call it a night. You look exhausted, Maggie. It's been a long day.' She wiped her lips with her napkin and dropped it atop her empty plate. 'A long couple of days.'

'Maggie?' Donna said, an edge to her voice.

'The chairs!' I blurted.

'What about the chairs, dear?' Mom asked.

I lifted a finger and counted all the chairs out front. 'Thirty!'

I counted again. Still thirty.

'Andy,' I said, my heart racing while my brain shifted through the gears. 'You unboxed all the chairs, right?'

'Yeah,' he answered, drawing the word out. 'Then I broke down all the boxes and left them in the recycle dumpster.'

I raced to the storeroom and looked everywhere, even the mop closet and walk-in fridge. 'So where are the chairs?' I scratched my scalp.

Mom, Donna and Andy had followed me into the storeroom. 'What chairs?' asked Donna.

'That's what I'm saying,' I said. 'Where are the chairs?'

They eyed one another nervously – looking at me like they anticipated a cozy white jacket in my near future – one I couldn't possibly escape from.

I took a deep, calming breath. 'Don't you see? There ought to be two more chairs.' I held up two fingers of my right hand. 'I ordered thirty-two chairs. They came in sixteen boxes. Rick Wilbur was inside one of the boxes. So,' I said, folding my arms across my chest, 'what happened to the two chairs?'

A Short History of the Beignet

Though associated mostly today with the French Quarter of New Orleans, Louisiana, the history of beignets extends back many hundreds of years. The Roman *scriblita*, moist dough leavened with sourdough and spooned into hot animal fat, was an early precursor to the modern New Orleans-style beignet. The Spanish later produced a similar pastry, the *bunelo*, balls of deep-fried *choux* paste (*choux* is a French word for a light, air pastry dough and is pronounced 'shoo').

French settlers brought the beignet with them as they migrated to North America, first to Canada, then later, to the continental States and, in particular, Louisiana. Many Acadians chose to settle in the Louisiana region when the British forced the French out of their settlements in Acadia, a region along the eastern coast of Canada, in the seventeenth century.

The Acadians brought their traditions, culture and cuisine with them. Their descendants eventually came to be known as Cajuns (a word derived from Acadians). And it's here that the beignet reached its culmination, becoming something of a tourist attraction in its own right.

As for the word, beignet, there are as many theories as to the origin of the word as there are theories as to the origin of the myriad mysterious vortexes that surround the Red Rock Country in which Table Rock sits. Some say the word beignet can be traced to the word 'bigne,' an early Celtic word meaning 'to raise.' Others say the Middle French term 'bignet,' which means a savory or sweet pastry surrounding meat or fruit, is the source. Other plausible sources include the Middle French words 'buyne' and 'beigne' which mean 'bruise' or 'bump' respectively and I can see how these, especially bump, could be used to describe the perfect beignet shape.

Call it what you want, I call it pastry perfection. And if you want a bite and are anywhere near Table Rock, come to Maggie's Beignet Café – Grand Opening tomorrow!

SEVENTEEN

Everybody began talking at once. Even the normally calm and laid-back Andy darted around the café, recounting all the chairs, verifying my simple math, then looking high and low for the two missing chairs.

We searched all around, even out back in the alley between the café and the stores on either side, but came up empty. Soon our excitement turned to disappointment and dejection.

'You need to mention the chairs to the police.' Donna was adamant.

'Good idea,' chimed in Mom.

I wasn't sure I agreed. Those two missing chairs might lead me to a killer. Because the police seemed intent on pinning the murder on me, they'd probably find a way to use my lead against me. It just might be best if I kept my thoughts to myself. If I found my missing chairs, I might find Rick Wilbur's killer.

'They may already know,' Andy suggested. 'Maybe that's what they were hoping to find at your apartment.'

A chill ran up my arms. If the police found those chairs in my apartment, things would sure look bad for me. But they wouldn't. They couldn't.

I promised my brother-in-law I'd fill the police in on my suspicions concerning the chairs – I didn't promise when.

It was late and we were clearly exhausted. The mystery of the missing chairs was a mystery best left for another day. Mom insisted on following me home as I pedaled my bike back to my apartment. She even insisted on coming inside with me while I made sure the coast was clear.

We checked behind the sofa, under the bed and in all the closets. And yes, Dad's ghost still wasn't hiding there. She even stuck around while I threw on my PJs and got ready for bed.

The place was a shambles, but I knew better than to blame the police search for that. And there didn't appear to be anything missing. The TV was still there, and the remote.

Mom then insisted on straightening the place up a bit. I would've complained but she was a mother and I just figure there's something in the mom gene that makes women do this.

Who knows? Maybe if or when I become a mother, my mom gene might kick in too. But not tonight. Tonight all I wanted was sleep. And plenty of it.

I fell asleep listening to the sounds of Mom puttering around in the kitchen. Thankfully, she hadn't decided to vacuum. Even more thankfully, I didn't own a vacuum.

I rose somewhat refreshed and dressed for business. My first day of business! My excitement was palpable. I was finally opening my very own business. My first business. My first day at my first business.

I'd already planned out what I'd wear – light

tan khaki slacks and a moss-green V-necked pull-over shirt with white sneakers. I'd be standing on my feet for who knew how many hours and I wanted to look professional yet feel comfortable at the same time. And any collateral damage, as in powdered white sugar cascading onto my feet, would blend in nicely with the white canvas sneaks.

I pushed open the closet door to fish out my intended outfit and my eyes fell on the big zippered garment bag shoved against the wall.

My brow shot up like a hand holding a winning card at bingo. Dare I? This could be the answer to all my prayers. Tentatively, I reached for the thick hanger, then pulled away. It felt wrong and it felt right.

I wasn't sure I should really do this. I wasn't sure I *could* really do this.

There was only one way to find out. I removed the bag from the back of the rack and dropped it atop the bed. That's when I noticed the pile of clean clothes on the seat beside the dresser. The chair was an extra chair from the kitchen table. I rarely needed all four so had brought this one into the bedroom.

I shook my head. Apparently, Mom had decided to run a load of laundry as well. At least I'd managed to sleep through the job. Something in the foot-high pile caught my eye, though. I reached into the stack of neatly folded tops, shorts, socks and undies and pulled out the shorts I'd been wearing yesterday.

Filled with dread, I flapped them apart in the air and reached a hand into the right-hand pocket.

I came up with a dried clump of paper. Just yesterday it had been potential evidence in a murder investigation, possible proof that someone was out to get me or at least scare me. Now it was a crumpled mess. Oh, where does the time go?

The wad looked like something a yak had chewed on then spat out. I tried to pry the lump of paper open with my fingernails, hoping to salvage something – anything – but it just fell away in my hand.

Finally, I gave up and tossed it all in the trash under the bathroom sink. What can I say? Mom always means well. So now I had a rolling pin that had been washed clean of any potential fingerprints or DNA or whatever it is the cops are always finding, and a wad of washed, rinsed and spun-dried paper that was very likely evidence of a threat on my life.

I yanked the curtains open and let the warm morning sun wash my face. I was determined to focus on the positive. Like getting to the café on time. I smothered a yawn as I checked the time on my cell phone. It was already five forty-five and I'd told Aubrey I'd be at the café by six. There was no time for a bracing cup of coffee out on the patio. I'd have to wait until I got to work.

I grabbed my purse, my garment bag and my keys and sped away.

Aubrey was already waiting for me outside the front door of the café. 'Good morning!' she called with a chipperness that I feared I could never match at this hour. Somehow, though, I was going to have to learn. After all, if you're going to offer coffee and beignets, you've got to catch the morning crowd and show up with a smile.

'Good morning,' I replied, jumping off my bike.

Aubrey grabbed the wardrobe bag. 'What's in here? Our new uniforms already?'

I laughed. 'Not hardly,' I said. She looked disappointed. 'Believe me, I don't think you'd want to come dressed to work every day in a ball gown.' I struggled with my keys, which had somehow gotten tangled up in my comb. 'Wedding gown, actually.'

'Wedding gown?' Aubrey stepped back, startled. 'Are you getting married? Today? That's totally, totally awesome!'

I shook my head. 'No, no way.' I thrust my palms out. 'Long story,' I said as I unlocked the door. I stuffed my keys in my purse and wheeled the Schwinn inside while Aubrey held the bag in one hand and the door open with the other. 'I'll explain later. Right now, we've got a lot to do. Thanks for coming in early.'

As I twisted the lock, I looked up and down the street. It was pretty quiet out there, but it was very early for a Saturday. I tried not to be disappointed that there wasn't already a line of customers waiting to get in and sample my beignets.

I noted Aubrey had selected a collared black polo shirt and a comfortable-looking pair of black slacks. She even had a black visor atop her head. She looked more professional than I did. And none of the pieces were stamped Karma Koffee. Sweet.

Unfortunately, we didn't match at all. Aubrey was right: we were going to need uniforms.

'No problem.' Aubrey spun around. 'Hey, you got everything set up!' She ran her hands over the back of one of the chairs. 'Even the chairs.'

I relieved her of the garment bag and explained how my family had unexpectedly come by to lend a hand.

'That was totally, totally nice of them,' she said, following me into the back where I hung the bag on a hook in the mop closet.

'Do you have family here?' I asked.

She nodded. 'Mother, father and brother. I live with them.'

'Well, you'll have to tell me all about them sometime.' I motioned for her to follow me back out front. 'Right now, we've got to get the fryer turned on and start making some dough.'

'I can't wait to try my first beignet!' Aubrey said excitedly.

'You've never had a beignet before?'

Aubrey shook her head. 'I'm dying to try. Sorry, poor choice of words?'

I rolled my eyes and decided to let it pass. This was no time to focus on dead guys; it was time to focus on business. Beignets before bodies. 'You're in for a treat, believe me.'

I heard a low rumble and looked out toward the street. One of the big tour buses that frequent Table Rock passed slowly by, probably on its way to one of the resorts outside of town. 'Oh, the sign!'

'Huh?'

I grabbed the new section of banner from under

172

the counter where I'd set it to keep it from getting damaged last night. 'Can you run and get me the tape and scissors, Aubrey? They're in the top right drawer of the back counter.' I realized I'd just asked a young woman to run with scissors and hoped nobody reported me to OSHA.

I nudged a chair up against the window and climbed up. I gently pulled down the far side of the banner and cut off the last word. Aubrey handed me several pieces of transparent tape and I spliced on the new section.

I replaced the chair and stepped back to admire my handiwork. It might have been backwards from where we stood, but it still said 'Grand Opening Today!' for all the world to see.

Aubrey high-fived me and we got back to work. 'That ought to bring the customers in,' I predicted. And make Rob and Trish hot under their respective Karma Koffee-logoed collars, if I was lucky.

I gave Aubrey the short version of the beignet-making process. Later, when we had more time, I'd go through each step with her more slowly. It would be good to have a second beignet maker on the premises. For now, I figured I'd do the cooking and she'd do the cashiering.

She definitely had more experience in that department than I did. She'd cashiered at Karma Koffee, after all. The electronic cash register on my counter with its touchscreen controls and credit card scanner still confounded me. The nice man who'd installed it had very patiently gone over all its functions with me for more than an hour. I'm afraid my eyes had glazed over like a couple of raised yeast doughnuts halfway through.

He'd kindly left me his business card and told me I could call him if I had any questions. I had lots of questions but every time I called him I got his voicemail. Funny, that. I was beginning to think the man was avoiding me.

Maybe Aubrey could explain the thing to me sometime.

A bang on the door got my attention. I looked up from the fryer, pushing a stray lock of hair away from my face. I smiled. It looked like we had our first customer.

Aubrey was at the register unwrapping coins and dropping them in their respective drawer trays. She checked her watch. It was ten to seven. 'He's early. What do you want to do? Unlock the door?'

I rubbed my hands together. Future, here we come. I grinned. 'Let's do it!' No way was I going to make my first customer on my first day of business wait. What if he never came back?

'Doctor Vargas!' I shouted from behind the fryer station. 'You made it!' He wore a sharply creased pair of charcoal slacks and a crisp white shirt. I almost didn't recognize him without his doctor's garb.

He ambled past Aubrey at the door and on up to the counter. Aubrey connected her thumb and forefinger into an A-OK sign and mouthed, *He's hot.*

I tried to ignore her. Besides, as cute as she was, she was no match for this six-foot Latin looker.

'You did invite me.'

I nodded dumbly and pulled an order of beignets from the fryer.

'Maggie, right?'

'Yes. I'm glad you could make it.'

'Are you kidding? The big grand opening?' His voice sent shivers up my toes. 'I wouldn't miss it. And please, call me Daniel.'

There's something about that accent. Hot oil splattered my fingers. 'Ouch!' I shook my hand. Note to self: never lose focus when standing over a hot, deep fryer.

'Are you all right?'

I nodded. 'Occupational hazard.'

He nodded back and scrutinized me. 'How have you been feeling? Any dizziness or lightheadedness?'

'Nope. Nothing at all.' Well, I was getting a little dizzy now but I chalked that up to pheromones. 'Wait a minute, you didn't come here just to check up on me, did you?'

Was he still concerned about my mental state? Had Highsmith been talking to him? If Doctor Vargas was going to do any checking I'd rather it was of the checking me out variety than the 'Is the woman mentally stable to be walking the streets of Table Rock?' variety.

'Of course not. It's the doctor in me,' he said. 'It's hard to turn it off.'

His big smile weakened my knees. His charm didn't seem to have an off switch either.

Aubrey scooted back behind the counter after turning on the rest of the overhead lights and the Open sign. 'Welcome to Maggie's Beignet Café. What can I get you this morning?'

The doctor studied the chalkboard menu while I studied him. Who had sculpted that chiseled chin of his – Michelangelo?

'I'll take two dozen beignets and the ten-cup coffee box to-go.'

I ran the roller over a sheet of dough and squared it off. 'Wow, you must be hungry this morning.' I groaned inwardly. Had I really just said that?

Daniel grinned. 'I'm working the early shift at the hospital this morning and thought I'd surprise the staff.'

'Aw, that's totally, totally sweet,' Aubrey said. She rang up Dr Vargas' tab and handed him back his change. Two more customers had already slid into line behind him. They looked like tourists, with bright shirts and digital cameras in hand. Things were looking up.

I handed him a bag filled with beignets. He leaned his nose toward the opening and inhaled. 'These smell amazing.' He shot a look at me. 'I'll bet they taste amazing too.'

I swallowed my tongue. 'Thanks,' I sputtered. Aubrey giggled and I shot daggers at her.

'Well,' he rubbed at the leather strap of the watch around his wrist, 'I'd better be off. My shift starts soon. Good luck, ladies.' He grabbed up his second bag of beignets and took the coffee carton by its handle.

'Here, let me get the door for you.' I dropped my tongs, wiped my hands on my apron and held the door open.

'Thanks,' he said again as he brushed closely past me. So close that, despite the scent of sweet fried dough, I caught a faint whiff of an earthy cologne.

'You know,' he said, 'if these pastries taste as good as they smell, you are going to be very successful.'

'Thank you.' This guy was so sweet. Highsmith could – should – be taking charm lessons from him. Maybe I'd suggest it the next time I saw Table Rock's lone detective.

Daniel stepped out to the sidewalk and set his purchases on the seat of a dusty navy blue Grand Cherokee. 'And I wouldn't worry at all about what my sister says. Folks around here are open-minded. They'll give you a chance. Look, you've got a line forming already.'

I turned. Sure enough, there were now four customers standing on queue. My heart jumped. 'Wow, I'd better get back. Wait.' I frowned. 'Your sister?'

He walked to the other side of his Jeep and climbed in. 'Yeah, Veronica. She hasn't stopped talking about your café.'

My stomach dropped. Vargas, of course. 'VV? You're related to VV?' I could sort of see the resemblance now that he'd said it, especially around the nose and eyes.

But they were so different! And he had such a lovely romantic accent. VV must have gone to an otolaryngologist to have hers excised.

His hands gripped the wheel. 'You know her?'

'We've met.' We've met, we've clashed, we've become mortal enemies . . . there were so many answers I could have given.

Daniel must have noticed my expression

177

because he laughed and said, 'She's not so bad once you get to know her.' He turned the ignition and the engine sprang to life.

Sure, wasn't that kind of like Californians said about earthquakes? Pity, he was so good looking too. And a doctor! But VV . . . I shivered. I couldn't picture the two of us hanging out at the family picnic together. I could picture her hanging me from a makeshift gallows thrown up in the middle of Laredo Street for the murder of Rick Wilbur.

Heck, she'd probably take my hand and lead me up the rickety pine steps and tell me where to plant my feet for when the trapdoor fell open. VV would probably call dibs on pulling the lever.

EIGHTEEN

I lingered at the door a moment longer, enjoying the cool, dry morning air. A customer carrying a small bag of beignets nudged past me.

'Maggie!' cried Aubrey. 'We're out of beignets. I need you!'

I hurried back inside, feeling terribly guilty. 'Sorry,' I mumbled, putting my head down and setting up a fresh batch of dough.

'No problem.' Aubrey smiled my way and shoved back a stray lock of hair using the side of her arm. 'Oh, and this guy's been waiting to talk to you.'

I looked up. A tall, slender-waisted man about my age with swept-back wavy brown hair smiled my way. He had a slight gap between his two front teeth. 'Be with you as soon as I can.' I grabbed a premade ball of dough, dusting the prep counter with a bit more flour, then began rolling out the dough ball.

'No problem.' His electric-blue eyes rolled over me then swept to Aubrey. 'I'll have an order of beignets and a large coffee.' He looked comfortable in a relaxed pair of blue jeans and an unadorned white T-shirt that hung below the belt.

'Coming right up.'

He stood in front of the glass that fronted the fryer and watched me work. It made me a bit self-conscious and nervous, but I was going to have to get used to it. After all, it had been my idea to make the beignets in front of the customers like I'd seen at several places around New Orleans. It makes the whole experience more tactile and interactive, like going to the candy maker and watching them make fudge or pull taffy.

He carried his order to a free table and I didn't pay much attention to him until twenty minutes later when there was a lull in the action and I looked up to see him eying me. He grinned. 'Have some time for me now?'

I smiled back. 'I'll be right with you.' I washed my hands and toweled them dry, poured myself a cup of coffee, dumped in some extra cream and joined him at his table near the wall. 'Sorry it took so long.'

'No problem.' He played his now-empty coffee cup in circles on the tabletop. 'It looks like your new business is off to a good start.'

I smiled proudly. 'It looks that way,' I agreed.

He dipped a finger into a trail of powdered sugar on his plate and brought it to his lips. 'Tastes just like the real thing.'

'You've been to New Orleans?'

'A couple of times.' He wiped his finger on his napkin and held out his hand. 'Brad Smith, by the way.'

I shook his hand, firm but gentle. Just the way I liked it. 'Maggie Miller.' Brad Smith had those classic All American looks that some women find attractive. Not me.

I find it *very* attractive. Then again, my dead husband Brian had those classic All American good looks and look where it had gotten me.

Divorced.

He leaned toward me. 'Tell me, Maggie, is it true that you found Rick Wilbur's body in your storeroom?'

A shiver ran up my spine and I looked quickly around the café. Half the tables were occupied so I kept my reply low. 'Yes,' I admitted, 'but I'd rather not talk about it.' I sipped my coffee.

He nodded and placed his elbows on the table. The man oozed self-confidence. 'I understand completely, Maggie.' He laced his fingers together. 'Still, it's weird, huh?'

I watched Brad over the edge of my cup, wondering where he was going with this conversation. 'I guess. Sure.' Of course it was weird. It sure as heck wasn't normal to find a dead guy in a box in your storeroom. Even in Table Rock I was pretty sure this was considered extraordinary.

He nodded once more. 'Do you have any idea who would have wanted to see Rick Wilbur dead?'

I sighed and set down my cup. 'Not a clue,' I said. 'Believe me, I've tried to think of who might want him dead – his wife, disgruntled clients, maybe some other family member.' I shrugged. 'Anybody who might have something to gain.'

He pulled a pen from his front pocket and a small spiral-bound notebook that opened at the top. He pushed back its black cover, thumbed to a clean sheet and began writing. 'Wife, you say?'

I pulled my eyebrows together. 'Maybe. I mean, who knows?' I twisted my neck and looked out at Karma Koffee, also open for business this morning. 'Personally, I'm hoping it's the Gregorys.'

'The Gregorys?'

I nodded toward the street. 'Rob and Trish. They own Karma Koffee.' Brad grunted and scribbled some more.

What was he doing? Making out his grocery list while we talked? I tried to discreetly follow his writing, not easy since it was upside down from where I sat. But then I deciphered some of his pigeon scratching. He'd written my name and the names of several others under a category he'd labelled and underlined as potential suspects.

My eyes widened. 'Who are you exactly?'

'Brad Smith.' He smiled. 'We met already. Remember?'

'Very funny.' I crossed my arms over my chest. 'You know what I mean.'

He was silent a moment. He closed his notebook and slapped his pen down atop it. 'OK, you got me. I'm a reporter with the *Table Rock Reader*.'

'What?' I huffed. 'So you came here hoping to spy on me? And what? Maybe get an interview with a murder suspect?' I was standing now and didn't care what my customers heard. I didn't care how nice looking this guy was, he was a jerk. With a capital ERK.

He waved his hands, motioning me to sit. 'No, no. It's not like that at all. The editor sent me to get a story about you. About your grand opening.' He leaned back and looked at me with a sly expression. 'It'll be good for business. What do you say?'

182

'Well . . .'

'Don't make me go back empty-handed,' he pleaded, his eyes softening.

I bit at the inside of my cheek. A free story in the newspaper would be good for business. 'Fine,' I said. 'You've got five more minutes. Then I've got to get back to work.'

'Sure,' Brad said, quickly regaining his composure. 'So, you've got a brand-new business. Tell me, have you ever been in the beignet, coffee or even restaurant business before?'

I wagged my head. 'Nope. I used to be a hair stylist. I decided to try something new.'

Brad nodded. 'Hair stylist. Right. Interesting.'

If it was so interesting, why wasn't he writing anything down?

'Expensive, though, isn't it? Starting a new business, I mean.' He ran strong fingers through the waves of his hair.

'Oh, yeah,' I said. 'Tell me about it. I've got everything I own tied up in this place.' I thought about all the money I'd borrowed from the bank, and the additional bucks I'd borrowed from my mother, sister and brother-in-law. 'And more.'

'I expect it will be devastating for you if your café has to shut down.'

A chill went through me. 'What do you mean?'

'Well, there's the murder, for one thing.' He toyed with his pen. I was getting the feeling he was toying with me too. 'The bad check you wrote to Wilbur Realty, for another . . .'

'How on earth did you hear about that?' My volume and my blood pressure were rising.

183

He grinned triumphantly. 'I have my sources. Besides, Table Rock is—'

'A small town,' I finished. 'Yeah, I know.'

'So it's true?'

I leapt from my chair. 'I think it's time you left, Mr Smith.' I pointed to the door.

'But what about our interview? Our story on Maggie's Beignet Café for our *Table Rock Reader* readers?'

'Now!'

'Tell me,' he said, still not giving up as he grabbed up his notebook and headed for the exit, 'are the police operating on the notion that the fact that Wilbur Realty was threatening to shut you down gave you a motive to murder Mr Wilbur? Do you expect charges to be filed anytime soon?'

I gave him a push out the door. 'Sorry about that,' I said to my remaining customers as I figuratively and, I hoped literally, wiped my hands of Brad Smith.

NINETEEN

'Are you OK, Maggie?' Aubrey asked as I stepped back behind the counter, my knees shaking.

'Yes, I'm fine.' The door opened and I jumped, my eyes darting to see who was entering. But it was merely a few strangers, not Brad Smith redux. 'I only wish I had a subscription to the *Table Rock Reader*.'

'Why?' Aubrey asked.

'So I could cancel it,' I said, slamming my rolling pin down on a ball of unsuspecting and undeserving beignet dough.

After that, things got busy and steady, never a mob but never a dull moment. All in all, I was quite satisfied. When I checked all the cold hard cash sitting in the register I was *more* than satisfied.

I relieved Aubrey around eleven when things quieted down and sent her to the storeroom with a fresh hot plate of beignets and a lemonade. She'd managed to snack on a couple beignets earlier, but this would be her first real serving, her first true opportunity to sit down and savor the moment. I had a suspicion the girl would soon be totally, totally hooked.

While she was in the back, I whipped up a couple dozen beignets, slid them onto the warmer and turned on the dual overhead heat lamps.

I was handing a customer her change when Aubrey returned, a dab of powdered sugar on her nose. I tossed her a napkin. 'You're supposed to eat them with your mouth, not inhale them through your nose!' I said with a smile.

Her finger went to her nose and she blushed. 'Oops!' She folded the napkin over her nose and rubbed. 'Better?'

I nodded. 'Do me a favor and hold down the fort for a minute, would you? I've got to see a man about a horse.'

'Huh?'

I grabbed my gown from the mop closet. 'I'll be at The Hitching Post.'

I tossed the garment bag over my shoulder and walked next door to Clive and Johnny's wedding shop. Johnny was wearing a dark suit and talking to what appeared to be a mother and daughter. They had two gowns spilled out over a blue velvet loveseat and seemed deep in conversation.

Personally, I thought the bride-to-be should go with the dress on the left. I couldn't picture her in a mermaid dress. With a figure like hers, bigger at the hips than the shoulders, I was sure she'd look better in the empire silhouette.

Johnny Wolfe glanced over his shoulder at me as I passed. He didn't look happy to see me but I shrugged it off. I seemed to be running into a lot of that lately.

Besides, I wasn't exactly getting a chill in my toes seeing him again. I just hoped he didn't bring up my offer to replace those fancy designer jeans of his.

This was my first time inside the elegant dress

shop and I was duly impressed. They had a lovely inventory and my nostrils picked up a subtle hint of sweet gardenias. I remembered when I had gone wedding dress shopping with my mother. It seemed like a lifetime ago – and somebody else's life . . .

Clive sat behind a large, elegant oak desk near the back of the store. He looked much healthier today than he had the last time I'd seen him. He had some color back in his cheeks and that redness around his left eye had disappeared. He was looking quite dapper, too, in his gray suit and red bowtie.

'Hi, Clive.' The expansive desk sat atop an expensive-looking Persian rug in shades of muted reds and browns, a sharp contrast to the hand-scraped walnut floors. Johnny and Clive must have dropped a pretty penny remodeling this place.

He looked up from the bridal magazine he'd been thumbing through. 'Maggie!' The glow from the brass lamp on the corner of his desk made his red hair glisten.

'It's good to see you. Welcome back.' I still needed to ask him what hair care product he was using to achieve that shine. I could Turtle Wax my own locks and they'd still look dull and lusterless.

He waved to the pair of tall wingback chairs facing his desk. 'Have a seat.' He closed his magazine and pushed it to the side. 'So, what brings you here?'

'I heard the hospital released you,' I said, settling into the upholstered chair on the left. 'You look well.'

He waved a hand. 'It was nothing really. I do suffer a bit with my blood pressure. And to tell you the truth, I'm embarrassed that I fainted like that.' He dropped his eyes.

I put forth my friendliest smile. 'Nothing to be embarrassed about. To tell *you* the truth, I felt like fainting myself.' I draped the garment bag across my lap. 'In fact, the only reason I didn't was because of you.'

'Because of me?' He looked puzzled.

'Sure, I mean, if I fainted, who was going to catch you?' We shared a laugh. I noticed Clive's green eyes dart nervously to Johnny. Johnny probably wasn't big on people having fun.

'I was going to come see you today. I saw the banner.' He spread his hands in the air. 'Grand Opening Today!' He sighed. 'I remember our grand opening.'

'Oh? How long's it been?'

'Almost three years. We opened The Hitching Post not long after we married. It had always been a dream of ours.'

'That's great. I hope Maggie's Beignet Café is still open for business three years from now.'

'I'm sure it will be.' He tented his fingers atop the black leather blotter. 'Can I get you some refreshment? A cup of chamomile tea, perhaps?'

I shook my head no. A tall, tapered glass vase of pink angel's trumpets occupied the left corner of his desk. Hadn't I read somewhere that those flowers were poisonous? Was old Clive trying to kill me? Put a little angel's trumpet juice in my tea, perhaps?

I suppressed a shudder.

188

'A coconut macaroon?'

'Thanks, but I don't think I'd better.' I patted my belly through the garment bag. 'I think I'm becoming my own best customer.'

Clive arched his brow and glanced meaningfully at the bag on my lap. 'So, what's in the bag? I suspect it's rather too large to be an order of beignets.'

'Well . . .' My hands stroked the dark fabric of the garment bag. 'This is what I came to see you about.' I suddenly was feeling nervous. After all, I barely knew Clive and since we'd met I'd been responsible for him ending up in the hospital. Not to mention, I'd run his husband, Johnny Wolfe, over with my Schwinn. Now I was about to ask them a favor.

A very big favor.

An expensive favor.

I sucked in a breath. 'Let me show you,' I said, getting to my feet. I draped the garment bag over the back of my chair and slowly pulled down the zipper.

I heard Clive gasp as I pulled out my wedding gown.

He pushed back his chair and came around to my side of the desk. 'Oh, Maggie,' he exclaimed, pushing his cheeks together in his palms, 'it's magnificent!'

I gathered up the folds of fabric, carefully extracted the gown and held it aloft. It was magnificent.

Clive waved. 'Johnny, come see!'

Johnny shot us a dirty look, said a word or two to his clients and walked over. I swear, the way he was swinging those slender hips of his around, you'd think he was a runway model.

Johnny looked at Clive, then at me and then fingered the gown. 'Quite nice.' He regarded me up and down. 'You're getting married and need the waist let out.'

'What—' Need the waist let out? He hadn't even posed it as a question!

Johnny turned to Clive. 'No problem. We can do the alterations for you even if you did not purchase the gown here. Clive can write you up. I'm afraid our calendar is quite full this time of year, but if you can give me a few weeks—'

'But—' I looked at my hips. OK, maybe I'd put on a few pounds, but still, who did this skinny coxcomb think he was making comments like that? 'I don't need—'

I was about to suggest some rather unladylike alterations I'd like to make to Johnny Wolfe when I suddenly remembered what I was doing in The Hitching Post.

I cleared my throat and started again. 'I mean, thank you, Johnny, that would be very kind of you, but that's not why I'm here.'

'I see.' He chewed his lower lip and his eyes angled to the mother and daughter at the other end of the showroom. 'Then you'll excuse me. The Burkes are on a tight schedule. I'm sure Clive can handle whatever it is you require. Clive?'

Clive nodded. 'Of course, Johnny.' Johnny swiveled silently and maneuvered his way back to his clients. I scored him a seven-point-five for the move because I didn't think he'd done a full rotation and had landed on the inside edge of his left heel.

'Sorry about that,' said Clive. He leaned against his desk. 'So, you're getting married again. How lovely for you. When is the wedding?'

I shook my head. 'No wedding. This is my old dress.'

Clive cocked his head.

'I want to sell it. More specifically,' I cleared my throat, 'I want you to buy it.'

'Oh, I see.' Clive chewed his lip and sighed. 'You know, Maggie, this is unusual. We don't normally buy wedding dresses, nor do we sell pre-owned dresses.' He was really wagging his head now. 'I'm not sure that Johnny would approve.'

'Don't think of it as pre-owned,' I said, waving the beautiful dress in front of him. 'Think of it as gently used.'

He rubbed the satin between his fingers. 'It is a beautiful dress.' He looked at me curiously and said in softer tones, 'Are you sure you want to part with the gown, Maggie?'

'Yep.'

He seemed surprised. 'The dress must hold very special memories for you. Perhaps you want to think about this before you do something rash? Sometimes, such things are all we have to hold on to, to remember our dear departed loved ones by.'

I shifted from foot to foot. 'You'd really be helping me out.'

He stiffened.

'Did I say something wrong?'

'No.' He shook his head. 'Some oaf has parked a gargantuan truck right out front, blocking our entire window display from the street. Johnny hates that. Whoever he is and whatever he is delivering, trucks are by law required to use the alley, you know.'

I knew. All my deliveries came in through my storeroom off the alley. There was a town ordinance about it.

He squinted out the window. 'The driver's even got one tire on the curb.' He read the name on the side of the trailer and tapped his teeth with his fingernail. 'Miller Transport. It's certainly not a delivery for us.'

Clive turned back to me. 'Hey, Miller – that's your last name, too, Maggie.'

'Yeah, quite a coincidence.' I raised the dress higher, hoping to get Clive to focus on more important things than trucks. Like dresses. 'Now, about the dress—'

'Do you suppose it's anybody you know?'

'No,' I said, rather too sharply. Miller is a common name, after all. Now if it had read Malarkey I might have been curious myself. Still, I found myself looking out the window. Human nature, I supposed.

Brian jumped down from the cab. He was wearing an old pair of loose-fitting Wranglers and a Sedona red Arizona Diamondbacks T-shirt. He'd always been into baseball.

My wedding dress hit the floor.

TWENTY

Brian angled to the right and disappeared. Clive scooped up the gown and handed it back to me. I white-knuckled the cedar hanger. If anything happened to the gown, he wouldn't offer me two cents for it.

'Are you all right, Maggie?' Clive said. I felt his hand on my shoulder. 'Perhaps you'd better sit.'

Brian burst through the front entrance of The Hitching Post. 'Maggie!' he shouted across the store. 'What on earth is going on? I went to the café and your employee told me I'd find you here.'

His eyes flew around the space. 'What are you doing in here instead of your own place?' He paced toward me and his eyes moved up and down my wedding dress. 'Hey, your wedding gown. What are you doing with that?'

'Brian—' I stuttered.

'Brian?' Clive matched me stutter for stutter.

I nodded.

'Your dead husband, Brian?'

'Dead?' Brian scratched his head. Why was he looking at me funny like that?

Clive stuttered again, apparently not going to let go of this. He swiveled to face me. His eyes full of questions. 'But you told me he was dead!'

'Dead?' Brian scratched his head some more. I was beginning to think the man had lice.

'Wow,' I replied, laughing nervously. 'Would you look at that – dead man walking. It's like the zombie apocalypse!' I ended my sentence with another nervous laugh and a glance at both men.

'What's going on, Maggie?' Both men said it together.

The force of their words sent me reeling. I smiled out of the side of my face. My knees felt like grape jelly. I turned to Clive. 'I guess I was wrong?'

Clive folded his arms across his chest and glared. 'Maggie.' He drew the word out. There was an edge to his voice. It wasn't the first time I'd heard the word 'Maggie' said like an accusation, but it was one of the best.

I took a step back.

Johnny rushed over. 'What the devil are you all doing?' he hissed. 'This is a bridal shop, not a saloon.' He squeezed his hands together. 'Show some decorum.'

I lowered my eyes.

'Sorry, Johnny,' Clive said.

'Hey, you're Johnny Wolfe, that ice-skating guy.' Brian stuck his hand out.

Johnny hesitated, then allowed him a handshake. What the heck? Hadn't Johnny refused to shake my hand the other day? 'Yes,' Johnny said curtly. 'You are?'

'Brian Miller. Miller Transport.' He dropped his arm over my shoulder. 'Maggie's husband.'

Brian stood a good seven inches taller than me and I felt his weight on my shoulder. I quickly wiggled away. 'Ex-husband,' I said.

Clive pulled a face. 'Dead husband.' He stared at me. 'Or so I'd been told.' He wagged his finger. 'Shame on you, Maggie.'

Brian grinned from ear to ear, making his round head look all the more like a pale beach ball. 'Yeah, shame on you, Maggie.'

I held out the gown. 'Look, Clive, are you going to buy the dress or not?' I turned to my dead ex-husband. 'Brian, leave.' With my free hand, I pointed to the door just in case he'd forgotten where it was located.

Johnny looked out the window of The Hitching Post. 'Is that your vehicle parked halfway up the sidewalk, blocking our—' He stopped and turned to me. 'Wait, what's this about buying your dress?' His eyes fell to my gown again.

Clive nodded briefly. 'Maggie would like us to purchase her wedding dress from her, Johnny.'

'We don't buy wedding dresses,' Johnny said sourly, 'we sell them.'

'That's what I tried to explain,' Clive replied.

'But you'd really be helping me out. Doing me a big favor. You see, there was a problem at the bank. My rent and security check got bounced for some reason and—'

Brian said, 'You're selling your wedding gown? Maggie, that's a twelve-thousand-dollar Pnina Tornai original!' He laced his fingers through his thick black hair.

'Yeah, well, if you want to give me what I originally paid for it, she's all yours.' I thrust the gown in his face. It was a beautiful dress, with a sweetheart neckline, a dropped waist and silk satin cathedral-length train. Part of me wanted to hang on to the dress; the other part wanted to keep my business afloat.

Brian sputtered and backed up. The cheapskate.

I pushed the dress at Clive. He took a step back and I thrust it in Johnny's face. He looked nervously to his customers and lifted a finger. 'I'll be with you in a moment, ladies.'

Johnny turned back to me. 'How much do you want?' he hissed brusquely.

I cocked my head and considered. 'Four thousand?' Hey, it was more than I needed but why not ask? A girl's got to think big.

He frowned. 'Two.'

'Three?' I said, arching my right eyebrow. That was as low as I could afford to go. I didn't know what I'd do if he said no. I held my breath and waited.

Johnny sighed. 'Fine.' He turned to his partner. 'Clive, write the woman a check and get her out of here. Quickly.' He turned, his eyes on Brian, his finger aimed at Miller Transport. 'And you,' he said, 'remove that monstrosity from my sight!'

Clive hung my gown on a nearby rack, then sat behind his desk and pulled open the middle drawer. He removed a large leather-bound ledger the color of dark chocolate. 'I'll prepare your check.'

He glanced up at Brian who still hovered. 'I really do suggest you move your truck, Mr Miller. Johnny has a very short fuse. He's liable to telephone the police.'

'Thanks, bud.' He shot Clive a thumbs up.

'I'll move the truck and meet you next door, Mags.'

'Go away, Brian,' I replied. I turned back to Clive as he put pen to check. 'You wouldn't happen to be able to give me the three thousand in cash, I suppose?' With the bank closed on Saturday, a check wouldn't do me much good. What if Natalie made good on her threat and had Maggie's Beignet Café padlocked today?

'Sorry,' answered Clive. 'We don't keep that kind of cash around.'

I fell back onto the chair and thought. 'I know,' I said finally. 'Make the check out to Wilbur Realty.' The Hitching Post had been a tenant of theirs for years, after all. Certainly they'd accept a three-thousand-dollar check from them. At least for the weekend. Long enough for me to keep my doors open.

Clive agreed.

He handed me the check. 'Thanks.' I folded it in two and slid it into my pocket. I'd run it over to the real estate office later. 'Say, Clive,' I said before leaving. 'You didn't happen to find a couple of chairs—'

He looked puzzled.

'Like maybe out back, in the alley?'

Clive shook his head.

'Oh.' That hadn't been helpful at all.

'Why do you ask?'

'No reason.' He looked doubly confused by my answer but I couldn't afford to let him know that I knew about the missing chairs. What if he and Johnny were in cahoots and had killed Mr Wilbur for some reason as yet unknown to me?

197

Where on earth were my two missing chairs? They definitely weren't out here on the showroom floor. Could they be in the back? They certainly appeared to have a good-sized storeroom, triple the size of mine. What I had to figure out was how to get a look back there.

'I notice that your air conditioner is working today. Didn't you say it was on the fritz? Did Rick Wilbur get it running?' That's it, Maggie, dangle the bait and see if the fish bites. Get him to admit maybe that Rick Wilbur had been in their store around the time of his death.

Clive stood. 'Like I said, it runs hot and cold. Today, giving that I read the temperature is going to rise to ninety-five, I'm happy to see that it seems to be working properly. Mr Teller promised he'd take a look as soon as he is up to the task.'

'Yeah, poor man.'

'That reminds me, I promised him I'd feed his cat.'

So Ed Teller wasn't quite so all alone in the world as I'd thought. That news eased my conscience a bit. 'Have you been taking care of him all this time?' With no wife and no kids, I was happy to hear that Ed at least had a cat. Sometimes a pet is all you need.

'It's a her. And no, someone from the office, Ms Eagleheart, the office secretary, has been assisting. But with her allergies, it's been quite a struggle apparently. Before I left Mesa Verde, Mr Teller asked me if I might be able to stop by his house once a day to help out. She's a house cat. Goes by the name Carol Two.'

Before I could ask, Clive answered, 'Carol One was his wife.'

I wasn't sure whether Ed's choice of names was meant to honor his dead wife or to diss her.

'Mr Teller doesn't like to leave Carol Two completely alone in the house. It wouldn't be so bad if all I had to do was fill her kibble dish, but that litter box . . .' He visibly shivered. 'Ick.'

'I could do it for you.' Good grief, had those words just come out of my mouth? I didn't have time to clean up after a cat. I didn't even like cleaning up after myself.

'Do what? The litter box?'

'The whole thing.' I spread my hands. 'Feed the kitty, empty the litter.' What can I say? I felt like I owed the guy.

'I don't know . . .' Clive tapped his fingers together. 'I told Mr Teller I'd do it.'

'Please, you did me a big favor buying the dress and getting me out of a jam. Let me do this for you to pay you back.' I folded my arms over my chest. 'He won't mind,' I wheedled. 'I insist.'

'Well, if you insist.' He reached into the top left-hand drawer and pulled out a Wilbur Realty logo key ring with several keys attached. 'Here are Mr Teller's keys.' Clive wrote out the address. 'It's a small bungalow on Prescott. It's a fixer-upper with cobalt-blue shutters. You can't miss it.'

I nodded. I knew the general area and it was definitely doable by bike.

'Whatever you do, Maggie, do not let Carol Two out of the house.' He wagged his finger at me like I was a schoolgirl or something. 'She is strictly an indoor cat.'

'OK.' I gave Clive a thumbs up and a smile.

'Seriously, Maggie. Mr Teller was quite explicit on the matter. Carol Two is not to be allowed out of the house.'

'I said OK already.'

'I know, but—' The tinkle of the string of bells attached to the front door announced a new arrival and Clive stopped talking. We both turned to look. Four young ladies entered. One of them was wearing an engagement ring, and the way the rock on it flashed even from this distance meant she probably had a healthy budget for a wedding dress. Maybe she'd like a slightly used Pnina Tornai original.

Clive stood. 'You'll have to excuse me, Maggie. I have to assist my customer.'

'Of course,' I said, waving him on. 'I'll let myself out as soon as I've used your ladies' room. You do have one, don't you?'

'What's wrong with yours?' His brows lowered.

I shrugged sheepishly. 'Can't wait?'

Clive pointed to the right and scurried over to intercept the group of young women who had begun riffling through the racks amid a chorus of gasps and oohs.

I went straight to the restroom. And turned left. A dark, narrow hall led to a small office on the right. Talk about neat. I've never seen an office without clutter. Part of me wanted to stop and admire it, maybe shoot a picture with my phone to post on Facebook. But if Clive or Johnny caught me, how would I explain myself?

I crept on, finally coming to a second open door. There was a light switch on the wall just outside. I flipped the switch.

Bingo, this was their storeroom. Boy, was it big. And loaded with rack after rack of wedding dresses and bridesmaid dresses. Shelves along two walls held veils, lace and every other accessory a bride-to-be could want. All very neatly arranged and organized, of course.

The industrial lights overhead cast triangular arcs of light down over the clothes racks. I stopped and touched a taffeta gown. Nice. This inventory must have been worth a bundle.

I tiptoed up and down the aisles, pushing aside dresses now and again, looking for my two missing dining chairs. They could be hidden anywhere in here.

I sighed. Searching this backroom could take hours. I couldn't spare hours. Not only was I supposed to be back at the café helping poor Aubrey, but Clive and Johnny were right out front.

My nerves were already shot and my heart pounding with fear of being caught. And what if I did discover my chairs back here? What would it prove? That Johnny and/or Clive are murderers? Then what?

Confront them?

Hopefully, even I wasn't that stupid. No, I'd have to get out without them knowing and phone the police. I had Detective Highsmith's cell number in my purse. Of course, my purse was back in the café.

I turned toward the back wall, perpendicular to

the alley. Still no sign of the chairs. Yet they seemed like the most likely ones to have taken them.

There was my neighbor on the other side of the café, Salon de Belleza, run by that butinski Caitie Conklin. I was still sure it had been her who'd ratted me out to the police about my little argument – non-argument – with Rick Wilbur.

Come to think of it, maybe Conklin had conked Mr Wilbur on the back of his head. No pun intended. After all, what did I really know about the woman? Besides the fact that she was a jerk, that is.

And charged fifty bucks a pop for a haircut. I know because I'd called the salon soon after arriving to schedule a cut. But not at those prices!

I mean, really, who charges fifty bucks a pop for a haircut? This was Table Rock for crying out loud, not Scottsdale. So far, I'd stuck to trimming my own locks. I used to cut the entire family's heads, but since moving to Table Rock, Donna's been cutting Andy's and my nephews' hair herself. And she was doing a pretty good job, too – for a grocer.

Yeah, Caitie Conklin. Maybe I was barking up the wrong tree. I added her to my list of suspects and turned back toward the showroom. Time to get back to the café. Even if the chairs were here I might never find them.

Something shiny on the floor caught my eye as I snaked through the narrow aisle of gowns. I bent and lifted it from the plank. It was a ballpoint pen with a Wilbur Realty logo. I'd seen pens like this before. Rick Wilbur handed them out like candy. I heard the sound of footsteps. I looked up.

'Looking for something?' Johnny Wolfe blocked my path.

Tips On Choosing a Flattering Wedding Dress

So, you're getting married. Good for you – just don't marry anyone named Brian. OK, maybe I'm being a little hard on the Brians of the world – don't marry my dead ex-husband Brian.

Though there are as many shapes and sizes of people and dresses as there are people and dresses, there are several general categories of each that you can use to guide your selection. Just remember, there are no right and wrong choices – well, I hate to sound like a broken record here, but do avoid Brian – other than that, if you love it, wear it!

Now, if you had to describe your figure, what would you select: an apple, pear, straight, triangle, inverted triangle, hourglass, even a circle, perhaps? Note: if you answered hexagon or polyhedron, I can't help you. You're on your own. Your problems may be bigger than simply trying to pick a wedding dress. I mean, I wouldn't even know what to advise when it came to socks for the polyhedronic! Tube? Anklet? I would avoid argyle – way too busy if you've got that many angles to cover.

Here are some thoughts on silhouettes you might want to try.

Ball gown: Let's face it, we all want to be a princess. This style of dress works especially well for the pear/circle body type. Me, I always wanted to be a princess.

A-line: Very similar to the ball gown but with more flare than poof. There's not a body out there that this gown won't flatter. Well, I'm not sure how Johnny Wolfe would look in this silhouette. Personally, I think he should stick with the ball gown. It not only suits his figure, it fits his personality.

Empire waist: With a waist line that sits right below the bust line this style is ideal for circle and pear shapes and the petite.

Mermaid: This dress hugs your body tight, then flares out below the knee, creating a mermaid silhouette. It's a good choice for you if you've got those hourglass curves. And yes, I'm jealous if you do. But you try standing on your feet all day in a beignet café and see what shape you are then. And despite its name, I wouldn't suggest swimming in one. I saw this once on a beach in Mexico and it wasn't pretty! I did get to see a lifeguard in action, though. It just goes to show what a lack of sleep, a hot sun and a couple of pitchers of strong margaritas can do to a woman's sense of judgment.

Sheath: This is just what it sounds like – slides right down your body and drops straight to the ground. Consider this if you are slim and/or tall.

Trumpet: Similar to the mermaid, the trumpet hugs the body but flares out above the knee, giving that trumpet-like silhouette. This might be your dress if you have a straight, hourglass or inverted triangle figure.

And the most important tip? Stay on budget. I didn't and look what it got me. I ride a Schwinn, ladies . . .

TWENTY-ONE

I stumbled backward, my hands clutching my chest. 'You nearly gave me a heart attack!' Great, instead of helping Mr Teller with his cat, I'd be sharing a hospital room with the man, probably end up feeding each other pabulum with plastic spoons. Wouldn't that be both chummy and yummy?

Johnny's arms were folded across his skinny chest. His feet were planted shoulder width. 'What are you doing back here?' His voice came out as a cold whisper.

I took another step back, my fingers wrapped tightly around the pen. I was alone in a dimly lit backroom with a potential killer. All these poufy gowns filling the space would probably muffle the sounds of my screams. And all this frilly fabric would be a great place to hide my body. Much better than an empty cardboard box. I looked at the pen. Maybe I could use ink defense – scribble the guy to death.

'Johnny, you surprised me. Tell me,' I said, my mouth getting the best of my brain, 'did you surprise Rick Wilbur, too?' Wow, I really might be dumber than I thought. Dumber even than my dead husband Brian thought. 'Is that why you killed him?' Yep, definitely proof there.

'Are you mad?' He came at me, grabbed me by the elbow and pulled me toward him. I yelped and pushed back. 'Would you please—'

I punched his arm. 'You don't think I'm going to let you murder me the way you murdered poor Mr Wilbur, do you?' I punched him again.

'Ouch! Stop it!' he said, chafing his arm up and down. 'You could hurt somebody like that.'

'What on earth is going on back here?' Clive leapt in front of us. 'Maggie! What are you doing?'

I freed myself from Johnny's clutches. 'Trying to get away from this mad serial killer!' I panted. 'And I found this!' I thrust the pen toward them.

Johnny turned to Clive. 'I caught your friend rummaging through our backroom. I'm trying to get her to leave.'

Clive said softly but sternly, 'I think you'd better go, Maggie.'

'Yes,' shot Johnny. 'Please do leave. You are disturbing our clientele.' His eyes danced toward the showroom. 'Don't you have customers of your own to pester?' His eyes were dark clouds of thunder.

'I'm leaving,' I said, my eyes on Johnny. 'But don't think you've heard the last of me.' I waved the pen in his face.

'I'll take that.' Johnny snatched the pen from my hand. Wow, reflexes like a cat. The guy must still keep in shape. I'll bet he could swing a rolling pin at someone pretty good.

'OK, OK.' I held my palms up. 'No need for all this tension, guys. I was just taking a look around. All these lovely gowns, what girl could resist?'

'Try harder next time,' said Clive.

'There won't be a next time,' was Johnny's reply.

I nodded and edged past the two men, then headed quickly for the exit. My shoulders tightened as I heard Johnny hiss to Clive, 'I can't tolerate having that woman as our neighbor. What are we going to do about her? She's just crazy enough to—'

'Don't worry, Johnny. I believe Maggie is suffering from post-traumatic shock.'

It was all I could do not to turn around and yell at the two men. In the end, I figured that would just be giving them ammunition. Frankly, I was keeping their ammo belts pretty full already.

'She's your responsibility,' Johnny said.

I didn't hear Clive's answer. I was too far away.

I popped back into the café and told Aubrey that I had to run to the real estate office to drop off a check. There were two men standing in front of her at the register and she was looking flustered.

One of the men turned my way. 'No need,' he said. 'I'm heading that way myself.' He held out his hand. 'I can take that for you.'

I squinted my eyes together. 'You're Tommy, aren't you?'

He smiled. 'Right the first time. Tommy Henson.'

The infamous Tommy who wanted a job at his uncle's real estate office but apparently Uncle Rick had not wanted him. 'I remember you.' I also remembered his attitude. And his mole.

He slipped the check from my fingers before I could even think to protest. 'I remember you,

209

too. But then, it's hard to forget a pretty lady like yourself.'

I ignored the compliment and hurried behind the counter, dropping the hinged top down behind me like a defense mechanism. 'What are you doing here?' So far, I wasn't a fan of Tommy or his mother, Natalie – after all, she'd been the one to send that letter threatening to have my café padlocked.

'Isn't it obvious?' There was a mischievous twinkle in his eyes.

'If you're still looking for a job, sorry, but I'm not hiring.'

Tommy laughed. 'That's OK, I'm set.'

A sudden thought itched at my gray cells. Were Tommy and his mom involved in Rick Wilbur's murder? Were they mother and son accomplices? Weirder things had been known to happen. I'd have to dig a little deeper into their respective backgrounds as well. Suddenly, Table Rock seemed to be filling up with suspects.

Come to think of it, was it any coincidence that Natalie Henson was suddenly in Reno visiting her eldest boy, or had the trip been an excuse to get out of town while the police were investigating Rick's death? Natalie was Patti's sister. And Patti was taking a sudden interest in Wilbur Realty. I felt a headache unfold over my right eye.

He read the check. 'Wilbur Realty. Three thousand dollars. For Maggie Miller, but written on a Hitching Post check.' Tommy looked from the check to me. 'What's that all about?'

'I seem to be having a slight mix-up involving

the bank and the realty. Your mom knows all about it.' Come to think of it, had she written me that threatening note as well? Writing threatening notes seemed to be a favorite pastime of hers. Was she really even in Reno? 'Just see that somebody in the office gets the check.'

'Will do.' He folded the check in two and slipped it into his shirt pocket.

'Ouch.' I looked at my little finger. I'd managed to run the dough cutter over it. Fortunately, I hadn't broken any skin. I refocused my attention on the task of making beignets, aware of Tommy staring at me over the glass. He still hadn't told me what he was doing here. 'Are you going to tell me what you want?'

'You sell beignets, right?' He licked his upper lip. 'That's what I came for.' He leaned over the glass and faced me over the fryer. 'And to see where, you know, it happened.'

Wow, that seemed particularly gruesome. I resisted the temptation to drop an ice cube into the hot grease and give Tommy a burning sensation that he wouldn't soon forget. A sudden realization hit me. 'Wait, are you working at the realty now?'

Tommy shrugged. It was his turn to order. He ordered a plate of beignets and a small coffee and handed Aubrey a credit card before answering. 'Aunt Patti hired me herself.'

This was news. Rick Wilbur dies and the black sheep nephew finds himself in the line of the suddenly employed. It appeared Uncle Wilbur's loss had been Tommy's gain. I really wanted to learn more about Patti and Natalie. Why was

Patti showing an interest in the business that, according to Moonflower, she'd never shown before?

'Sounds like your uncle's death hasn't hurt you none.' My mind spun in larger and larger circles. I was beginning to wonder how well off the Widow Wilbur would now be with her husband gone.

Tommy lifted a shoulder. 'What can I say? I'm just lucky, I guess.' He scooped up his order and headed for the door. He waved my check from The Hitching Post in the air. 'Don't worry, Maggie, I'll be sure this gets in the right hands.'

Yeah, probably his, I thought. I'd call the office later and make sure those right hands belonged to someone more responsible. Tommy and Brian crossed paths at the door.

Great, one jerk leaves and another comes in to fill the vacuum. Nature in action, I guess. They do say nature abhors a vacuum.

But not as much as I abhorred my ex-husband, I'll bet.

TWENTY-TWO

I called out, 'We don't serve jerks!'

'Maggie!' Aubrey gasped in a loud whisper and shot me a funny look.

'Don't worry,' I waved a hand in her direction. 'It's only my dead husband.'

'Wait a minute.' Aubrey banged the register drawer shut. 'One minute you're walking in here with a wedding dress and a little while later you announce that that's your dead husband walking in the door.'

She pointed at Brian. 'Would you mind explaining to me what's going on?' Aubrey looked from me to Brian and back again.

'I'll be glad to,' said Brian, laying his hands atop the register. 'First, I think I'll have a cup of coffee and an order of beignets, please.'

'Your money is no good here, Brian!' I moved toward the register.

'Wow, really?' Brian rubbed his hands together. 'That's nice of you, Mags.' He winked at Aubrey. 'Guess I should've made that two orders of beignets. Too late to change my order?'

'Too late to change my answer when you asked me to marry you?' I growled in reply.

'OK,' Aubrey said, grabbing a glass of water. 'Things are getting a little crazy,' she said, heading for the storeroom. 'I think I'm gonna take a short break, if you don't mind. Call me when normal returns or if things get too busy out here for you.' She wiggled her fingers in the air.

I rested my hands on my hips and watched Aubrey go. I could have insisted she stay but then I might have felt compelled to watch my manners and my mouth in front of her. Impressionable young minds and ears and all that.

I filled a cup of coffee, then placed three fresh beignets on a plate and sprinkled them with sugar. 'That will be ten dollars.' I held out my palm.

'What?' Brian took a step back and looked up at the menu board. 'That's too much!' He pointed at the sign. 'That's double what it costs!'

I smiled. 'You want to go for triple?'

'Fine.' Brian frowned and pulled out his wallet. He grumbled the entire time but finally forked over the ten-dollar bill. 'Keep the change.'

I knew sarcasm when I heard it but it didn't bother me. I shrugged and dropped the money in the till. Brian headed for a table and I helped my next customers. I also kept one eye on Brian. I didn't place a lot of trust in the man. Could you blame me?

Brian had a degree in finance from Arizona State. When we'd met, he was working in a bank. Then one day, he came home and announced he was giving up banking to drive a truck, which was fine by me until he started parking that truck outside Anita Lawrence's house. He said they were just friends and maybe they were. But now they were man and wife.

When I'd found out Brian had quit the bank,

I had put it down to no ambition and disdain for the corporate world. When Mom found out he'd given up a solid career in banking to haul freight, she'd put it down to, and I quote, 'No brains.' She claimed two letters in his name only needed to be switched around to prove that. And since he'd dumped me for Anita Lawrence, you can see why Mom is, to this day, not Brian's biggest booster.

The way I see it, it serves him right that I tell everybody he's dead. So why couldn't he stay dead? What on earth was he doing here in Table Rock?

With no further customers, I grabbed a clean towel and a spray bottle of pink disinfectant and started wiping the tables.

Brian had polished off his beignets and half his coffee. 'Ah,' he said, patting his belly lovingly while looking at me. 'Brings back the old days.'

'If you're talking about our honeymoon, I'm under doctor's orders to forget.'

He shook his head. 'Still holding a grudge, eh? Just can't let go.' Brian shook his head some more. I felt like shaking his head myself, like a piggybank, and seeing what fell out. Probably not two cents' worth of brains.

'Don't you have someplace to be?'

He grabbed a paper napkin from the tabletop dispenser and wiped his chin. 'As a matter of fact, I do. I've got a truckload of computers to deliver.' He jerked his thumb toward the alley where his truck was parked. 'Then it's back to Phoenix.'

'Excuse me.' I picked up his empty plate and

215

tossed it in the recycle bin. Brian lives with his new wife, Anita, and two kids down in the Phoenix suburbs, along with that dog the size of Mom's Volkswagen. Brian looked like he'd lost a few pounds from his banker days. Driving a truck seemed to be requiring a little more muscle than working as a desk jockey.

'I was dropping off some medical supplies in Prescott when I heard about the murder in your café.' Brian rested his hand on my lower arm. 'I wanted to be sure you were OK. I came as fast as I could.'

I yanked my arm away. 'I'm fine. Everything's under control.' Well, sort of. The café was up and running and I had plenty of leads to go on concerning who'd killed Mr Wilbur.

He reached for my arm again but I kept out of range. 'Are you sure there's nothing I can do?'

'No.' I flapped my towel and retreated behind the counter to help four young men who'd just come in wearing soccer uniforms. 'Can I help you?' I scratched down their order and moved to the fryer. Aubrey returned from her break and I was glad to see her.

When the boys were seated and enjoying their food and refreshments, Brian ambled up to the fryer once more. 'Guess I'll be off. It was good to see you again.'

He stood there hesitantly. If he was waiting for me to say it had been good to see him, too, he was in for a long, long wait. ''Bye,' I said finally, glancing at him.

'If you need anything, just let me know.'

'Wait!' I said as Brian started for the door.

He turned around, a smile broadening his face. 'Yeah?'

'There is one thing you could do for me?'

'Yeah, what's that?'

My eyes sparkled as I grinned. 'You could say that *you* murdered Rick Wilbur.'

His brow deepened. 'Who's Rick—' He stopped. 'Oh.' The corner of his mouth twisted up. 'Very funny, Mags.'

I shrugged lamely. 'It was worth a shot.' I'd learned to stop complaining anytime he or anybody else for that matter called me Mags. It sounded too much like maggots said three times too fast.

Mom and my sister came in shortly after, bringing Andy and the boys with them. I treated them all. It was fun seeing the looks of joy on my nephews' faces as they bit into the sugar-covered treats. Donna and Andy weren't big on sweets and didn't allow a lot of refined sugar in their house. I half-suspected they were un-American.

But my joy at sharing my opening day with my family was spoiled when Detective Mark Highsmith walked in the door, after first holding said door open for dear old VV, Veronica Vargas, looking blazing hot in a sharp navy skirt suit, with a small black Chanel purse slung over her shoulder. She blew in on a perfumed waft of air like she owned the place.

For the first time I wondered if I was cursed. I shut my eyes for a moment, in search of my happy place, then opened them.

So, of course, that's when Brian had to come bursting through the door once again, leaving Highsmith still holding it open.

'What are you still doing here?' I huffed.

'Can you believe it?' He waved a piece of paper in the air. 'Some moron gave me a ticket.' Brian strode right up to my face, bristling. I'd always felt his ears were too large for his head. At the moment he looked like an angry blue-eyed koala. And that was not a compliment. 'You told me I was supposed to park in the alley. That's why I moved my truck in the first place. Now some idiot cop gives me a ticket.'

He waved the ticket around some more. I hoped Highsmith was enjoying this as much as I was. 'Yeah, cops,' I said, feigning commiseration. I glared at Highsmith. 'A royal pain.'

Brian shook his head. 'Tell me about it.'

I turned to the detective. 'Have you seen enough?'

'Enough for what?' VV had her arm laced through the crook in his elbow. While she was dressed to the nines, as I suspected she always was, he was in jeans and a polo shirt.

'Enough to arrest this guy, of course.'

Highsmith cocked an eyebrow. 'On what charge?'

'Disturbing the peace, making a public nuisance?'

'Hey, what are you talking about?' Brian asked.

I ignored my dead husband.

'I don't think so,' said Highsmith. He and Veronica shared a look.

'How about public stupidity then?'

'How about some food?' Highsmith said, leading VV to the counter where Aubrey described our offerings, which at this point included only the plate of three original French donuts, plus coffee, orange juice, hot and cold chocolate milk and soft drinks.

'Who is that guy?' demanded Brian as I shoved him out the door.

'Police officer,' I said, giving him a nudge toward the street. 'You'd better leave quickly before he changes his mind and throws the book at you. That one's got a nasty reputation!' I gave Brian another push.

'Thanks, Mags!'

I stood on the sidewalk grinning as I watched Brian turn the corner to the alley. I wiped my hands on my apron and shot back inside. What the devil were the detective and the prosecuting attorney doing here?

Detective Highsmith and Ms Vargas were just settling down at a table near the window when I returned. 'Have fun poking around in my underwear drawer?'

Highsmith reddened as VV's eyebrows inched up. 'Ran our search of Ms Miller's apartment last evening.'

Veronica bobbed her chin. I'd been hoping to get a bigger rise out of her. Dang, she was the coolest of cucumbers. 'Poor you.'

I wasn't sure if she meant Highsmith or me, so I let it slide. 'How is everything?' I inquired.

Veronica sipped slowly, lofting a ladylike finger. 'Interesting.' I studied her lips closely. Not so much as a smudge or a dab of powdered sugar. How the devil did she do it?

'Good,' said Highsmith. 'Really good. These beignets are delicious. I've got to say, it's the first time I've tried one and I'm a fan.'

I shifted my weight as I watched them. 'Is this the only reason you're here? For the food?' Were they spying on me? Maybe even about to charge me with the murder of Rick Wilbur? Had they found something in my apartment that, in their narrow minds, they thought implicated me? Did I need to phone Andy? Arrange bail?

Veronica returned my stare. 'What other reason could there be?' She batted her lashes at me.

Oh, how I hated this woman. 'None, I guess.' My mind's gears turned round and round. 'You know,' I said finally, leaning a hand on the table, 'I've learned some interesting things about Rick Wilbur, his wife, his nephew and a whole lot of other people in the last couple of days.' I directed my words toward Detective Highsmith.

He stuck an entire beignet in his mouth, chewed for several moments, then swallowed. I watched as the bolus moved down his throat, a sight akin to watching a bullsnake swallow a whole rat. 'You're not poking your nose into our murder investigation, are you, Ms Miller?' He raised his cup to his lips and drank, then set the cup down.

'Because that would be interfering with the law.' Veronica folded her arms in her lap, her face rigid.

'Of course not,' I said quickly. 'I simply heard

220

things. Table Rock's a small town. You know how it is.'

Highsmith nodded slowly. 'You leave it to us,' he said, rising leisurely. 'Ready to go, Veronica?'

'In a moment, Mark.' VV tapped at her perfect front upper teeth with a perfect fingernail. 'If there is anything you can tell us that would further the investigation – any evidence at all that you are aware of – we'd be very interested in hearing about it.'

My eyes lifted to the ceiling tiles. Was she really interested? Or was this a trick of some sort? I was still pretty certain that the delightful VV would like nothing more than to see me hang for the murder of Mr Wilbur.

Ignoring my better judgment in my urge to show these two chumps how much I'd discovered – and in the process prove my innocence – I grabbed a chair from the empty table beside theirs and slid into it uninvited. 'First of all, there's Tommy Henson.' The words spilled out. 'He's a nephew of Mr Wilbur's. He wanted a job but Mr Wilbur wasn't interested in hiring him.'

'So you think Tommy murdered his uncle over it?' That was Detective Highsmith.

I shrugged. 'Could be, right?' I waved my hand. 'But wait, there's more. I think Wilbur Realty might be in trouble, too. And then there's Johnny Wolfe—'

'From The Hitching Post?' VV asked.

I nodded. 'He and Rick were seen together having a heated discussion and I found a Wilbur Realty pen on the floor in their stockroom.' I went on quickly, ignoring the unfathomable look

221

that had just come from VV: 'He's got quite a temper, believe me. And then there's Patti Wilbur. And her sister, Natalie! They could be in cahoots!' I paused. 'Or Natalie and Tommy could be in cahoots.' I scratched my chin. I really wasn't sure. But my excitement was rising now. There were just so many possibilities!

My eyes jumped to Karma Koffee across the street. 'And don't even get me started on Rob and Trish at the coffee shop.' I pointed. 'Those two are a real pair of odd birds. They couldn't stand Mr Wilbur. Rob said so himself.'

My eyes dodged to Aubrey. 'She must have told you all about how the two men didn't get on and how she saw Rob and Rick arguing over here, right?'

Highsmith looked skeptical. 'In cahoots?'

'Who even uses that word anymore?' Veronica flashed an amused glance toward Highsmith.

A bolt of anger shot through me. He wasn't listening to a word I was saying. In fact, the two of them were mocking me!

Here I'd been planning to tell them all about how they should be looking for my two missing chairs. They could forget it now. More than ever, I was determined to solve this crime for them.

I slammed back my chair and stood up. 'I'm merely trying to point out,' I said, pressing my hands against my hips, 'that there were plenty of other people in Table Rock who might have wanted to see Rick Wilbur dead. Despite what you think, plenty of people actually thought he was a jerk! Maybe even worth killing!'

Both Detective Highsmith and Veronica Vargas were looking past me now. 'What's so interesting?' I snapped.

Veronica silently pointed behind me. I turned. My stomach fell. 'Oh, hello, Mrs Wilbur.' I smiled weakly. 'I didn't hear you come in.'

I did hear her go out.

That woman knew how to slam a door.

TWENTY-THREE

Things went downhill after that. I ran to the counter and grabbed the new marble rolling pin. 'Look at this,' I insisted. 'A brand-new rolling pin.'

'Congratulations.' Highsmith looked down his nose. 'So?'

I shook the rolling pin in the space between us. 'So, this rolling pin is identical to the one I had before. You know,' I said, 'the one that killed Rick Wilbur!'

'I repeat. So?'

Veronica tugged Highsmith's shirt. 'If we don't leave now, we'll be late for the movie.'

He nodded.

I dug in my pockets and fished out the wad of paper that had once been the rolling pin's accompanying note. 'So look at this.' I held the dried lump of paper in my hand. Seeing it lying there, it didn't look all that impressive. I could see by the looks in their eyes that they didn't think so either.

'This note, well, not this note.' I stuck the lump back in my pocket. 'I mean, it was that note, but Mom washed it.' I shook my head in a desperate attempt to sort my thoughts.

'Anyway, it was in my storeroom with the rolling pin. I don't know who left it there but I do know why.' I slammed the rolling pin down on the counter. I hadn't really meant to let it drop that hard, but dang that thing was heavy. Solid marble, remember?

'Because you needed a new rolling pin?' Veronica said.

'No,' I replied. 'It was a warning.'

'What sort of a warning?' asked the detective.

'Not to stick my nose where it doesn't belong.'

Highsmith was quick to reply. 'Sounds more like good advice than a warning.'

Veronica looked up at her companion. 'Do you think it's worth checking for prints, Mark?'

'Look at it.' He pointed down at the counter at the rolling pin. 'It's covered with flour and sugar. Good luck lifting any prints from that thing. Plus, she's been handling it.'

Veronica nodded.

'If you thought it was evidence why the heck are you even using it, Ms Miller?' He scolded me with his eyes. 'Why didn't you bring it straight to the station?'

'Well, in the first place, I was sort of busy at the time. In the second place—'

'Yes?'

I studied my shoes. 'My mother washed it.'

'What's that?' he asked.

I lifted my chin. 'My mother washed it. Are you happy now?'

VV draped her arm around Highsmith's slender waist. 'The movie.'

As soon as Table Rock's least favorite couple left, I accosted Aubrey. 'You never did tell me what happened when you went to the police station to tell them about how you saw Rob arguing with Rick.' I pulled her close. 'You did tell them, didn't you?'

Aubrey nodded. 'Yes, but not that guy. I explained it to a woman in uniform I met when I entered.'

I frowned. 'What was her reaction exactly?'

Aubrey scrunched up the side of her face. 'Not much. She thanked me and everything and said she would make sure to pass on the information to the officer in charge of the investigation.'

That would be Highsmith. I let out a deep sigh. It had been a long day, and if life was quicksand, I was sinking deeper with every move I made.

Was I the only person who cared about finding Rick Wilbur's killer? Or was everybody so certain that I had killed the guy that they weren't capable of looking any further?

I sent Aubrey home – it had been a long day for her too – and closed up early. I could see already that I was going to have to take my sister up on her offer of splitting one of her part-timers from Mother Earth/Father Sun Grocers to cover a shift. I couldn't expect Aubrey to put in twelve-hour days. I wasn't even sure how long I could keep up the pace.

Plus, I'd promised to feed Mr Teller's cat. I groaned as I climbed up onto the Schwinn and pedaled into the western sun. There was still plenty of light this time of year. Thank goodness for that. I dislike riding in the dark.

Clive was right: finding Teller's bungalow was easy – and those cobalt blue shutters. Ick. What was the man thinking? The yard was mostly dust.

A desiccated and browning three-armed cactus sat two paces from the porch. A tan Buick sat in the drive. I spotted two more scraggly little cacti growing from a corner of the roof.

I parked my bike behind the car, walked up and knocked on the door just in case Ed or anyone else was home. Two of the three front windows were crudely boarded up. Clive was wrong. This wasn't a fixer-upper. This was a tearer-downer.

I wished I'd brought a spray can of disinfectant to squirt myself down with afterward. Something told me this house would be just crawling with cooties. I didn't want them coming home with me.

I dug around at the bottom of my purse and pulled out the house keys. The key turned easily enough. I pulled open the door and was immediately accosted by a hot wave of stale air and the ever delightful smell of cat.

'Here, kitty, kitty!'

Whoosh!

I looked between my legs just in time to see Carol Two fly between them. 'Hey!' I ran after her as she turned the corner to the backyard. 'Come back here!' I panted. 'I've got kibble!'

Fortunately, Edwin's cat, Carol Two, hadn't gone far. I spied her licking her tail on a dirty patch of concrete that served as the back patio. A rusted charcoal grill and a green and white lawn chair with a couple of broken straps gave the patio a certain ambience.

Shabby eek.

Looking around, it was clear to see that the entire yard was in total disrepair. Had the previous occupant left it this way or was Ed one lousy housekeeper? Of course, he was in the hospital so I guess I had to cut him a little slack.

I trod slowly and carefully to the calico. She seemed content where she was and I did my best to speak cat to her as I approached, not wanting to spook her and spend the rest of my night chasing some cat I didn't know all around a neighborhood I didn't know, for a guy I didn't know.

I spotted a pile containing an odd assortment of lumber, some cement blocks, bags of cement and a roll of chicken wire. Either Edwin was remodeling on the cheap or he was building a chicken coop. Pity the poor chickens if he was. Out here, in the flat yard, with its distinct lack of shade and not a tree in sight, they'd be broasted in a day.

To call the detached one-car garage ramshackle was being very generous. Its pitched roof was more pitched to the left than could possibly be normal, the shingles were decaying and there was a depression on the near side of the roof that looked like a ten-ton boulder might have once sat there. The windows were clouded with dirt where the glass hadn't been busted out. I suspected it was going to take a younger, healthier man than Ed Teller to set this place right again.

I worked my way through the land field of debris and junk that cluttered the yard and scooped up Carol Two. 'That's a good kitty.' I rubbed her head and was rewarded with a purr.

As I set Carol Two down inside the front door, careful to pull it shut behind me to avoid going another round with her, I heard the ringing of a telephone from somewhere deep in the shadow-filled house. I walked quickly, following the sound and, after stepping through a short hallway, found myself in the low-ceilinged kitchen.

My eyes bounced off the walls. Yikes, what hideous wallpaper! Strips of pink gerbera daisies and purple pansies. How appetizing. I squinted. What were those lumps between the flowers? I looked closer. Cows? Were those cows?

By the looks of it, the wallpaper must've been original. It certainly wasn't something Mr Teller had newly pasted up, not with the tears and peeling and the nicotine stains that added a yellow tinge to the room and stink that my nostrils instantly picked up and started sending signals directly to my stomach creating an urgent desire to puke.

I reached for the phone, having spotted it hanging on the wall beside the refrigerator. Like the refrigerator, it was old. With its olive-green complexion, long, droopy coiled cord and rotary dial, it looked as tired as this old house. 'Hello?'

'Hi, who's this?' said the squeaky woman's voice at the other end.

'Maggie.' I was breathing heavy, partly from exertion and partly from the closed-up feel of the house. Maybe I'd open a few windows and air the place out before I left. I'd bet Mr Teller would appreciate it. 'Sorry,' I fanned myself, 'out of breath.'

'Huh? Is Daddy there?'

'Sorry, wrong number.' I hung up. Ed didn't have any kids – at least, not alive and breathing, from what I'd been told. He didn't even have a wife. Just the fur ball. Carol Two rubbed against my shin, tail up. 'I know, I know. Dinner time. I could use a burger myself.' I looked around the kitchen. I'd failed to ask Clive where the cat's supplies were kept.

The phone rang again. 'Hello, this is Maggie.' I could see the cat bowl and litter box set up in the utility room off to my right. Seems a mite unsanitary if you ask me. I mean, I don't go keeping my kitchen supplies in my bathroom, but it was his house, his cat.

Click.

I turned the receiver to my face. 'Moron.' I hung up. I refreshed Carol Two's water dish, poured out a generous helping of kitty kibble and approached that which I dreaded most.

The litter box.

Definitely in need of a little housekeeping. Business complete, I spent a few minutes with Carol Two then took a swing through the house. Not that I'm snoopy or anything; I was just curious as to what the place looked like.

I can report: the place didn't look like much. Two bedrooms, one bath. All in need of some extreme TLC. Ed Teller was going to have his work cut out for him if he wanted to renovate this place and flip it for profit. I'll stick to making beignets.

TWENTY-FOUR

My good deed done and my body spent, I locked up and headed home. But first I thought I'd swing by Mesa Verde Medical Center and see how the patient was doing. Partly to let him know that I was taking care of his cat for him and partly to assure him that he had nothing to worry about on that front.

More importantly, I wanted to see if he could offer me some insight into the staff and goings on at Wilbur Realty. After all, he'd worked there for years and was Rick Wilbur's close friend. If anybody could shed some light on things, I was betting he could.

If I was lucky – and let's face it, I rarely was – Daniel Vargas would be there, too.

He wasn't. Fortunately, the receptionist didn't give me any trouble and I soon found myself in Edwin Teller's room. The problem was that he wasn't there. A copy of the *Table Rock Reader* and a half-empty glass of water sat atop the bedside table. My eyes fell on a small headline: Police Continue Search for Killer. The article read: Police continue to interview Ms Margaret Miller regarding the discovery of local realtor, Rick Wilbur, in the storeroom of her newly opened eatery, Maggie's Beignet Café.

A growl vibrated in my throat and I threw the

paper back down without finishing. The story was written by Brad Smith.

If I was going to be responsible for killing anybody, it was going to be him. I mean, he deserved some sort of punishment for that first run-on sentence alone!

I moved out to the hall and looked up and down in each direction. Where does an ailing patient with a heart condition go? Didn't he have a stroke of some sort? OMG, he wasn't dead, was he?

I tracked down a man in a nursing uniform. 'Excuse me, I'm looking for Mr Teller, room twenty-two? Do you know where I can find him?'

'Sorry. I work in the emergency department. He could be in therapy. You'd have to ask at reception.'

I passed by Mr Teller's room on my way back to reception and this time caught sight of him lying in his bed. 'Mr Teller, there you are!'

I pulled to a stop and turned into his room. The bed Clive had occupied was still empty. 'I was looking for you earlier but you were gone.'

'Bathroom,' he replied gruffly.

I nodded. I should have thought of that. Why are the simple explanations in life always so . . . well, simple? 'You look great!' I patted his knee through the covers. Truth be told, he looked like a troop of cannibals had been boiling him in a pot of some unsavory goop.

'How are you doing? Are you feeling OK?'

He pinched his eyes together. 'Of course I'm feeling OK.' He leaned toward me. 'Why shouldn't I feel OK? Nurses tell you something?'

I shook my head. 'No, no.'

His eyes pinched even closer – any more and they'd change places. 'Who are you, anyway?'

I gave the guy my best 'I'm surprised you don't remember me' face. 'It's me, Maggie Miller. I own Maggie's Beignet Café. I lease the spot from Wilbur Realty. Rick himself showed me the property.'

I didn't seem to be getting through to him. 'We've spoken before.' Gee, whatever he'd suffered from was having some lingering effects. I pointed to the bare mattress on the other side of the smallish room. 'My friend Clive was your roommate.'

'Oh.' Recognition filtered up to his eyes. 'You're the loudmouth.'

I grimaced. Not exactly the descriptor I'd choose to describe myself. But he was the patient, I told myself. Play nice, Maggie. 'I'm taking care of your cat, Carol Two, while you're laid up.'

He ran his fingers through his beard. 'What happened to Clive? He die or something?'

'What?' My back stiffened. 'No! Nothing like that. He's busy is all and I told him I would take over the responsibility for him.'

He looked me up and down. 'You ever have a cat?'

'Uh, no.'

'Ever take care of one before?'

'Well, again, no, but—'

'Doctor says I can go home soon.' Ed cut me off. 'Maybe tomorrow.'

'That's great news,' I said, reaching out to pat his hand, surprised to discover how clammy it felt. Had a doctor, a licensed doctor, actually told this man he might be going home tomorrow? It seemed unlikely. If Edwin Teller went anywhere tomorrow, I wouldn't be surprised if it was to take a long nap in a pine box.

'You think you can keep her alive till then?'

'Sure, of course.' I mean, come on, did he really think I could kill his cat in less than twenty-four hours?

'Fine.' He crossed his arms over his ribs. 'Job's yours.'

What a sweetheart. I pulled up a chair. If Ed Teller could provide me with any answers, this might be my best chance to ask the questions. 'Speaking of Rick Wilbur,' I said, my knees touching the mattress, 'who do you think killed him?'

'Personally,' I said, without waiting for an answer, 'my money is on Tommy, Patti or Natalie.' I bit my lip. 'And Rob Gregory. It definitely could be Rob Gregory. Or my shop neighbor, Johnny Wolfe.'

Ed looked at me, his eyes wide and white. 'Wow, that's a lot of suspects. I just figured it must have been a robbery gone wrong.'

I gave Ed's idea some thought. 'Could be,' I admitted. But that wouldn't help me find the killer. In fact, that might mean that Rick Wilbur's true killer would never be brought to justice.

That left me looking like the most likely suspect. Even if I was never arrested and formally charged, folks in town would always suspect. It's hard to live and work in a small town when everybody thinks you're a murderer.

I sighed bitterly. 'I just wish I knew why Mr Wilbur was murdered in my café. I mean, why me? Why not someplace else?'

Edwin rubbed his fingers. 'No way of telling, I suppose. Just one of those things. I know Rick had gone over to take a look at your AC.'

That would explain what he'd been doing at the café. I had mentioned to him that the air conditioner was on the fritz. 'Speaking of which . . .'

'Don't worry.' His pallid hand cut through the air. 'As soon as I'm feeling up to it, I'll check it out. Everyone's been complaining. You should hear some of the unkind words Caitie Conklin has had to say since her AC has been acting up.'

He chuckled. 'You see, all those air conditioning units are interconnected. All those little shops used to be part of a large department store. But it closed up and the space got subdivided years ago.'

Of course, the hairdresser. I still needed to have a word with her. 'She was angry?'

'Oh, yeah,' said Ed, his head wagging. 'And she's got a mouth on her. Always been a difficult tenant, that one.'

'So why didn't Wilbur Realty simply evict her the next time her salon came up for renewal of her lease?'

'It's complicated,' Ed said. 'Seeing how Caitie used to be married to Rick.'

My head twisted so fast I heard a click. 'Caitie Conklin is Rick Wilbur's ex?'

'That's right.' He chuckled some more. I was glad to see it. They say laughter is the best medicine. 'I guess that's why she's gotten away with sassing him all these years. Rick always was afraid of that woman.'

'Afraid?'

Ed shrugged. 'You know what I mean.'

I didn't. Not exactly. But I was dying to find out.

'I also heard some rumors about Wilbur Realty,' I said.

'What sort of rumors?'

A nurse came in to check Mr Teller's vital signs. 'A little high, Mr Teller. Let's not overdo things.' She cast a meaningful look my way and I squirmed. I waited until she was finished to answer Ed's question.

'I hear the agency may be in financial trouble.'

Ed waved a hand in front of his chest. 'Please, Rick was always crying famine. I mean, I loved the guy, but he was as cheap as they come.'

I sat straighter. 'So you don't think Wilbur Realty is having money trouble?'

He chuckled. 'Not unless Patti's having trouble trying to figure out how to spend all Rick's money.'

I gave this some thought. Ed's opinion didn't jive at all with what I'd been hearing, but who would know better than him? I tapped the edge of the chair with my fingernail. And it did jive with appearances. Wilbur Realty owned and managed plenty of properties. If that was financial trouble, please let me have some!

'I went by your house. It's looking good.'

Ed snorted. 'Please, it's a dump.'

I contained a sigh of relief. Thank goodness he

knew that. I was afraid he'd developed mental problems to go with his physical ones.

'But once I get done with it, I'll be able to get top dollar.'

I nodded and rose. 'Don't worry about Carol Two,' I said. 'You can count on me.' No way that cat was going to die on my watch.

As I left, Ed said, 'Let me give you some advice, Miller.'

'Yes?'

'If you do talk to Caitie, watch your back.'

A frisson ran up my spine. Did he mean that figuratively, literally or both?

Should Rick Wilbur have been watching his back?

TWENTY-FIVE

Exhausted, I pulled open the refrigerator door, reveled in the blast of chill air that came my way and nosed around. For lunch, I'd sent Aubrey for a couple of burritos and a bag of homemade taco chips from Senor Sapo's, the Mexican restaurant a few doors down. She'd come back with a pair of half-pound rattlesnake burritos, chips and spicy guacamole. I thought the name, rattler burrito, was kind of cute but wanted to puke when Aubrey explained to me that there was real rattlesnake meat in my half-eaten burrito.

'It's good for you,' Aubrey said. 'Haven't you heard of the medicinal and nutritional benefits of snake meat?'

I considered throwing the rest of it at her, but in the end was too hungry to put up a fuss. Besides, if I hit her with a half-pound of rattlesnake meat, I'd probably send her to the hospital. And I needed her working.

Of course, if rattlesnake was as good for you as Aubrey reported, she could use it as a poultice after I knocked her upside the head with it and save herself an expensive trip to the ER. That was a big plus, seeing as I didn't offer employee insurance.

I kept my thoughts to myself. I did keep an eye out for loose fangs or rattlers while I finished it off, however.

Though I'd missed dinner, I wasn't all that hungry – I don't think that rattler was sitting well in my stomach – so I snagged a pint of Safeway-brand vanilla ice cream and spooned a couple of globs of strawberry jam overtop. Hey, it hit two of the major food groups – fruit and dairy.

I still got queasy thinking about the rattlesnake sitting in my gut, pulling itself together, getting ready to strike at my stomach lining and gnaw its way free.

Before I could make myself any crazier, I grabbed a pad of paper and a pen from the junk drawer, then pulled out a chair at the kitchen table and sat. Time for a list. There were so many ideas, suspects, clues and motives swimming around in my brain that if I didn't write them down I might never recall them, let alone sort them out.

I savored the creamy coolness of the ice cream as it slid over my tongue and down my throat. Now *this* was dinner. After a couple of spoonfuls – I'm not sure why the carton looked three-quarters empty, I'd only had a bite or two – I got down to business.

I needed to start at the beginning. Get my suspects in order. I chewed on the end of my pen and thought. First, there was Clive Rothschild, of course. He'd been with me when I'd discovered Mr Wilbur's body. Could he be the culprit? Had he set me up? Maybe he knew about the body because he'd left it there himself and knew the police would never suspect him of murder if he'd been there when the body was discovered. Ooh, crafty. I jotted his name down on the top of the sheet. He could have been faking that fainting spell, too.

That led me to his partner and spouse, Johnny Wolfe. What did I really know about him? I tapped the tip of the pen against the notepad. Former Olympic skater, bridal shop owner, pain in the patooty . . . And he'd been seen arguing with the victim.

I drew a connecting line between him and Clive. The two of them could be in cahoots. Yes, I'd said the word 'cahoots.' In your face, Detective Highsmith. I pushed the pen harder against the paper, thickening the line.

Who was next?

Tommy Henson, Natalie's son. The one who desperately sought a job with Wilbur Realty but Rick wasn't having him. Now he had a job and Rick Wilbur was pushing up proverbial daisies. He was a definite suspect.

What about his mother, Natalie? I still wanted to talk to her, not only about the threatening letter she'd sent me about my check, but about Wilbur Realty's finances. She was currently out of town, but had she been out of town at the time of the murder? That still wasn't clear to me and I was going to have to ask around. Maybe Moonflower could tell me.

That led me to the Widow Wilbur. Spouses make the perfect suspects. I hadn't heard any talk about discord in the marriage but that doesn't mean there hadn't been any. What marriage doesn't have bumps in the road?

My marriage had had a bump in the road called Brian. Had Patti's bump in the road been called Rick?

I added her name to my growing list. A definite maybe.

I leaned back in my chair. The problem here was that I didn't know who anybody's alibis were so far. I had learned that Mr Wilbur had definitely been killed sometime during the late evening hours of the day before I'd discovered him. What I needed to find out was where all these people were on Wednesday night.

I hunched over and thought some more. I added Rob and Trish Gregory's names to my list. They were categorically no fans of Mr Wilbur. Aubrey had seen Rob arguing with him recently. With the prices they were charging at Karma Koffee they were certainly thieves, so why not murderers to boot?

Of course, when I was in Karma Koffee, Rob had mentioned something about hearing that Mr Wilbur's body had been found in my walk-in cooler. Maybe he had been intentionally misleading. Rob Gregory had those devious eyes. He could have said that just to throw me off, knowing all along that the body had been in the chair carton. Oh, that man was crafty, too.

I polished off the ice cream, rose and tossed the empty carton in the trash. I yawned and stretched. Who else could have had a motive?

I flopped back in my chair. The chairs! I still had to figure out who had the café chairs! I chewed at the bottom of my lip. There was something I was missing . . . what was it about the chairs?

I could feel it ticking inside me, like a snaky tongue liking my stomach lining. Ugh.

241

I straightened. My chairs. Of course. I'd seen those missing chairs of mine. I'd sat in those missing chairs of mine.

Laura's Lightly Used. The day I'd taken the Schwinn in to get the chain fixed, Laura and I had sat in those chairs. They'd been right up by the register.

I swallowed hard. Was Laura Duval, meek, kind, Laura Duval, a cold-blooded murderer? My hand shook as I added her name to my list. She was strong and capable. Was she capable of murder?

I'd be paying Laura's Lightly Used another visit tomorrow.

I yawned once more. Must've been something in the ice cream. Fatigue coursed through me. I read my list over. Who else was I missing?

There was the ex-wife, Caitie Conklin. Ed Teller had warned me about her. I knew almost nothing about the woman. She was a complete unknown. But exes sometimes aren't a big step removed from perpetrators.

I put a question mark next to her name. The Salon de Belleza was open Sundays. I could pop in on her, too. Ask her about her relationship with Rick and where she was at the time of the murder.

A last yawn just about swallowed me whole. I stumbled to the bedroom and pulled off my shorts and shirt, leaving them in a pile on the floor. The maid could pick them up in the morning. Note to self: hire maid.

I threw on a clean T-shirt and tumbled into bed. The room was stifling and the bed was as warm as tepid tea. I groaned and tossed back the covers. I crossed the floor, turned on the room air conditioner and flopped back down head first into the pillow.

Rest. A good night's sleep. That was what I needed.

I coughed and opened my eyes. The room was swirling with ghosts. My eyes burned. I choked and coughed some more. My eyes darted to the bedside digital clock. Though the numbers glowed red, I couldn't make out the time. I could make out the flames spilling from my AC unit, however, as they tried to lick the ceiling.

I screamed, kicked off the covers and tumbled to the floor. 'Ouch!' I pushed myself off the floor and half-crawled, half-ran out of the bedroom. Smoke filled the living room and kitchen as well. I fumbled for the light switch along the wall. Nothing. The power had gone out.

I needed to call the fire department! Where was my purse? I coughed and coughed, choking on the thick, acrid smoke that filled my apartment. Then I saw it: on the floor near the kitchen table. I scrambled on my knees, crashed head first into the leg of the kitchen table and felt for my purse. I dragged it with me by the strap to the front door and fell onto the stoop, breathing hard and heavy.

I dialed the operator. 'Fire! Emergency!' I coughed as the man on the other end asked me my address. Finally, I managed to blurt it out, but by the time I had the fire department had already arrived.

Two firemen hauled me up by my armpits and led me to the fire truck. A third handed me a metal water bottle. I drank. The cool water spilled down my throat like the elixir of life from ancient Hindu mythology or one of those Harry Potter novels.

'Anybody else inside?' An older man with ruddy cheeks and a gristly salt-and-pepper beard peered down at me. He had on a blue T-shirt and matching trousers. He wore a badge that identified him as the fire chief.

I shook my head no and trembled.

'No pets?'

I shook my head once more. There was a bottle of margarita mix that kept me company when my spirits were low, but I didn't think that was the kind of companionship he had in mind.

He handed me a blanket. 'Thanks.' I pulled it close. 'How'd you get here so fast?'

'A neighbor saw the smoke and called it in. I'm Terry Stillman,' he said. 'Head of the Table Rock Volunteer Fire Department.' The flashing red lights of an ambulance caught my eye and I turned as the vehicle raced up to the curb. At least they didn't have their siren going. I really didn't care to have my neighbors out enjoying the show. I mean, I was in my worst old T-shirt and underwear!

I lowered the blanket across my knees. Two firemen decked out in their firemen's gear tromped out my front door holding fire extinguishers. 'All clear!' cried one as he approached the fire truck.

Chief Stillman nodded. 'Much damage?'

'Nah,' the fireman replied. 'The wall holding

244

the AC unit is a bit singed but nothing major. More smoke damage than anything. We opened up the windows to air the place out.'

The AC unit. 'So that's what caused the fire?'

The man shrugged and set down his extinguisher. 'It's too soon to tell, but if you ask me, yeah.'

All the while, the team of paramedics had been prodding and poking me, checking my vitals and shining bright lights in my eyes. I felt like a lab specimen. I recognized one as the woman who'd checked me out and pronounced me as suffering from shock the day I found Rick Wilbur's body.

'How are you doing? Maggie Miller, right?'

Aw, she remembered my name. Not that that was necessarily a good thing. I managed a smile and a thumbs up. 'Shock-free.' The blanket slid down my knees and I pulled it up. A lady has to protect her reputation, after all. And her private parts.

'I'm Luann Pendley. Call me Luann. If we're going to keep running into each other like this, we may as well be on a first-name basis.' She gently lifted one eyelid after the other. 'You seem to have suffered no external trauma.'

Tell that to my knees. I'd banged them both up pretty good crawling full speed toward the nearest exit.

'It might be good to take you to Mesa Verde, just to be on the safe side.'

'I'll be OK, really.' Though I wouldn't mind playing doctor with Dr Vargas, I did not want to spend the night in the hospital. 'All I need is some sleep.'

'We could all use some sleep.'

My head jerked around. Highsmith. 'What are you doing here?' He wore blue jeans and a short-sleeve plaid popover shirt with dress shoes.

'I got a report of a fire,' he said. 'It's my job to be here.' He looked at his watch. 'A little late for a barbecue, isn't it?'

A flash went off in our faces and I threw my hands up in front of my face as a second one followed. The stars before my eyes cleared and I saw a sight I could live without. Brad Smith, the *Table Rock Reader*'s intrepid reporter. The *Table Rock Reader*'s uncouth reporter.

'Hey, Brad,' Highsmith said.

'What are you doing here?' I said for the second time, my words coming out like acid.

'I'm a reporter. I heard about the fire on my scanner.' He snapped several more shots then let his camera fall to his chest, hanging by its strap. I noticed he wore a gray Phoenix Coyotes T-shirt. Obviously a hockey fan.

Brad folded his arms, looking from me to the smoke coming out of my apartment door and windows. 'It's what I do.' He turned to Chief Stillman and extracted a notepad and pencil. 'Is it bad, Terry? Any deaths? Can you give me a property damage estimate?'

I stood, clutching the wool blanket around my waist. 'I estimate that if you don't get out of here you're going to be in some serious pain!' Hmm, that might have been a poor choice of words to use in front of a cop.

Detective Highsmith looked me up and down. 'I see you've made yet another friend in town,' he quipped.

246

'We are not friends!'

'Hey,' said Brad, snapping another unflattering shot of me – bed hair, smoky complexion and in my nobody's-business-but-my-own underwear. 'I'd like to think we're friends.'

'Stop that!' I threw a hand in front of my face and the blanket fell off my hip, exposing more flesh than I usually liked to bare during any group activities, let alone a house fire. I snatched the blanket back up.

By now, several neighbors, not only from my fourplex but from up and down my block were milling about the sidewalk and street, taking in the show. What, not *Saturday Night Live* fans?

I turned to Chief Stillman. 'Are we about done here?'

'We're just wrapping up. Two of my men are just pulling out the AC unit.'

Sure enough, two firemen came out grappling each end of the burnt out appliance.

'I'd like to get a look at that,' Detective Highsmith said, stepping over to the unit. 'You think it's the source of the fire?'

The chief repeated what he'd told me earlier. 'I'll tell you what, Mark,' replied Chief Stillman, 'why don't we drop it off at the police station for you? We can analyze it there as well as anywhere and two heads are better than one.'

In Highsmith's case, I was beginning to think that one head would never be enough and that there should be a minimum order of two. 'I can tell you exactly what you're going to find.'

'Oh?' said Detective Highsmith.

All three men looked at me. Under other

circumstances, that could have been flattering, now it was simply nerve-wracking. I thrust my chin out. 'I'm sure it's attempted murder!' I blurted.

Chief Stillman took a step back. 'Are you sure, miss?'

Brad wrote madly on his pad. 'Oh, man, this is great.'

Detective Highsmith looked skeptical so I focused my attention on him. 'Somebody is out to get me, like they got Rick Wilbur.'

'Why?' asked the detective, a goofy smirk sticking to his face. 'Were the two of you in *cahoots* on something?'

My face reddened like a party balloon. 'Listen, you—' I aimed my index finger at his nose and my blanket fell again. 'Would somebody please get me some pants!' I pulled the blanket tighter. 'Or at least a belt?'

Chief Stillman was thrusting the business end of a screwdriver into the face of the air conditioner. 'I suppose it could have been tampered with. This is a pretty old unit, though.' He turned to Highsmith. 'The wiring looks shot.'

Highsmith nodded. 'Faulty wiring. Happens all the time.'

'Or maybe the killer just wants you to think that,' I insisted.

'You have anybody particular in mind?' asked Brad. He was like a hungry wolf.

That's when I saw Rob Gregory holding open the passenger-side door of a minivan for his wife, Trish. 'Them!' I pointed. I rushed to the duo, my naked feet complaining as I raced over the rough, bare ground. I could hear footsteps behind me racing to keep up.

'What are you two doing here?' I demanded. 'Come to see if you've succeeded? Make sure I'm really dead?' I drew myself up to my full height, my hands on my hips. I wasn't about to lose the stupid blanket again, not in front of all my neighbors. 'Well, I've got news for you. I'm alive.'

Rob turned to Chief Stillman. 'What's she talking about? Has she lost her mind? Are you taking her to the psychiatric ward for observation?'

I scowled. That had sounded more like a suggestion than a question.

'Easy, Rob,' said Trish, giving Rob a squeeze around his waist. 'Let the chief talk.'

Yeah, Rob, let the chief talk.

'Nothing to worry about,' the chief answered. He had a deep, slow-moving voice, perfect for calming fire victims. 'A small appliance fire. Everything is under control.'

'What is your interest in this?' asked Detective Highsmith.

I smiled. It was about time this guy did his job and asked somebody besides me some questions.

Rob and Trish were both in shorts and T-shirts with sandals on their feet. 'We received a call from our agent in Sedona.' Despite the smoke clogging my nostrils, I caught a distinct whiff of sage. The two of them smelled like they'd been rolling in it. I'd heard it was popular with the New Age crowd and was supposed to possess

249

magical properties. I could only hope it made the two of them magically disappear.

'We own the building,' explained Trish.

'You own the – you own my—' I turned and looked at my apartment. 'You two are my—' I felt my ribs collapsing like the internal structure of a skyscraper that had been carefully laced with TNT, then instantaneously detonated.

'We're your landlords.'

Tips on Fire Safety

Disclaimer: I'm no expert. In fact, I'm the person people point to and say, 'Don't do what that woman did!'

So, don't believe a word I say, or rather, don't *trust* a word I say. Do keep a fire extinguisher handy and know your emergency exits.

That said, if you do get yourself in a situation like the one I'd gotten into, here are some tips that might help keep you safe:

If you smell smoke or your smoke detector goes off, get yourself, your family and your pets to safety first (leave the margarita mix behind). Next, call the fire department and activate the nearest pull-station at once.

- Before opening the door, lightly feel the door with the back of your hand.
- If the door is hot or warm, DO NOT open the door.
- If the door is cool, open it just enough to check the hallway or next room. If you see more smoke out there, do not enter.
- If there is no smoke in the hallway, leave and close the door. Go directly to the stairs to leave.
- If you cannot escape, use wet towels to seal the door and any room supply vent.

251

- If you have a balcony and there is no fire below it, exit this way.
- If the fire is below you, go to the window but do not open it. Simply stay near the closed window.
- If there is no fire below you, go to the window and open it. Stay near the open window.
- Hang or wave a blanket or a towel out of the window to let people know that you are there and needing help.
- Remain calm and wait for someone to rescue you.
- Never use an elevator. The power could go out, leaving you trapped.

Don't worry about your pants. Chief Stillman assures me he's got plenty of blankets on his fire truck.

Caveat: If you are currently renting from the Gregorys, check the batteries in your smoke detector once a month.

TWENTY-SIX

I stumbled numbly to the gaping door. Chief Stillman, Detective Highsmith, Brad the reporter and the Gregorys followed.

I stopped at the transom. Everything looked pretty normal. I felt Detective Highsmith's hand on my upper arm. 'All right to go in?' he asked the chief.

Chief Stillman nodded and we went inside. Detective Highsmith stopped at the door and inspected the lock. 'No sign of a break-in.'

I looked at Rob and Trish. 'I'll bet they have a key.' I'd rented from an agent over in Sedona. I knew the agent I'd worked with wasn't the property owner but I'd had no idea that I was renting from my competitors, the Karma Koffee duo!

Now it all made sense. TR Properties, LLC. I'd thought the initials stood for Table Rock when in reality they obviously stood for Trish and Rob. Suddenly the twelve-month lease I'd signed was looking more like a twelve-month jail sentence.

'Of course we have a key!' Rob said with a sneer. He swung around to face the detective. 'We're her freaking landlords!'

Did he have to gloat like that when he said it?

The smell of smoke filled the air and I expected it would for days to come. There was a gaping hole in the bedroom where the AC unit had once sat. I turned angrily to Rob and Trish. 'You owe me a new air conditioner.'

Chief Stillman glanced up at the ceiling. 'I wonder why your smoke detector didn't go off.'

I shot around and yelled at Rob and Trish. 'Yeah, why is that? Isn't it your responsibility to see that I have working safety equipment?' Unless they'd sabotaged the smoke detector as well.

Rob pursed his lips. 'The batteries are probably dead.' He looked at me with obvious distaste. 'You're supposed to check them occasionally.'

Trish nodded. 'It's in your lease.'

'Still,' I began, showing off my high-school debate team skills – of which I had none. Who reads leases?

Rob plucked at the damp drywall. 'I'll get someone over in the morning to board this up.' He turned to his wife. 'Remind me to call the agency.'

Trish nodded. 'It may take a day or two to have a new air-conditioning unit installed, Ms Miller.'

Of course. Were the two of them trying to make me sweat? 'That's OK,' I replied. 'You have a guest room, don't you?' Neither of the Gregorys laughed. But then again, I may have just spoiled their plans by surviving their attempt to burn me to death. They might just not be in a laughing mood.

Detective Highsmith took a few pictures with his cell phone – souvenirs, I guess.

'You sure you want to stay here, Ms Miller?' Chief Stillman asked.

As much as I wanted to stick it in all their faces

and brave it out, no way I was spending the rest of the night in this acrid-smelling apartment. Especially with no AC. I was having enough trouble sleeping as it is. In this heat, sleep would be next to impossible.

'No.' I let out a breath of surrender. 'Guess I'll stay with my sister.' They didn't have an extra bedroom, but they did have a sofa in the living room with my name on it.

After the fire truck rolled away, Detective Highsmith zoomed silently off in his vehicle and the Gregorys disappeared down the road hand in hand to their minivan, I was left on the front porch with Brad Smith.

'So I guess I'll be reading about this in the *Table Rock Reader*.' Great, now everybody in Table Rock would know what a lousy housekeeper I was.

'Sorry, but—'

'It's your job.'

He fingered his camera. 'I got some great shots of you.'

'Yeah, I'll bet.' I could see the headline now: Scantily Clad Murder Suspect Sets Bedroom Ablaze.

I'd be the talk of the town – and not because of my mouthwatering beignets. 'Be sure to save a good one for the police. I'm sure they'd be happy to use it for my mugshot.'

'I'm sure that won't be necessary,' Brad said.

'Oh? Does that mean you think I'm innocent?' Maybe he wasn't half the jerk I thought he was.

'Nah, they've got their own photographer on staff.'

I stood corrected.

'Can I give you a lift?' he inquired as I locked the door behind me.

'Thanks,' I replied. 'But I've got my bike.' Not that I was in any mood to ride all the way to Donna and Andy's house at this hour. It was nearly one in the morning. Only spooks and aliens and murderers should be out and about at this hour. Besides, every bone in my body ached and every muscle squawked. Maybe it was merely the rattlesnake in my stomach talking, but I was beginning to get a little depressed.

I mean, how many more things could go wrong?

And what if somebody out there really was trying to kill me? I looked around the dark street, a now malevolent-looking spot where murderers could be lurking behind every cottonwood, under every boulder – maybe inside every mailbox if they were capable of folding themselves up into extra dimensions.

This being Table Rock, I wouldn't put it past them. If there are aliens around here, I'll bet they're whizzes at origami.

'Suit yourself,' Brad replied. He stuffed his hands in his pockets and started up the walkway toward his car.

A coyote cried in the distance. 'Wait up!'

He stopped and turned. 'Yeah?'

I gave him my sister's address.

A few minutes later we were sitting at the curb in his Honda. I had a small suitcase that I'd tossed a couple of things in and I'd traded my Property of Table Rock Volunteer Fire Department blanket for a pair of gray sweat pants.

'So your sister owns that health food store downtown, huh?' He stared at the dark house.

'My sister and her husband, Andy,' I answered, fingering the grip of the suitcase on the floor between my legs. 'And they don't like you to call it a health food store. Simply a food store.' Believe me, I'd made that mistake once and gotten the lecture to prove it.

Donna and Andy considered what they sold to be normal, real food, and that calling it 'health food' implied that it was something other than normal.

The two of them considered the stuff that regular supermarkets sold to be the unnatural, unhealthy stuff. In fact, they had a name for such places: food factory outlets.

Personally, I'm not so particular. As a matter of fact, I could have gone for another pint of Safeway's finest vanilla ice cream about now. All that smoke was still torturing my trachea. I rubbed my throat for good measure.

'I'll have to check it out sometime.'

'You should,' I replied. 'Try the veggie haggis.' He said he would. Sucker.

I wrapped my fingers around the door handle, then paused. 'Seeing as how you're a reporter,' I began, 'what can you tell me about Rick Wilbur?'

Brad's hands rested atop the steering wheel. 'Not much. Wilbur Realty is about the biggest advertiser the *Table Rock Reader*'s got. Other than that . . .' He shrugged.

I could believe it. I'd seen page after page of real estate listings in the paper. 'No skeletons in Rick Wilbur's closest, eh?'

He smiled. 'Not that I know of. Why?'

'Because I'm trying to figure out who killed the guy. Contrary to what seems to be popular opinion,' I looked at him hard, 'I didn't.'

'Hey.' He shifted his body toward mine. 'I never said you did. I'm only doing my job.'

'So?'

'So what?'

'So what have you managed to find out?'

A smile filled Brad's face. 'You're asking if I've uncovered any fact that might be pertinent to Rick Wilbur's murder?'

My eyes said I was.

Brad's hands drummed the dark dash. 'Nothing. Mr Wilbur's time of death is within a two- to three-hour window and it seems that anybody, including you, is a suspect in the eyes of the Table Rock PD. Where were you, by the way?' Brad asked point-blank.

I frowned. 'Running errands. Then home.'

'Can you prove it?'

'No. What about you?' Two could play this game.

'Covering a wedding.'

'A wedding?' This was interesting.

'The marriage of Faith Parker and Jaxon Johnson.' Brad's hands strung a make-believe banner in the air between us. 'I was there all night. The ceremony took place at the Enchantment Resort in Sedona.'

OK, that might be true. But I wondered if

Johnny and/or Clive had been there as well. They were in the wedding business, after all. 'What about Clive Rothschild or Johnny Wolfe? Were they at the wedding?'

'The guys from the bridal shop?'

I nodded.

'I'm not sure.' Brad scratched his cheek. 'Should they have been?'

'I don't know,' I replied in frustration. Did wedding gown and accessory sellers attend the weddings of their clients? Had Faith Parker even been a client? 'Clive was with me when I discovered the body. Johnny was seen arguing with Rick recently. I found a Wilbur Realty pen in their storeroom when I was poking around.'

'You were poking around in the back of The Hitching Post? I'm impressed.'

'Don't be,' I said. 'I got caught.'

His eyes grew. 'What happened?'

I explained how I thought Johnny was going to kill me. Brad shook his head in disbelief. 'Did you tell the police?'

I lifted a shoulder. 'Nah. What could I tell them?' It was all rather nebulous. I couldn't prove anything.

'I'd be careful if I were you. Maybe Johnny Wolfe, maybe somebody else, but somebody might be trying to put you out of commission – permanently. It will be interesting to learn what the police and the fire department conclude regarding that AC unit.'

Finally, maybe somebody besides my immediately family believed me. But did it have to be this obnoxious reporter?

I threw open the car door and put a foot on the curb.

'There is one thing,' Brad said.

I stuck my head back in the car. 'What's that?'

'This is strictly confidential,' he said. 'My buddy would kill me if he knew I was passing along privileged information.'

'So let's not tell him.'

Brad nodded. 'I have this friend, an old college roommate, actually. He works for a large insurance company down in Phoenix.'

'And?'

'And he says Mrs Wilbur is about to become a very wealthy woman.'

Well, well. 'I wonder if the police know.'

'Probably,' answered Brad. 'My guess is that checking out the surviving spouse and how much they might gain is standard operating procedure.'

Brad was probably right. But this still bore further looking into. 'What can you tell me about Mr Wilbur's ex, Caitie Conklin?'

Brad's brows went up. 'She cuts a mean head of hair, if you can afford her.' He ran a hand through his locks. 'Personally, I go to the barber. She's been in trouble with the police a time or two, but nothing significant.'

'Such as?' I dropped my suitcase and rested my arms against the roof of the Accord.

Brad shrugged. 'Fights with customers mostly. I hear you don't want to get on her wrong side and that she has no good side.' He laughed. 'Another time, I remember she and Rick nearly came to blows. The police came out and broke up the argument before either of them did any real damage. She packs a mean right.'

And a mean rolling pin? I wondered. I picked up my suitcase. 'Goodnight, Brad.'

'Wait a sec—'

'Yeah?'

'You're open till three tomorrow, right?'

'That's right.' My right foot had fallen asleep and I swung it in small circles.

'So you want to get some dinner after? Let's say six?'

My mouth was hanging open for the flies again. Thank goodness they sleep at night. At least I hoped they did. 'Are you asking me out?'

Brad smiled, the gap between his teeth glinting off the streetlight. Oh, brother, I hadn't realized before how much his smile reminded me of Brian's.

'Thanks for the ride,' I said, turning on my heel and hightailing it to my sister's door before I said something I might regret.

TWENTY-SEVEN

I didn't know what had shaken me more, almost being burned to death in my own bed or Brad Smith asking me out on a date.

Whichever it was, as I turned the key in my sister's lock and wiped my feet on the mat, my knees turned to jelly and my hands quickly followed. The suitcase fell from my grip and thwacked the hardwood floor.

I muttered a curse, picked up my bag and tiptoed toward the sofa. My nerves were frayed to gossamer threads. My eyes and throat were still feeling the effects of all that smoke.

'What's going on out here?' Andy stood in the doorway between the living room and his and Donna's bedroom.

My heart jumped to my mouth. 'Sorry,' I whispered. 'Didn't mean to wake you.'

Andy stepped closer, stifling a yawn with the back of his closed hand. He wore yellow-and-blue striped pajama bottoms and a University of Northern Arizona sleeveless T-shirt. 'Are you OK, Maggie?' He shot a glance toward the boys' rooms, then lowered his voice. 'What are you doing here?'

Seeing him there, all warm and caring, the house snug and inviting, something in me collapsed like the wall of a sandcastle against the incoming tide.

'I think I'm in over my head,' I said softly, listening to the gentle click-click of the antique grandfather clock in the corner of the room. I wiped a tear from the edge of my eye with a pinkie.

'You want to tell me about it?' Andy padded over the rug in bare feet.

'If you don't mind, I'd just as soon get some sleep.' I set my suitcase beside the sofa and sat. 'We can talk about it in the morning.'

'Sure thing,' said Andy.

'Oh, no you don't.'

I looked up. 'Hey, Sis.'

'I'll fetch a pillow and some blankets.' Andy left the room.

Donna sat beside me on the couch, our knees touching. 'You tell me what's going on right this minute.'

I knew better than to argue when Donna got like this. Heck, if I didn't start talking she might start feeding me. Who knew what she had in the refrigerator? Veggie rattlesnake, maybe?

'There was a fire at my apartment.'

'A fire!' Donna gasped. 'Maggie, are you sure you're OK?' She grabbed my arms above the wrists.

'A small fire,' I said. 'A very small fire. More of a giant smoke bomb, really.'

Donna's face scrunched up in apparent confusion.

'It started in my bedroom. The fire department thinks the AC unit shorted out or something.'

'Oh, Maggie.' Donna shook her head.

Andy returned and dropped a pillow and blanket

263

behind me on the couch. 'Don't worry,' he said, 'you can stay here as long as you need.'

'Absolutely,' said Donna. 'I'm sure the boys will love having you.'

Sure, so they could torture me more facilely. 'It's only for tonight – maybe two nights,' I replied. 'My landlords . . .' Why was I having trouble saying that word? 'My landlords promised me they'd get the wall patched up ASAP and a new air conditioner put in.'

Andy fell into the recliner across from the sofa. 'So it was an accident?' His face showed concern. And a need for sleep. The poor guy usually gets up with the chickens. In this case, literally, since they gather the fresh eggs then.

'Well—'

'What?' said Donna, edging closer.

I shrugged. 'What if it wasn't an accident? What if somebody is trying to—' I glanced down the hall toward Connor and Hunter's rooms. 'Shut me up for good.' I told them all about my suspicions regarding Rob and Trish Gregory, Tommy Henson and his mom, Patti Wilbur and even Johnny Wolfe and Clive Rothschild.

'And I still have to interview Caitie Conklin, Rick's ex, over at Salon de Belleza.' Despite my nerves, I felt my eyelids sagging.

Andy and Donna shared a look. 'I'll see what I can find out about the cause of the fire tomorrow,' Andy promised. He stood. 'Until then,' he yawned, 'I think it would be best if we all got some sleep.' He stepped over and tousled my hair. 'You look like you could use it.'

'You're safe here,' my sister said. 'And we're

going to have to have a long talk about all this nosing around you're doing. Whether someone is out to shut you up or not, I don't know. I do know that if you keep poking your nose into other people's business, well, there are some people who may take a strong dislike to that. They may be willing to do whatever it takes to stop you.'

'And,' said Andy, picking up the thread of his wife's tale, 'if it turns out your air conditioner was tampered with, that would mean somebody has access to your apartment. And they mean business.'

I nodded slowly. Not exactly the most soothing bedtime story I'd ever been told. As Donna and Andy retreated to their room, I stretched out on the sofa and tossed the blanket over my legs. The most obvious suspects with the key to my apartment would be the Gregorys. After all, they owned the entire fourplex. But I figured just about anybody could get into the apartment if they'd a mind to.

Plus, who knew how many previous renters might still be running around with a key to my door? How often did the lock get changed? Had it ever been changed? Was there any way I could learn who any of those previous tenants might have been? Asking the Gregorys was probably out of the question.

I thought it might be good to sleep with one eye open, just in case. Unfortunately, the eye I'd left in charge wasn't cooperating.

I woke to see two glowing green eyes boring into me. A cold hand clutched my right arm. I stiffened.

'Mom, what are you doing here?'

Mom's hand went to my forehead and rested there. Why, I wasn't sure. I'd had a house fire, a small house fire, not a fever. I pulled her hand away. 'Are you all right? Donna and Andy filled me in. I came as soon as I heard.'

I smelled pancakes and maple syrup coming from the kitchen. Thank goodness, normal food. Hopefully factory outlet food, like Aunt Jemima's, bless her heart.

'I'm fine, Mom.' I sat up and rubbed the sand from my eyes. A little freaked out to be sure, but nothing a cup of coffee, a stack of pancakes, four ounces of maple syrup and a session with a psychiatrist couldn't fix.

'I can't believe you spent the night on this sofa,' Mom scolded me with her eyes, 'when you know I have a perfectly good guest room at my condo.'

Oh, I knew all right. 'It's only for a day or two. Besides, it was the middle of the night. I didn't want to disturb you.'

Mom rose, folding her arms over her chest. She was dressed casually in loose-fitting shorts and a white blouse. 'Tonight you're staying with me.'

I sat up and stretched, not quite with yoga grace, but it was something. 'Thanks, but that won't be necessary,' I explained. 'I'll be back in my own place tonight.'

We were still debating my short-term living arrangements over breakfast.

'Boy, breakfast sure smells great. Looks great, too!' I said, peering over my sister's shoulder as she flipped pancakes from the skillet to a large serving tray.

'Mom always makes us pancakes on Sunday morning, Aunt Maggie,' said Hunter.

'Yeah,' chimed in Connor. Both boys were still in the short PJs. 'She says it's an American tradition.'

'Count me in.' I pulled up a chair. 'I'm famished.' Andy brought an extra chair from the living room for Mom. I rose and grabbed the coffee pot.

'Tell us about the fire, Aunt Maggie!' Connor said, tightly clutching his fork.

'Yeah, cool,' said Hunter. 'A fire.'

'Boys,' admonished Donna. 'Please, Aunt Maggie could have been badly hurt.'

Connor looked half-confused and half-apologetic. 'But she wasn't. I mean, you weren't, were you, Aunt Maggie?'

He looked at me, eyes wide, as if waiting to hear an exciting story of blazing buildings, policemen creating order out of mayhem and firemen chopping down doors with razor-sharp giant axes.

Unfortunately, I expected the biggest thrill the night before had been the embarrassing glimpses of me that all my neighbors and everybody else got seeing me prancing around in my underwear. The biggest damage to me personally was to my reputation.

I smiled. 'The fire department came and put out the fire before it got out of control. It was cool to see all those flashing lights, though,' I added for the boys' benefit.

A phone chirped in the distance. 'Sounds like

my cell,' Andy said. He rose from the table and went off to the bedroom to answer it.

I scooped two spoonfuls of sugar into my coffee and stirred as my sister served up breakfast.

The pancakes I'd been yearning for turned out to be a blend of whole wheat, pea and artichoke flour. That explained the unnatural greenish-brown color.

Even Aunt Jemima let me down – the woman was a no-show. The syrup was something called Magave, a combination of agave and maple syrups that Donna blended herself.

Words cannot begin to describe what breakfast tasted like, so I won't even try. The good news was that I figured the meal had killed that rattle-snake that had been slithering around in my tummy since yesterday.

Andy returned. He glanced at my sister, then set his cell phone down on the kitchen counter. 'That was the police,' he said. He turned to me. 'It looks like your AC unit was tampered with.'

I jerked in my chair, a forkful of pancake smothered in Magave halfway between my lips and my plate. 'Then that means—' I gulped.

Andy nodded. 'Somebody tried to kill you.'

Mom screamed.

'Wow!' the boys shouted as one, looking at me with newfound respect.

Well, the good news was that somebody had tampered with my air conditioner, somebody was trying to kill me . . . I could stick that in Detective Highsmith's chiseled yet smug face. VV's too.

The bad news was, well, somebody was trying to kill me!

TWENTY-EIGHT

Andy explained that the police and fire investigators had quickly found evidence of foul play once they'd cleaned the smoke smudges and debris from the unit. They'd discovered clear signs that the wiring had been tampered with. Andy said I was lucky I hadn't burned to death or died of smoke inhalation.

Mom had immediately gone right off the deep end, insisting I get round-the-clock police protection. Donna insisted that Andy follow me around all day.

The boys, Connor and Hunter, pleaded that they be allowed to follow me around all day. I guess they wanted to be close by in case the killer decided to strike again.

I couldn't blame them. Boys will be boys. And it wasn't like they wanted to see anything bad happen to me. They just wanted some excitement. I mean, if those abominable Sunday morning pancakes were one of the best things they had to look forward to every week, then they were seriously excitement deprived.

I promised myself that I'd take them to that wild animal park that I'd heard about over in Camp Verde, let them feed a tiger or two and zip line over the alligators while tossing down chicken parts.

I also promised Donna I would not let the boys

269

tag along with me when I went to work. I told Andy I did not need an official escort; the poor man had better things to do with his time.

I explained to Mom that I most definitely did not need round-the-clock protection. 'Besides,' I said, knowing it would end the argument, 'I've got this!' I tugged at the crystal around my neck. 'What more protection do I need?'

Mom nodded as if that had meant something. See what I mean?

Without the Schwinn, which was still back at the apartment, I did accept a ride to Maggie's Beignet Café from Andy after breakfast. 'You want me to come in with you? Make sure everything is OK inside?' Andy's eyes swept over the storefront and up and down the quiet street.

I looked too. I didn't see any signs of potential killers. 'That's OK.' I climbed out of the pickup. 'Aubrey's here.' I watched as she climbed out of her car and headed up the sidewalk with a bounce in her step.

Thank goodness. Despite my show of bravado, I really didn't want to face going into the deserted café alone.

Fortunately there were plenty of tourists around. I'd been worried about it being slow on Sunday but as it turned out there was a hot-air balloon race going on outside of town that had brought in flocks of tourists from nearby Sedona and other parts.

The first chance I got when there was a break in the action, I marched straight across the street to Karma Koffee. 'Where's that new air-conditioning unit you promised me?' I demanded. I felt the twinge in my back acting up. It had been a rough night on the couch.

Rob and Trish sat at a table in the corner, sharing a newspaper. Rob looked up and flashed a scowl. 'It's Sunday,' he said icily. 'You're going to have to wait until Monday.' He returned his eyes to the sports section. 'At least.'

'What was that?' Monday, at least? My psyche couldn't take it – my back couldn't take it!

He looked up once more, his eyes meeting mine. 'I said, "at least."'

'Don't worry, Ms Miller. We've called our property agent.' Trish looked Sunday comfy, with her hair hanging in loose folds, minimal makeup and wearing a simple off-white shift. 'She'll make arrangements with the electrician and the painters to get everything back in shape.' She ruffled the arts section. 'Shouldn't take more than a week.'

'A week?' I couldn't wait a week. A week of sleeping on Donna's couch, forced to feast on Donna's vegan nightmares. And there was no way I was surrendering and going to live in Mom's guest room!

'That just won't do,' I said loudly. The place was filled with customers but I didn't care. The three servers behind the counter shot nervous glances at me while busily frothing up coffees and plating pastries. If their nerves were that bad, they should cut down on their caffeine intake.

'So,' said Rob, folding the sport section from the *Arizona Republic* newspaper across his lap, 'unless you've come to steal another employee, I believe we're done here.'

'I didn't steal her, she escaped,' I replied. 'And

271

believe you me, she has plenty to say about the two of you.'

Rob cocked his brow, a look of condescension and amusement blending together on his face. 'Oh, what a surprise. Disgruntled ex-employee bad-mouths bosses.' He stretched his hands out like a banner.

'I always knew that girl was troubled,' Trish said, gently pulling apart a blueberry muffin that looked good enough to dive into. 'Her energy was all wrong. You could see it in her aura.'

'Oh, yeah? Well, Aubrey saw some things concerning the two of you.' I pointed a finger at Rob Gregory. 'Especially you, mister.'

He scooted back his chair and faced me. 'Such as?'

'Such as how she saw you arguing with Rick Wilbur the night he was killed.'

I felt every eye in the store on me now but I didn't care.

Rob tossed a hand in the air. 'Oh, that. Please, is that the best you've got?'

My jaw fell.

Trish smiled and stood. 'The police have already questioned my husband about Mr Wilbur's murder.' Her smile grew. 'He has an alibi.'

'And the police bought it?' I rolled my eyes.

'They had to,' said Rick. 'You see, I was teaching one of my yoga classes upstairs.' His eyes rose to the ceiling.

Boy, those were some nice tin tiles they had up there. Maybe I should have some of those installed one of these days. 'Maybe you slipped out.'

'I have a dozen witnesses.'

'Please, they could be lying to protect you.' I was pretty sure that twelve people wouldn't all be willing to perjure themselves to the police in order to protect their yoga instructor, but this is Table Rock, so you never know.

'One of my students is a Table Rock PD patrol officer.'

I felt deflated and needed to sit. No way was I going to though. The next thing you know, I'd be ordering coffee and one of those mouthwatering blueberry muffins. I had to do something, and quick.

'What about you?' I demanded of Trish Gregory. 'Where were you when your husband was teaching yoga? Were you here? Working?'

'I-I was home,' Trish stammered. 'I mean, you can't think I'd have anything to do with murdering Mr Wilbur.'

'Leave Trish out of this. My wife wouldn't harm a spider,' Rob insisted. He stepped in front of her. 'You're barking up the wrong tree.'

He took three steps to the door and opened it. 'Speaking of bark, I hear that's what your beignets taste like. Shouldn't you get back to your place and peel some more off the trees?'

I yelled back: 'I've got you pegged – the way you tricked me, pretending you didn't know where Rick Wilbur's body was found. I'm still giving dollars to doughnuts that you're mixed up in this.'

He could have made up the whole story about teaching yoga and there being a police officer in the class. It was all too pat.

273

Trish grabbed her husband's hand. 'And yet, Rick Wilbur was found dead in *your* establishment,' she said. 'We hear you'd had an argument with him as well.'

Darn, how had she heard that? This small town stuff was beginning to get under my skin.

'So you still seem like the most likely person to have murdered him,' Trish went on. 'You probably stuffed him in a box, waiting for an opportunity to dispose of his body.'

'Yeah,' Rob said, his lips curved into a snarl as he passed his eyes over his customers, 'maybe chop it up into little bits and use it in your beignet dough.' He laughed at his joke.

I don't know what upset me more, the thought of Rick Wilbur in my pastry dough or the Gregorys in my face. Either way, I'd had enough.

As I stepped out, Rob said, 'If you didn't kill Rick Wilbur, and I'm not saying you didn't, then the only other person I can think of with the nerve and the desire to punch his clock would be Caitie.'

I turned. 'Caitie Conklin?' My eyes shot across the street to the beauty parlor next door to my café.

'You know another one?'

'What makes you think she might be involved?'

Rick growled. 'I don't think she might be involved. I think *you* might be involved.'

'But you just said—'

Trish Gregory came to the open door and squinted into the sun. 'Rob, let's not let all this negative energy infuse our day.'

274

'Yeah, Rob,' I quipped. 'Infuse too much negative energy and you just might blow a fuse.'

Rob Gregory shouted some four-letter epithets my way as I crossed the street that I'm certain weren't in any mantras I'd ever come across. I ignored them as I headed back to the café then cut a diagonal toward Salon de Belleza.

Unfortunately the door was locked. The sign on it revealed that she'd be opening at two. Perfect. I was closing at three. At three-oh-one I'd be going *mano y mano* with the overcharging – fifty dollars for a trim, talk about your scalpers – tempestuous and notorious former Mrs Wilbur.

The more I thought about it, the guiltier she looked. Picturing Rick Wilbur's head sticking out of that carton, it did seem like he might have recently had a haircut.

Did Caitie Conklin cut his hair that day?

Had they had a falling out?

Did she forego giving him a blow dry in favor of a rolling pin blowout?

TWENTY-NINE

It had taken longer to clean up than expected but I knew better to leave the café a mess at the end of the day. That was a slippery slope of sloth I knew I'd never recover from once I'd slid down that path. One look at my apartment, even before the fire, was proof of that.

Speaking of apartment, I sure hoped I didn't have to sleep too much longer at Donna's house. I was pretty sure if I did that Mom would be offended, seeing as she has a perfectly good guest room at her house.

The only answer might be to move back to the apartment. If it got too hot in the bedroom, I could always sleep on my own sofa. The AC unit out there was working. I hoped. Come to think of it, how did I know it hadn't been tampered with too? Had the police checked?

I was going to find out before I used it. And what about the rest of the apartment? Could there be other booby traps lying in wait for me? An exploding water heater? A leaky gas stovetop?

I hung my apron on a hook in the back, then checked my hair in the bathroom mirror. I fluffed it up with my fingers. Leaning over a vat of hot oil hadn't helped it any. I hated the idea of interviewing Caitie Conklin on her own turf, the beauty salon, without my hair looking its absolute best.

I fished around in my pocketbook and pulled out my brush. Once I was satisfied and my lipstick was just so, I locked up and walked next door.

Lo and behold, who do I see sitting in a chair near the back, sharing a laugh with Rick Wilbur's ex? None other than one of my other neighbors, Johnny Wolfe. Were the two of them up to something? Clandestine lovers, even?

She was so much older. He was so much, well, Johnny Wolfe-ier. What could they possibly have in common?

Murder.

I stood on the sidewalk watching for a minute. Johnny was facing the mirror and Caitie had her back to me.

I could hear every word they said. The door was being held in the open position by a small round granite rock with the word Beauty etched into its face. Three bamboo fans whirled overhead the six chairs. I didn't see any other stylists on the floor at the moment. Maybe Conklin worked solo on Sundays.

'Are you sure he doesn't suspect anything?' Caitie asked. She had a wicked-looking pair of shears in her hands.

Johnny sneered. 'Not a bit.

I watched her hand dance around his head.

Jiminy, I knew those scissors. There was no mistaking that distinctive Japanese design. Those were Kamisoris, made from molybdenum and as expensive as gold. No wonder she charged so much for a haircut. She was probably making payments on those scissors.

And no wonder she'd chosen a rolling pin rather

than the scissors to murder her ex – who'd want to take a chance on messing up a pair of shears like that?

Johnny turned to see his profile. 'If we can keep things tight for a few more days, we'll be home free.'

'I hope so. This whole thing's got me nervous. I hear that Miller woman has been asking all kinds of questions.'

Johnny turned again to catch his right profile. 'Don't worry about her. She doesn't realize it, but she's actually helping us.'

'How do you figure that?' Caitie grabbed an electric razor and trimmed around his ears.

Johnny waited until the razor stopped buzzing to answer. 'The way I see it, she's making such a pest of herself, getting in everyone's way, it can only be good for us. She's certainly keeping Clive occupied. The poor man's a wreck.'

Hey! Was it my fault Clive was with me when I found a dead guy in my storeroom and fainted? Was it my fault that my dead ex-husband showed up at The Hitching Post? Was it my fault Clive was there when Johnny caught me snooping in his stockroom?

Caitie nodded. 'And like you said,' she pulled the smock from Johnny's neck and grabbed a brush, 'it's only for three more days and then . . .' She flicked hair from his shoulders.

'Hi, can I help you?'

I twitched and looked in the direction of the sound. A dark-haired young woman in a smock stepped from behind a three-paneled cedar room divider with half wagon wheel tops.

278

A silver-haired woman followed behind, her hair bunched up under a fluffy white towel.

I swallowed. 'Oh, hi.' I thought quickly. And, as it turns out, stupidly. 'Do you take walk-ins?'

Caitie and Johnny shared a look. Johnny jumped from his chair and dusted himself off with meticulous care. 'We'll talk more later,' he said. 'Miller.' Johnny nodded slightly as he brushed past me.

Wait, I thought. What's happening in three days?

Caitie Conklin headed straight to me. She stopped, folded her arms across her chest grandly and studied my head. Without asking permission, she reached out and pulled at my hair. 'I figured you'd show up sooner or later.' She had a voice sharp enough to cut brick.

Why? Did she think I was on to her? Maybe I should watch my step. 'You did?'

She nodded several times and took a step back as if to assess me further from a distance. 'Yeah, with that rat's nest I knew it was only a matter of time.'

'What?' My hair? She was talking about my hair! Why was she talking about my hair? My fingers went to my long red strands. What was wrong with it? I cut it myself. If I'd been clutching a pair of Kamisoris I'd have taught her a thing or two about hair and the many uses for scissors.

'How long's it been?'

I pinched my brows together. 'How long has what been?' Was she asking about the murder? Killer or not, she knew the answer to that question.

279

'Since you got a decent cut.' She reached for my head again and I pulled back. 'Five months? Six?'

'It hasn't been that long.' A couple of weeks at most. 'I cut it myself.'

Caitie laughed. Somewhere, I think I could hear bricks breaking. 'Hey, Belinda. Get this – this one cuts her own hair!'

The young girl in the smock was plucking curlers from her client, her back turned to us. 'You know what they say,' she shouted back, 'a lawyer that represents himself has got a fool for a client!'

She suddenly swung around. 'I mean, no offense or anything, ma'am, but I don't even cut my own hair!'

No offense? She's just called me ma'am and I couldn't have been a decade older than her. I drew myself up. 'I used to be a hair stylist myself back in Phoenix,' I said to Caitie.

'What happened?' She pulled a pair of reading glasses from the front pocket of her smock and squinted at me. 'Eyesight go? You gotta get glasses. That's what I did.'

If only to end this bloodbath, and at the risk of causing a new one, I said, 'Yes, that's a good idea.' I tugged at my locks. 'So, do you think you can squeeze me in?' I smiled hopefully.

'Sure,' Ms Conklin said. 'You go on back to my chair. I'll be with you in a sec.'

Not only had I been made to swallow my pride, but now I was going to be shelling out over fifty dollars or more that I could ill-afford. But if I wanted a chance to question the former Mrs Rick

Wilbur about his death, what better opportunity than sitting in here getting my hair cut by my suspect?

I was a bit nervous, truth be told, partly about what she might do to my hair and partly that she'd slit my throat with those scissors if she thought I was on to her, but I expected I was safe as long as there were witnesses around.

'Well, I'll be going now!' shouted the young woman as she pulled off her smock and hung it over her chair.

My head swung around. What happened to the silver-haired woman? Had she snuck out already?

The young woman disappeared out the back. I was alone with Caitie Conklin. I bristled as she tightened the ends of the smock around my neck.

She swung the chair around and lowered my head to the sink. 'Sorry about the heat. I've got the door open but I'm not sure if it's helping or hurting.'

I nodded as best I could as I felt the stream of water hit my skull.

'The air conditioner is on the fritz again. It's been sputtering and stopping for a week now. But I guess you probably know that, seeing how you've got the café next door.'

'So, you know me,' I said, feeling Caitie's hands massaging shampoo deep into my scalp. Strong fingers. Strong enough to hold a rolling pin and swing for the cheap seats.

'Sure, you're Miller, right?'

I nodded. I wasn't hearing so well though because my ear canals were filling with soap. It smelled like chamomile and neroli and tickled my nose.

'Anyway, the AC's normally the kind of thing Ed would take care of, but . . .' Her voice trailed off as she hosed me down. 'Water temp OK?'

I nodded and picked up where she'd left off. 'I know. I heard all about his stroke. In fact, I've been taking care of his cat for him.'

'Carol Two.' Caitie Conklin rinsed out my hair and expertly applied a cream rinse.

'You know her?' I cracked open an eye and looked up at her. A drop of soapy water fell in it and I blinked.

'Sure, heck, I knew the original,' clucked Caitie, 'Carol One.' She held up her index finger. 'A fine woman, that one.'

'What happened to her?'

'Died young. Car accident, as I remember.'

Once again, my heart went out to Ed Teller. Maybe I'd stop and pick up something special for Carol Two. Maybe some canned tuna.

She toweled me semidry then got to work on my hair.

'I hear you and Rick used to be married.'

Scissors froze in the air, mere inches from my nose. I gulped.

'That's right,' she answered. Her hand started moving again and I breathed more easily. 'It's no secret. Why?'

I shrugged. 'I was wondering if you had any ideas who might want to see him dead.'

Caitie spun the chair around and faced me. 'You shouldn't go sticking your nose into places it doesn't belong. Table Rock is a small town.

282

Folks around here don't like it much when you go getting in their business.'

I stared her down. 'Do you think that's what happened?'

'What do you mean?'

'I mean, do you think your ex-husband, Rick Wilbur, was getting his nose in somebody else's business and that person didn't like it?'

'And killed him, you're saying.' Caitie pulled my hair up in a comb and clipped the ends. She repeated this on the other side.

'I was married once,' I said. 'I know what it's like to have to deal with an ex-husband. Of course, mine is down in Phoenix.' At least, he should be. Why couldn't he stay there? 'I can't imagine him living here in Table Rock with me.'

Caitie grunted, focusing on my bangs. Wait! Since when did I have bangs? I groaned. What the heck was this woman doing? 'What was your relationship with your ex like?'

'Rick and me divorced over twenty years ago. It took a while, but we were friends eventually.'

'Did you cut his hair?' Recently?

'As a matter of fact,' Caitie answered, 'I did.'

'What about Johnny Wolfe?'

Caitie stood behind me now, facing the mirror while she worked in the back. We looked at each other's reflections. 'Yep, I cut his hair, too. You just saw it.'

'I was wondering if you thought Mr Wolfe might have had any reason to want to see your ex-husband dead.'

Caitie stepped back and looked directly at me.

283

'Why on earth would Johnny want to kill Rick?'

I shrugged lamely. I honestly had no idea. But what was going on between Caitie and Johnny? And what was going to happen in three days? Were they going to be skipping town? Getting out before the police caught up to them?

I tried another tack. 'I couldn't help noticing your salon hours before I came in. Weird, huh? You must have been open at the time of the murder.' I watched her face.

She wiped around my ears with a small towel, then dried her hands. 'I guess that's right.' She nodded. 'I guess I was here.'

'So did you see or hear anything?' The room seemed to have an electric charge suddenly.

'Not a thing.' She untied my smock and shook it out. I watched my beautiful red hair fall like silent rain drops. She grabbed a boar bristle brush and combed me out.

'How about your other stylists?' I asked. 'Did any of them see anything?'

Caitie smiled at me as she laid down her brush. 'I think we're done here.'

'Oh, OK.' I rose.

'And to answer your question, I was alone in the salon. No staff, no customers.' She led me to the cash register. 'I didn't see anything and I didn't hear anything.' There was a hard edge to her already hard voice. 'That'll be sixty-two dollars and fifty cents.' She held out her hand, palm up.

As I paid and headed for the open door, Caitie said, 'Rick and I split up years ago, Miller. So I had absolutely nothing to gain killing the man.'

We stared at one another for a long moment. She really was one tough cookie.

Caitie slammed the register shut, my hard-earned money in its bowels. That was sixty-two fifty I'd never see again.

And now I had bangs! I hate bangs!

She grinned slyly. 'Now, that vixen, Peggy, on the other hand . . .'

THIRTY

By the time I made it to Laura's Lightly Used, it was nearly six and I was completely deep-sixed, drained. I'd have been sweating profusely but this darned 'dry heat' wouldn't allow me the pleasure.

With the Schwinn back at the apartment, I'd been forced to walk. The last time I'd walked this much it had been at the Scottsdale Fashion Square – two million square feet of paradise – the week before Christmas. I could have detoured back to the apartment for my bike, but I knew Laura closed at six on Sunday and I really wanted to catch her before she left for the day. The side trip might have been cutting it close.

I'd seen what very likely had been my missing two chairs – the two chairs that would have had to be removed from the box to stuff poor Rick Wilbur inside – the other day at Laura's Lightly Used.

Heck, I'd sat in one of those chairs crying my eyes out and sipping iced tea.

Not a pleasant thought at all.

I hung under the big turbo-sized fan at the store entry for a moment, luxuriating in the blast of cool air as it pummeled me. Who knew when I'd get this much cool air in my bedroom again?

Feeling recharged, I went in search of Laura. An assistant was stacking flower pots near the door.

'Is Laura here?'

The floor clerk looked about and pointed toward the far corner. Following her arm, I spotted Laura chatting with a customer in the women's clothing section. She caught my eye and nodded in my direction. I waved and headed for the back. That's where the two chairs were.

Who knew? Maybe the killer had left fingerprints on the chairs. I couldn't wait to telephone Detective Highsmith and tell him to get his butt down here and tag and bag them or whatever it is that detectives do with evidence the size of dining chairs.

But when I got there, the chairs were gone. I stood staring at the spot, my head down, my hands drooping at my sides.

Laura laid a hand on my shoulder and I looked up. 'Something wrong, Maggie?'

'The chairs,' I wheezed. 'What happened to the chairs?' Not even the table that had been set between them was there. The whole area had been rearranged. There was a freaking canoe with a couple of paddles sticking out filling the space where the chairs had been just a couple of days ago.

I felt her arm across my shoulder. 'You need to sit?' She guided me toward the right side of the store. 'Come on, Maggie. I've got some chairs back here. You poor thing. You really do look like you need to sit down.'

She led me to the furniture section and pushed me gently down in a brown leather recliner. Laura took a seat in a matching loveseat and patted my knee.

'Feeling better?' She looked at me with concern written on her face. 'Can I get you anything?' She leaned forward. 'What happened to your hair?' She gasped. 'Did somebody attack you?'

This was not the time to discuss Caitie Conklin's butchery. I pointed to the aluminum canoe. 'Laura, there were two chairs over there the other day. What happened to them?'

She looked at the space I was pointing to and shrugged. 'Sold them, I guess. Why?'

'I think – no, I'm certain those were my chairs.' A sick feeling filled my stomach. Once again, proof of my innocence, this time in the form of potential fingerprints that might point to the true perpetrator, had slipped from my grasp.

'Your chairs?' Laura tugged at her ear. 'I don't understand.'

I took a deep breath and stood, my eyes scanning the cluttered store. Perhaps the chairs were still here. They could have been moved. 'Are you sure you sold them? Maybe they're around here someplace else?'

Laura stood with me. 'No, I remember now. I'm certain we sold them. We've sold a number of chairs today.' She shrugged. 'Some days are like that, you know? What's so important about those chairs?' She spread her arms. 'You need chairs? I've got plenty of chairs around here. Let's pick out a couple.'

I shook my head. 'You don't understand.' I grabbed her arm, as much to get her to listen as to steady myself. 'I think those chairs were the chairs Rick Wilbur's killer removed from the carton to make room to stuff the body in.'

Laura sucked air through her teeth. 'Oh, no!' She shook herself. 'That's awful!' Her hands compressed her cheeks.

I nodded. 'Think, Laura. Who sold you those chairs?'

Laura paced the shop floor up and down, then stopped, shrugging helplessly. 'I wish I could tell you, but I'm not sure.'

Wasn't she? Or was she hiding something? I watched her closely for signs of prevarication. She might have taken the chairs herself, making her the killer. What better plan than to take the chairs with her after murdering poor Mr Wilbur and then hiding them in plain sight in her vintage store?

It was perfect. And I'd been fool enough to sit in one of them, oblivious to the fact that I was sitting on evidence. Oh, how she must have been laughing at me.

I groaned inwardly.

Laura went to the checkout counter and pulled out a big book. 'This will tell me who we bought the chairs from and when. I note all the store's transactions here.'

She flipped the lined ledger open on the counter and ran her finger down the page. 'Hmm.'

'What is it?'

'The chairs came in the day after the murder. See?'

I glanced at the ledger. There it was, in thick blue ink. Assuming Laura wasn't so clever as to have doctored the ledger in case anyone came checking, this meant she was no killer.

That would be a relief, because I was really

growing fond of the woman and I'd hate to have to continue this friendship via visits to the state pen. I wasn't certain, but something told me that was more than a bike ride away.

'It doesn't say who you bought them from.' That was disappointing.

'No, it doesn't,' Laura answered. 'But it does tell us who conducted the sale. 'See these initials?'

I nodded once more. The ledger also revealed that Laura's Lightly Used had only paid out ten bucks for both chairs! Sheesh, I'd paid forty apiece for them. Laura's Lightly Used appeared to be quite the little goldmine.

'RP. Robin Pahe.' Laura snapped her fingers and called over the clerk I'd seen earlier by the front door. 'Robin,' she said as the young Navajo woman looked at us expectantly. 'You remember those two dining chairs – the ones that were right up front by the counter?'

'Of course, I took them in myself.' Robin wore denim shorts and a loose black tank top with moccasins and had liquid brown eyes.

'That's right,' Laura said. 'Do you remember who brought them in?'

'Gosh, Laura.' Robin rubbed her nose. 'Can I see that?' Laura handed her the ledger. She shook her head slowly side to side, then looked up at her employer. 'Sorry,' she said. 'I guess I forgot to write it down. I know you say we're always supposed to.' Her eyes fell to the floor.

'That's OK,' Laura replied. 'But do try to remember in the future.'

I stepped forward. 'Think, Robin. Are you sure you don't remember who sold you the chairs?'

She shrugged helplessly. 'Sorry.' She shook her head some more. 'He was just some guy, you know? Sort of scruffy.'

Some guy. Well, that was something. Now we were cutting the field of suspects in half!

Laura thanked Robin and told her she could get back to what she'd been doing. 'Sorry I couldn't be more help,' Laura said, putting the ledger back in its place.

'Hey, you tried. What more can I ask?'

Laura smiled. 'Are you sure you're OK?' She looked at me inquisitively.

I brushed at my bangs. My bangs! 'Yeah, I'll be fine. Thanks for trying.'

'Anytime.' Laura walked me to the entrance. 'It's too bad you don't want to know who *bought* those two chairs,' she chuckled. '*That* I could answer.'

I stopped under the big fan, feeling the air run up and down my flesh. I bunched my brows together. 'Who bought the chairs?'

Laura laughed. 'Trish Gregory. And you should have seen the look on her face when she saw them there. You'd have thought she won the lottery! She was so excited.'

'That's right,' put in Robin. 'Said she just had to have them. I helped her load them into her van.'

Trish Gregory. A woman, not a man. So much for cutting down the field of suspects.

THIRTY-ONE

'Let me get this straight,' I said. 'Trish Gregory from Karma Koffee came in here and bought my two dining chairs?' Why on earth would the woman do that? It couldn't be because she and Rob needed a couple more seats at their coffee shop. Even if they did, they wouldn't want my chairs. My chairs didn't match their fancy décor at all.

'That's right,' Laura answered. 'She offered me fifty dollars apiece for them before I could even name a price.' She leaned in. 'To tell you the truth, that's double what I would have asked.'

I realized then and there that I might be in the wrong business. Maggie's Modestly Used. Yeah, it had a certain ring to it. 'When exactly was this?'

Laura looked at Robin. 'What do you think, about two hours ago?'

'Sounds about right,' Robin replied.

'No offense, but Trish Gregory doesn't strike me as the type of woman who shops at second-hand stores.'

'None taken,' Laura replied. 'Trish comes in every once in a while and browses around. Occasionally buys a dress or some other bit of clothing.' Laura looked again at Robin.

Robin nodded. 'Mrs Gregory is into vintage stuff.'

I twisted my lip up. There was certainly nothing vintage about those chairs. They were brand new, generic restaurant chairs.

'She'd tried on a vintage eighties pair of Calvin Klein jeans – like the ones Brooke Shields made famous in those ads – and was bringing them up to the register when she spotted the chairs,' Robin explained.

'I was standing behind the register.' Laura looked at her watch and turned the Open sign to Closed. 'Mrs Gregory spotted the chairs and squealed. The next thing I knew, she was buying them, too.'

A car honked. Donna waved from the Mini Cooper. I'd called her on my way over knowing that she was at Mother Earth/Father Sun Grocers and would be closing at six p.m., too. Most businesses downtown closed up early on Sunday.

'That's my ride,' I said. 'One more thing,' I cried, climbing in on the passenger side. 'What can you tell me about Rick Wilbur's relationship with his ex-wife, Caitie Conklin, or his widow, Patti?'

'From the hair salon?'

I nodded.

Laura shrugged. 'Sorry,' she said with a shake of the head, 'that's all before my time. I didn't even know Caitie Conklin was his ex.'

'That's OK.' I waved. 'Thanks, you've been a big help!'

'Any time!' Laura said, pulling the door shut after me.

'What did you do to your hair?' Donna asked, taking her eyes off the road to get a better look at me.

'I'm trying something new,' I answered between gritted teeth.

Dinner was waiting for us when we got to the house. With Donna having been minding the store most of the day, we'd be eating Andy's cooking.

Tonight it was grilled cheese sandwiches on fresh sourdough bread with homemade French fries. The potatoes were organic, of course, and tasted like they'd been fried in used motor oil, and the 'cheese' was something made out of compressed soybeans curds or something equally suspect. Sadly, Andy and Donna didn't believe in Velveeta or good old American – but still, not bad. I'd take it over rattlesnake any day.

Andy and the boys kept stealing looks at me and I knew exactly what they were thinking. My eyes dared them to say anything at all about my hair – just one word. Lucky for them, they remained silent. Donna must have warned them.

The boys ate up or got sick of eating and disappeared to their rooms to play video games. 'So,' said Andy, 'you look like you've been itching to talk since you got here, Maggie. What's going on?'

'Should I tell him or you?' I said to my sister.

'Definitely you,' Donna said, reaching for a homemade flaxseed and carob chip cookie.

I nodded. I'd already filled her in on all I'd learned. I got Andy up to speed, telling him about my conversations with the Gregorys, Caitie Conklin and Laura Duval.

'Wow.' Andy leaned back in his chair. 'You've been busy. Not that that's a good thing. You really need to let the police handle this, Maggie. Don't you have enough to do just trying to manage your new business?'

I blushed. He was right, of course. Open only a couple of days and already I was neglecting what should have been the most important thing in the world to me – my business, my livelihood. My one chance to save up enough money to move out of the apartment I was renting from the Gregorys.

But how could I concentrate on running my business when there was a vicious killer running around Table Rock?

A killer who had left his or her victim stuffed in a box in my storeroom!

'You're right,' I said. 'Maybe I got carried away.'

Andy barked out a laugh and the legs of his chair hit the ground. 'You think?' He laughed once more.

He pointed a half-eaten cookie at me. But I wasn't afraid of any cookie. I was afraid to try one – was that bits of chopped up zucchini sticking out of that middle layer? – but I was not afraid of it on an intrinsic level. 'You need to go to the police and tell them your theories and what you've discovered. Let them handle things from here on.'

'I agree,' Donna said softly. She covered my hand with hers. 'Someone has already tried to kill you once,' she said. 'What if they try again?'

Donna was right. They were both right. Even Caitie had warned me that if I kept sticking my nose in where it didn't belong, I might get hurt. I might end up dead. Worse yet, Donna, Andy,

Mom or even the boys might get caught in the crossfire.

I promised to change my ways. I pushed back my chair and turned to Donna. 'Can I borrow the Mini, Sis?' I knew better than to ask Andy to borrow his precious truck – not that he'd say no, he was far too nice for that – but I knew that every second I was gone he would be worrying to death.

She raised an eyebrow. 'Whatever for?'

'I'm going down to the police station. If Highsmith isn't there, I'll talk to whoever is.' I also planned on doing a little snooping on Trish Gregory. I couldn't very well tail a suspect on a Schwinn.

'Keys are in my purse.' Donna pointed to the small table beneath the phone.

I dug out her keys and shook them. 'Thanks. Then I'll swing by the apartment and pick up a few more things. But this is the last night I'll impose on you two.'

'You're not imposing,' Donna scolded.

'Not at all,' chimed Andy.

'I know, I know. But I should have a new air conditioner any time now and it will be good to sleep in my own bed.'

I also couldn't live with myself if the killer tried to strike again while I was camping at Donna and Andy's house. If anything happened to them or the boys . . .

THIRTY-TWO

I swung by my apartment and grabbed a change of clothes and some toiletries and tossed them all in a pillowcase. I'd left my one and only suitcase at my sister's house. The entire apartment still smelled like smoke and not the smoky, mouthwatering barbecue kind – the 'I could have been burnt to a crisp in my bed' kind.

I closed the place up, leaving the air conditioner in the front room running with the hope that it might help clear the air.

Next, I stopped at the minimart a block over and selected a nice can of tuna for Carol Two, along with a bag of cheese doodles. If the cat wouldn't eat them, I would. Donna might have a fit but I figured I'd hide the bag behind one of the couch cushions until she went to bed.

I pulled up in front of Ed's house as the last remnants of the sun disappeared in the damson western sky. Ed's car wasn't in the driveway so I parked in the drive myself. I still didn't know if Ed had been released from the hospital yet. Until then, I was going to keep that cat of his alive if it killed me.

Walking up the path to the door, I wondered if maybe Ed had been released and that was why there was no sign of his car. He could be out for a drive somewhere. Grocery shopping, for all I knew.

With that in mind, I knocked on the door. There was no answer. I pressed my ear against the warm wood. Not a sound. I pulled his key ring from my handbag, unlocked the door and went inside.

Carol Two, surprisingly, wasn't there to greet me. I headed for the kitchen, then stopped. Were those noises I was hearing coming from down the hall? I cocked an ear and felt a chill scurry up my arms.

Definitely.

I tiptoed down the hall, careful not to make a sound. What if there was a burglar in the house? What if I caught them in the act? What would they do to me?

How mad were they going to be once they discovered there was nothing in this dump worth stealing?

The door to the master bedroom was ajar. I leaned low and peeked through the crack.

I sighed with relief. Ed was lying in bed, a portable computer on his lap. 'Mr Teller!' I called. 'I didn't realize you were back!'

'Huh?' He looked up, startled, and closed the laptop. 'What are you doing here?'

'I came to feed Carol Two,' I explained. 'I'm sorry, I didn't know you were here. I didn't realize you had been released.'

He frowned and wiped his forehead with the back of his hand. 'They let me out around noon. Been here ever since.'

'Again, sorry. I didn't see your car—'

'I put it in the garage. Not supposed to drive. No point in having the sun beat down on it.'

'Of course.' I went to his side of the bed and

briefly clasped his hand. 'I'm so happy for you that you've come home. You must be thrilled. I'll bet she is, too.'

His bushy eyebrows formed a V and he sat up. 'She? She who?'

'Carol Two.' I pointed to the cat, asleep on a rattan papasan chair with a brown cushion in the corner near a small television.

He shrugged. 'I guess so. You get a haircut?'

'Salon de Belleza,' I answered. 'Do you like it?'

He lifted a shoulder. 'I've seen worse.'

That was OK. I'd heard worse. 'Caitie cut it for me.'

'I'm not surprised. The woman has a way with a pair of scissors.'

Yeah, the wrong way. I reached into my purse. 'I brought Carol Two a treat.' I swung the tuna can around so he could read the label.

'Thanks,' he replied, running his hands over the dark bedspread. 'I'm afraid she's already had her dinner.'

I curled my lip. 'A treat for later?'

'I suppose,' he gave in gruffly.

'I guess I'll be off then.' I fluffed his pillow for him. 'Is there anything I can do for you before I leave? I'm on my way to the police station. I've got some great news about Rick Wilbur's killer.'

'You do?' He scratched at his beard. I wondered what he'd look like without it. Probably fifty years younger.

I nodded. 'I've got all kinds of suspects. One in particular. And,' I said, talking quickly, 'I know

299

what happened to the chairs. At least, I think I know.'

'Chairs?' His eyes were glazed over and his cheeks flushed. I was beginning to get concerned. It may not have been a good idea for the hospital to release him quite yet. 'What are you talking about, Miller?'

'My chairs,' I said. 'From the café. The ones that were in the box but the killer had to take out of the box to put the dead guy – Rick, I mean – in the box after he, *or she*, killed him.'

I looked at him triumphantly. 'Those chairs.' I still hadn't made up my mind if Trish had been working solo or with her husband, Rob. They probably committed the murder as a team, the Deadly Duo. Better still, the Karma Koffee Killers!

I could see the headline now. I'd get that Smith character from the *Table Rock Reader* to use my title. As long as he gave me credit for catching the killers, I'd let him have credit for the catchy headline.

Ed's jaw fell. His hands held the sheet tightly to his chest. He shook his head. 'Miller, I'm not sure what you just said,' he chuckled, 'but OK.'

I handed Ed his house keys. 'I guess I won't be needing these anymore.'

Ed eyed me a moment. 'Actually . . .'

'Yes?'

'Well, I heard about the fire at your place.'

'Oh?'

He nodded slowly. 'The fire chief, Terry Stillman, is an old friend of mine. He grew up here, like me. We went to school together.'

300

Ed fidgeted in his bed. Carol Two looked up from her catnap then laid her head back between her paws. 'Anyway, I've got a spare bedroom you can use if you need a place to stay for a day or two.'

'Oh, no, I couldn't do that.' I patted his arm. 'Really.' Could I? What harm could it do? It sure beat sleeping on Donna and Andy's sofa. It also meant I'd be keeping them out of harm's way if any harm came my way. 'I wouldn't want to impose.' And I wouldn't have to smuggle in the cheese doodles.

'You wouldn't be,' he answered. 'In fact, you'd be helping me out. The doctor recommended I get some sort of nursemaid. I told him no. You could stay here as long as you need. Help me out a little?' He looked at me with those tired, helpless-looking eyes of his.

I tapped my foot and smiled. And nobody – no killer, anyway, would think to look for me at Ed Teller's house. What could be safer?

I stuck out my hand. 'Deal.' I promised I'd be back after taking care of my errands.

The first thing I did was swing by the café. I was going to take a picture of my chairs just so it was clear what I was talking about. There seemed to be a certain lack of understanding between Detective Highsmith and myself. The man was dense as a pound cake.

I unlocked the door, pulled out my cell phone and fired off a couple of shots. Proof positive. I stuffed my cell phone back in my purse. I noticed the light blinking on the café phone behind the counter and pushed the play button.

'Maggie, this is Brad. Brad Smith. Call me back as soon as you get this. I've been digging around into Rick Wilbur's murder and I've got some important information.'

I heard loud sounds in the background, then the reporter's voice continued, 'Oops, gotta go! Wish I had your cell number—'

Well, that was weird. Digging around? Important information? I had his card in my wallet. I looked at the number and dialed. 'Hi, this is Brad Smith, I'm—'

Great, I'd gotten his voicemail. 'Maggie Miller here,' I said after the prompt. 'Got your message and will try you later. I've got big news of my own.' Bigger, I'll bet. I'd beat that nosy reporter at his own game.

I locked up and headed straight for the Table Rock Police Department. I'd called Detective Highsmith from the driveway and asked him to meet me there. He'd agreed but didn't sound too happy about it.

When I got to the station, I could see why. He was sitting at his desk in his office in the back, wearing charcoal trousers and a gray sport coat over a white polo shirt.

'What's this all about, Ms Miller?' He swung a hand through his hair and scowled to show his displeasure, as if his tone of voice wasn't enough of a giveaway. His brown hair was impeccably coiffed. Obviously, the man wasn't a client of Caitie Conklin.

As if reading my mind, Highsmith said, 'What happened to your—?'

My fingers went automatically to my scalp. 'I

don't want to talk about my hair!' I snapped. 'Can we talk about more important things, like who killed Rick Wilbur?'

He motioned for me to sit as he leaned back in his chair. 'Do you know who murdered Mr Wilbur?'

I sat down and set my purse on my lap. 'Not exactly.'

He sighed. 'Then what did you drag me down here for? It's my day off.'

'What's the matter, have you got a hot date?' I said. 'With VV, perhaps?'

Highsmith cracked a smile. 'Perhaps.' He folded his hands atop the desk. 'So what's this all about?'

I told the detective all about how I'd spoken to Rick Wilbur's ex, Caitie Conklin. 'And she and Johnny were conspiring.'

Highsmith looked dubious. I got a lot of that from this guy. 'Conspiring? To do what?'

I shook my head in frustration. 'That's just it. I don't know. I was listening to them talk when one of the stylists noticed me. Then they shut up and Johnny left.'

'That's not a whole lot to go on.'

'I do know that whatever it is that they are *conspiring* on,' I stared at him, 'is going to happen in three days.'

He raised his chin. 'You know that Rick Wilbur's murder was days ago. They can't be conspiring to kill him again now, could they?'

'I also talked to the Gregorys.'

Highsmith waved his hand at me. 'I already know all about that. Rob Gregory's got an alibi. A good one.'

Right, a Table Rock police officer in his yoga class. 'But what about Trish Gregory? Do you have an alibi for her?'

He leaned forward. 'Why would Trish Gregory want to murder Rick Wilbur?'

'Like I've said before, the Gregorys disliked Mr Wilbur. They weren't happy that he'd leased me a shop for my beignet café right across the street from Karma Koffee either. I could be taking a good bite of their business,' I conjectured. 'Money is always motive for murder.'

'Then why didn't they simply murder you?'

Why did I get the feeling he didn't think that would have been such a bad thing? 'I don't know. I guess you'll have to ask them yourself when you arrest them.' I paused for dramatic effect, folding my arms over my chest. 'And then there's the chairs.'

Highsmith squeezed his eyes shut. When he opened them, he said, 'What chairs?'

'My chairs, of course. The two that were missing from the storeroom.'

'Your chairs were missing from your storeroom?'

I nodded vigorously. 'Don't you see? Whoever killed Rick Wilbur had to get rid of the chairs first if they were going to stuff him in that box.' I smiled in triumph. 'And I know where the chairs are.'

Highsmith tilted his head to one side. 'I'll bite. Where?'

Just then, my phone went off in my purse. I pushed the flap aside and looked at the number on the screen. It was not a number I recognized.

304

'Must be a wrong number.' Even if it wasn't a wrong number, whatever it was could wait.

'The chairs?'

'Right. I got to thinking about those two missing chairs and suddenly I remembered where I'd seen them.' I pulled out my phone, called up the pictures of the chairs and played them for him.

'A little fuzzy,' he said, squinting. 'Don't you think you should have turned on some more lights?'

'Are you going to be a critic or are you going to be a cop?'

'Maybe swiveled the chairs so you could see them more head on?'

'Must you be so—'

'Right?'

'Ha ha. Mind if I continue?'

Highsmith started making small circles with his index finger, trying to get me to move along, I guess. 'Laura's Lightly Used. I'd seen them there the other day. Sat in them, even.'

'Why didn't you say so then? I don't remember you notifying us.'

'I didn't realize it then,' I said, getting testy. 'I realized it later. And when I went by the store today, I learned that the chairs had been purchased.' I folded my arms across my chest. 'Guess who bought them?'

Highsmith covered a yawn with the back of his hand. 'Somebody who needed two chairs?'

'Very funny,' I said. 'Trish Gregory.'

'So now you think she killed Rick Wilbur?'

I shrugged. 'Maybe. Though I'll bet it's the

two of them. Trish and Rob.' One had the perfect alibi, while the other committed the murder.

'Are you sure you aren't just upset because you've learned they're your landlords?'

OK, that did bug me a little bit. Heck, it bugged me a lot! 'Of course not,' I said. 'I am not that petty!'

'But you do think she bought the chairs to cover up the murder?'

I planted my hands on my hips and nodded. 'That's right.'

'If that was the case,' he smiled, 'why didn't she simply take them with her after she killed him?'

I hadn't thought about that. 'I thought about that,' I said. 'The way I see it, she must have been in a hurry. Maybe she saw something, heard something.' I shook my head. 'I don't know. Maybe she panicked and ditched the chairs in the alley and hightailed it out of there. Then later,' I continued before he could cut me off, 'she real-ized her mistake, went back to get them to destroy the evidence and discovered they were gone!' I looked at him triumphantly.

'What evidence did she have to destroy?'

'Fingerprints, of course.' Sheesh, did I have to do all the thinking around here? 'Don't forget,' I added, 'the Gregorys are my landlords. That means they've got the keys to my apartment. Who better to have sabotaged my air-conditioning unit? They had the perfect means.'

For once, he looked impressed. 'Somebody did mess with your window AC unit. Still, you'd think they'd have more sense than that. Like you said, they are the landlords and do have copies of your keys. The Gregorys would have to know they would be the first people we might suspect.'

'I never said they were smart.'

Highsmith plucked a pencil from the holder at the corner of his desk and doodled on his blotter. 'You know, there was a time when you were suggesting that Mr Wilbur's widow was involved. In fact, if I remember correctly, and I do,' he said, his M&Ms focused sharply on me, 'you also suggested that Natalie Henson and her boy, Tommy, might be involved . . .'

I bit at the inside of my cheek. Dang, he had a good memory. I suppose that was a good thing to have in a detective, but it was a trait I could live without at the moment.

'Maybe they are,' I replied defiantly. 'Maybe Rob, maybe Caitie Conklin and Johnny Wolfe, maybe Patti Wilbur, her sister, Natalie and her son, Tommy.' I threw my arms in the air. 'Maybe the whole town is involved! After all, Wilbur Realty seemed to own or have a finger in half the town. Maybe everybody had a reason to want Rick Wilbur dead.' I gasped and pointed an accusing finger. 'Maybe even you.'

Oops, I might have taken things too far. I lowered my finger and locked my hands together. I formed a weak smile. 'I mean, it's just a theory . . .' I felt a bead of sweat tumble from my forehead to my nose.

Detective Highsmith watched me sweat for a moment, then rose. 'I'm going to try to forget you said that.'

I hoped he would. I stood, too.

'I will have a talk with Ms Duval tomorrow.'

'But, Trish—'

'Goodnight, Ms Miller. If I find anything out, I'll let you or your attorney know. In the meantime,' he loomed over me, 'stay out of police business.'

Highsmith escorted me to the door. 'And do not call me again unless it's a true emergency.'

'I knew it. A big date, right?'

The corner of the detective's lip turned down. 'If you must know, I was watching the game at the Vargas house when you called.' He looked at his watch. 'If I'm lucky, I just might catch the last quarter.'

I slumped off to the Mini Cooper and climbed inside. As I pulled into traffic, a black minivan sped past.

Trish Gregory was behind the wheel.

THIRTY-THREE

There was nothing I could do but chase her. She was going at a good clip, so I floored it. There were two cars between us but that was OK. The last thing I wanted was for her to notice me following her.

I smiled. I'd forgotten how much fun driving a car could be, especially in hot pursuit. I looked at the speedometer – wow, Trish was really flying over the speed limit – stomped down even further on the gas pedal and the car sailed ahead. I was going to owe Donna some gas money.

The miles flew by and we were getting further and further from the lights of Table Rock. By now, I figured we were halfway to Sedona. There were still a couple of cars and a semi between me and the minivan but I hadn't lost sight of her.

Eventually, traffic ahead slowed as Trish turned right onto a narrow blacktop road that wound through the dark hills, turned to gravel, then to dirt.

I turned off my headlights and followed at a distance, bouncing up and down, my head banging the roof. I cursed every hundred yards or so and prayed I wasn't doing any serious damage to the Mini.

How much abuse could this vehicle take? How much abuse could I take if I wrecked my sister's prized car?

Where the devil was she going? She couldn't possibly live out here in this rocky desert, could she?

Her brake lights blinked and I could see her decelerating as she rounded a far turn near a large outcropping of rock. I didn't recognize the area at all. I coasted to a stop a few hundred yards away and cut the engine.

A few moments later, the overhead light inside the minivan came on. I could see Trish clearly as she stepped down from the van. She was dressed as I'd seen her earlier today but for the addition of a denim jacket. The desert gets cold at night.

She walked around to the side of the van and slid open the big door. A minute later, she pulled out one chair, then another.

My chairs.

I couldn't be certain from this distance and in the dark. But what other two chairs could they possibly be?

I strained against the windshield trying to imagine what she might be up to. She pulled the door shut, picked up one chair and disappeared up the hill. She held a flashlight in one hand. I watched its light bounce randomly over the uneven ground as she walked.

As I sat there trying to make up my mind whether to follow or not, she came back down the hill. She grabbed the other chair and went up the hill again.

Once I was certain she was out of sight and wouldn't notice the lights coming on in the Mini, I opened the driver's-side door and snatched my purse off the floor. I softly shut the door behind me. My heart was pounding. It was deathly quiet out here. And way too dark for comfort.

Especially since I was alone out here with a crazed killer!

I hurried over to her minivan and stole a look inside. All quite ordinary. Like any minivan should be. No dead bodies, no weapons of individual or mass destruction.

I turned and looked up the hill, my mind churning. There was no sign of Trish but I could just make out a rutted track. I hunched over and followed it.

After about five minutes of walking, the trail levelled off. There was a gap between two large egg-shaped boulders. I moved to the side and slowly approached. Peeking around the edge of one of the giant red rocks, I saw where Trish had led me.

She was standing in the center of a medicine wheel. I'd come to learn that these are fairly common monuments in Red Rock Country, originally constructed by early indigenous cultures. Medicine wheels are ceremonial circles of stones usually laid out in a particular pattern with a center stone or cairn and an outer ring of stones with spokes – lines of rock radiating out in the four cardinal directions: south, east, north and west.

Apparently they come in all sizes. Some may be as small as six feet in diameter, others twenty feet or more. This one was on the large size.

Native Americans used medicine wheels for meditation, prayer, healing and spiritual rituals.

Believers consider medicine wheels to possess a true physical connection with the spiritual world. I tugged at the crystal around my neck. Mom would love this.

Some medicine wheels are said to be quite ancient. I had no way of knowing how old or new this one might be. For all I knew, Trish had constructed it earlier herself.

But why did the medicine wheel need chairs? Did Trish think the aliens might need a good rest? Someplace to sit down after their long flight from the Whatchamacallit Galaxy to Earth?

Trish had placed my two dining chairs in the center, within the small central circle. Her flashlight sat on a small stone facing the middle. She looked around for a moment, picked up her flashlight, then headed back my way.

That was it? She was leaving the chairs? My mind panicked. Should I race down the hill ahead of her to my car? Should I wait where I was?

I heard the crunch of feet over gravel and pressed myself against the rock, praying she didn't see me. It was too late to make up my mind on a plan. I was going to have to let Trish go first. I groaned as I watched her disappear. I just realized she was going to pass the Mini Cooper on her way out to the highway.

She'd get suspicious. But at least she wouldn't know it was me. She must know I ride a bike and don't even own a car. Surely she wouldn't recognize the Mini as my sister's vehicle.

But what would she think suddenly discovering a second car out here when there hadn't been one on her way out?

I waited until she was out of sight and crept after her. As I started down the hill, I spied Trish heading back up. I gasped softly and quickly covered my big mouth with my fist. I ducked down hastily. She held the flashlight in her left hand, but had something else in her right. I recognized it.

It was one of those red plastic gas cans.

I scurried back up the hill, hid behind a cluster of small boulders and waited for her to go by.

I heard noises coming from the medicine wheel and crept back around the corner, sticking my head out just far enough to see clearly. She was tossing gasoline over the chairs and mumbling some sort of incantations. If Mom was here, she might know what that mumbo-jumbo meant. I knew one thing . . .

She was going to destroy the chairs!

I retreated and flattened myself against the rock. As soundlessly as possible, I dug around in my purse until my fingers wrapped around my cell phone. I could only hope I'd be able to get some kind of signal out here.

I tapped the phone and it sprang to life. Bingo! I had bars. I hit the menu for a list of recent calls and tapped my finger on Detective Highsmith's number.

'Hello?' It was a woman's voice.

'VV?' I whispered.

'Who is this?'

'It's Maggie Miller. You know, the beignet café lady.'

'The murder suspect.'

Ouch. That hurt. 'Who said I'm a suspect? I

can name any number of better suspects. In fact,' I said, and then, suddenly aware that my voice had risen, I gulped and brought it back down several notches, 'I've got one of them here right now,' I whispered.

'What are you talking about? Please make yourself clear.'

'That's what I'm trying to do,' I snarled. 'Listen, I'm out here at some medicine wheel between two big rocks and Trish is immolating the chairs.'

'What? What chairs?' I was catching a tone of impatience. 'And who is Trish?'

I sighed into the phone. 'Where's Detective Highsmith?'

'Who is it?' I heard the detective holler from the distance. It sounded like a TV was going in the background too.

'It's the Miller woman,' I heard Veronica reply. 'Saying something about some woman named Trish and some chairs.' I sniffed. The smell of smoke came my way. If he didn't get here soon, the evidence would be toast. Literally.

'What? Tell her I said to give it a rest. Tell her I'll talk to her tomorrow, like I told her earlier. That's if I don't lock her up first tonight.'

Boy, he sounded tense. I had a feeling whatever team he was rooting for was on the losing side of things. 'Then hang up!' I heard him shout.

'Mark said that you should call him tomorrow.'
'I heard.'
'OK, then. Goodnight, Miss Miller.'
'Don't you dare—'
Click.
I stared at the phone. The screen read 'Call

314

Ended.' 'Hang up.' Ooh, that woman. Oh, that man!

I noticed I had a message on my phone. I'd forgotten about whoever had called while I'd been talking to Detective Highsmith earlier at the police station. I pressed the play button and held my ear to the phone. It was a call from Mesa Verde Medical Center, asking me to call back.

What on earth could that be about? Maybe Dr Vargas was telephoning to ask me out on a date?

A woman can dream, can't she? Then I remembered the nightmare that was his sister.

Some dreams are best left unfulfilled.

No way was I calling back out here where Trish might see or hear me. I ran back to the Mini. There wasn't much reason to stay now. The damage had been done.

And there was no way I was calling Detective Highsmith again. Besides, there wasn't much left to see but a pile of ash. Can you dust dust for fingerprints?

I didn't think so. I mean, those CSI guys are good, but I don't think they're that good.

I stopped at a gas station and convenience store out on the highway and dialed the Mesa Verde number. I yawned as I waited for someone to pick up on the other end. I was exhausted and had to be up early to get to work. After this call, I was heading straight back to Ed's house to catch a few hours' sleep.

A sharp male voice answered. 'Mesa Verde, can I help you?'

'This is Maggie Miller. Someone from there called me?'

'Oh, yeah. Ms Miller, right. One of our patients was asking about you.'

'Oh, no! Has Mr Teller been readmitted?' I'd been expecting the worse and now it had happened.

'Who? No. Mr Smith.'

I scrunched up my face. 'Brad Smith?'

'That's right. He was real anxious to talk to you.'

'Brad Smith is one of your patients? What happened?'

I heard a deep sigh on the other end of the line. 'We don't know for sure. But the paramedics brought him in here pretty busted up.' There was a short pause. 'He asked for you before he went into a coma.'

'A coma?'

'Yes.' There was sadness in the man's voice. 'Sorry to be the one to break it to you like this. Are the two of you close?'

I stood there, listening to the cars streak by as I sat in the lot of the gas station. Brad Smith had called the café trying to reach me. What had he said? Had he discovered something? Had he some big news about Rick Wilbur's murder?

Was that why he was now lying in a coma in a hospital bed?

And was it my fault?

THIRTY-FOUR

'They said it was a car accident,' I said to Ed when I got back to his house. Though it was late, Mr Teller was awake and lying in bed watching television on his laptop.

'Tough break,' grunted Ed.

'Yeah,' I said, wearily. 'Do you know him?'

He shook his head. 'The newspaper's not one of our properties.'

'I think I'll give Carol Two that little treat I promised her, then hit the sack.'

'Good idea,' he agreed. Ed rubbed the back of his neck. 'Mind hitting the light on your way out?'

I nodded, flicked off the ceiling light and closed his door behind me. Carol Two mrowled at my feet. I'd forgotten all about her treat earlier. 'Come on,' I said wearily, 'let's get you some tuna. Then,' I said, looking down at the cat at my feet, 'I suggest we both get some sleep.'

She mrowled once more. I like it when a cat agrees with me. I dug around through the drawers looking for a can opener and found drawers full of assorted knives, one full of old brochures for Vegas and Reno and one chock full of what looked like mostly expired coupons.

I finally found a can opener mixed in with a drawer full of cheap silverware.

A knock on the front door scared the living

daylights out of me. And that was something, considering it was practically the middle of the night.

Was it Trish? Had she figured out where I was staying? Had she spotted the Mini? Should I have parked up the street or the next block over?

I shivered. Had she come to get rid of me like she had Rick Wilbur?

I stole to the front room and peeked out the window through a crack in the slats. The living room was one place where the windows had been boarded up. A couple stood under the grimy porch light. For a moment, I feared it was Trish and Rob.

Me, an invalid and one scrawny cat would never be able to fight those two off. But as the man knocked again, I realized this pair was too young to be the Gregorys.

The young man was thin and wore baggy blue jeans and a blue T-shirt that was way too large for his frame. His companion had short dark hair. Though a few pounds overweight, she was quite pretty, and was flaunting what she had in a pair of denim short-shorts and a pink tube top.

'What if he's not here?' I heard the girl say.

'He's here,' the young man said, a hard edge to his voice. 'Where else has he got to go?' He pushed a black lock of hair from his forehead.

Were they talking about Ed or did they have a wrong address? The banging got louder. I knew I had to answer it before they woke Ed and the whole neighborhood!

'Can I help you?' Carol Two came up to the door and I shooed her away with my foot.

318

The young woman had light-toned skin and gray-blue eyes. She used way too much mascara. 'Who are you?' she asked, looking up at me. She couldn't have been more than five-two, standing. 'I'm Maggie.' I looked up and down the block. An old Mazda sat directly across from the house. 'Can I help you?'

The young man and woman looked at each other a moment. The girl didn't look much more than eighteen. He may have been a few years older.

A dark van rounded the corner and crept slowly along the otherwise quiet street. We all turned to watch it pass. Was that Trish? Had she found me? I was so jumpy I was seeing the woman everywhere! Was that her behind the neighbor's sycamore?

'We must have the wrong house,' the young man replied. 'C'mon, Blaire.'

'But I'm tired and we don't have any money—'

'I said, come on.'

He grabbed her hand and led her to the Mazda. I shut the door and headed for bed. I took a quick shower in the bathroom between the bedrooms and pulled out a pair of gym shorts and a T-shirt to sleep in.

As I stepped barefoot into the hall, I heard noises coming from the direction of Ed's room. A slit of light was visible under the door.

I rapped lightly.

'Come in.'

I opened the door and Carol Two came in with me. What was it with this cat following me every-where? 'Are you OK in here?' Ed was under the covers, the ever-present portable computer resting on his lap.

'Sure, why?'

'I thought I heard shouting.'

'I couldn't sleep. Streaming *MasterChef* on the laptop.'

I nodded. 'I like to watch TV when I can't sleep, too.' I stepped closer to the rumpled bed. 'Are you sure you're OK?' He definitely didn't look OK. He was whiter than a ghost wearing bed sheets. I flipped on the bedside lamp.

Ed sighed with obvious exasperation and shut the computer. 'Yes. I'm fine. It's late; I think I'll try to get some sleep.'

'Oh, my gosh!' I exclaimed. 'You're all sweaty. The bed's soaked too.' I felt his clammy forehead. Sheesh, before I was simply worrying about Carol Two dying on my watch. Now I had to worry about Ed dying on my watch!

'Should I call the doctor?' As in Dr Vargas. Hey, if I had to call a doctor it may as well be a handsome one.

Ed shook his head. 'Nah.' He waved his hand then punched his pillow. 'I tell you what. If I'm not feeling better in the morning, you can call the doc.'

I reluctantly agreed and pulled the bedroom window shut. 'I'll crank the air down a few notches and see if that gets you cooled down.'

I shut Ed's door and adjusted the thermostat in the hall. Poor Ed. Carol Two twisted between my legs and I remembered the can of tuna I'd brought for her. I'd left the can open on the counter when those kids had knocked on the door.

The cat followed me silently back to the kitchen, where I prepared her a nice midnight snack. I rinsed the empty can and added it to the hill of refuse rising from the recycle bin. Both the bin and the trash can were overflowing.

I yawned loudly. I suppose it could wait until morning but I didn't want Ed to get up and see this mess. Heck, I didn't want to face it myself in the light of day. Besides, I'd be getting up early tomorrow if I wanted to make it to the café on time to prep for opening. I couldn't have Aubrey think I tolerated tardiness.

I picked up the overspilling trash can and pushed open the laundry room door with my knee. 'Hey!' I cried as Carol Two shot between my legs. I dropped the can on the stoop and gave chase.

'Oh no you don't!' I muttered, jumping out into the star-filled darkness. It was chilly and smelled like a junkyard.

Fearful of waking Ed, I tread slowly and carefully, fully aware of all the junk that littered the yard. And me in bare feet!

I really did not want to cut myself. I could live without getting a tetanus shot any time soon. Shots were scary. Shots hurt. Shots were to be avoided at all costs. Whoever invented shots should be, well, shot!

'Here, kitty, kitty!' I called in a loud whisper. 'Here, kitty, kitty!'

A black smudge shot past me. 'Hey, Carol, Carol Two! Come here, you!'

I squinted, wishing I had some of those night-vision goggles. Instead I had a pair of eyes that wasn't all that good during the daytime, let alone the dead of the night.

The middle of my foot landed flat on a sharp rock. 'Ouch.' I hopped on one foot while rubbing my injured foot with my fingers. 'This is why I don't have pets!' I shouted at the cat.

I heard a movement over near the garage. 'Gotcha now,' I said.

I approached the side door of the garage. There was an old pet door that the previous homeowner had built into the bottom of the side door. It was large enough for a medium-sized dog, so it was definitely large enough for one ornery cat. Carol Two had obviously gone inside. In fact, I could still see the flap moving ever so slightly.

I tried the handle. Locked, of course. I stamped my foot. There was a broken pane of glass just above the door handle. 'Looks like someone else had the same idea.' Though it must have been long ago, judging by the aged look of the glass shards on the ground.

I carefully snaked my hand through the jagged opening and wiggled the lock free. 'You can run but you can't hide,' I said playfully.

The door opened with a creak. I looked over my shoulder to make sure I hadn't disturbed Ed. I didn't want him struggling out of bed to come out here and check on the noise. He had enough problems.

Come to think of it, so did I.

Ed's tan Buick and a century's worth of junk filled the one-car garage but I saw little detail through the dim light of the stars and the half-moon overhead. My hands fumbled for a light switch and found it. I could only hope it worked.

Click. It did. Carol Two sat quietly in the corner licking the nose of the young man I'd seen on the porch earlier.

Ick.

Not that he minded.

Because I believe he was dead.

I smothered a scream with my hand. 'Come here, kitty,' I whispered, my voice tremulous. What the devil was this guy doing in here? The side of his face was covered in blood and a short-handled sledge hammer lay beside him. Had he broken in? Had the hammer fallen on him from the junk-filled rafters above?

What would a dead guy be doing in Ed's garage? I backed up a step.

Unless . . . unless.

'Trish,' I whispered. Had this poor guy been wandering around in the wrong place at the wrong time and Trish had murdered him instead of me? The girl had said the two of them were tired and had no money. That meant probably no place to sleep. So they came back here, thinking maybe they could sleep in the deserted garage.

Looking for me, Trish had stumbled into him and . . .

A chill scurried up my arms like a pair of furry little brown mice.

Where was the girl? Where was Trish? What about Rob?

Was I next?

While all this was running around in my mind I didn't hear who was creeping up behind me.

'Oh, dear,' said Ed. 'What am I going to do with you?'

I spun around. I hoped he was talking about that naughty cat of his, but that gun in his hand told me he wasn't.

THIRTY-FIVE

My eyes darted anxiously around the small garage. Nowhere to run, nowhere to hide. My gaze fell on the front of Ed's car. There was a big ugly dent in the driver's-side front fender and bumper. I didn't remember seeing that there when I'd seen the car in the drive, and it was really too big to miss.

'Stupid punk,' spat Ed.

'I don't get it,' I said, struggling to buy time. 'That's the boy that came to the door earlier. He was with a girl.' My eyes whipped around the garage. There was, thankfully, no sign of a second victim. 'What did he do? Try to break in?'

Ed laughed. 'Punk wanted money.' He aimed his pistol at the corpse. 'Banged on the bedroom window and started whining for a handout. Like I'd give him anything. But he believed me. Followed me out here like the lowlife imbecile that he is.' Ed grinned. 'Was.'

'What about the girl, Blaire? Did you kill her, too?'

'Nah.' He waved his free hand at me. 'When she saw what was happening, she took off like a scared rabbit. But she'll be back. She always comes back.' There was a sick leer on his lips.

I was beginning to quake from head to toe, and it wasn't just the chill night air and lack of sleep. This guy was beginning to scare me big time.

Something told me I was going to be next on his hit parade if I didn't come up with a plan soon.

Regrettably, I didn't have a clue what that plan might be. I was alone, unarmed and in bare feet. 'Wait,' I said, inching further from Ed. Unfortunately, this also put me further and further from the side door. 'You killed Mr Wilbur!'

'Think you're pretty smart, don't you?'

'He was your friend! How could you do that? Why would you do that?' Why had I agreed to spend the night in a murderer's house?

Ed shrugged and scratched his beard with the barrel of his pistol. I prayed the darn thing would go off in his face.

No such luck as he lowered the weapon and held it loosely toward me. 'Yeah, killing Rick was kind of a shame.'

Kind of?

'I guess there's no harm telling you,' he said with a low chuckle. 'Dead men tell no tales.' He took a step closer, leveling the gun in my direction. 'That goes for women, too.'

'Now wait a minute, Ed,' I said quickly. 'You don't have to do this!'

Ed ignored my plea. 'Me and Rick went way back.' He looked at me through watery eyes. 'I'm gonna miss him, you know?'

'Too bad you didn't miss him with that rolling pin.' I instantly shut my mouth. There I went, being a smart mouth again. And the look on Ed Teller's face told me he didn't appreciate my sense of sarcasm. Mom always said my mouth would get me in trouble one day. Why did that day have to be today?

'You don't understand, Miller.' He paced the small cluttered floor. 'I had no choice. Rick found out how I'd been stealing from the company. You see, I needed money and Wilbur Realty had it, and plenty of it.

'I didn't think they'd miss it if I helped myself to some. I was responsible for maintenance on all the properties. It was easy. I funneled the money that was supposed to be used to make repairs to my own account.' He smiled. 'It was simple, really.'

'But Mr Wilbur found out?' My brow furrowed in alarm. I needed to come up with some way out of this. How much longer could I stall him? How long would it be before I'd be joining Blaire's companion on the garage floor?

Ed frowned. 'Yeah. He confronted me about it. We were at your place and he was screaming about how he'd given me sufficient funds to fix the building's AC and wondered why I'd barely done any work at all.'

Ed thrust his chest out, his voice growing strident. 'He told me his sister-in-law, Natalie, had spotted me over in Reno a couple of times throwing money around with a young girl on my arm. Like it was any of his business.' Ed lashed out and kicked the back tire of the Buick.

I swallowed hard. Carole Two tensed in the corner. 'Let me guess,' I said, 'Blaire?'

'That's right. She and I met on the internet, one of those online dating sites, you know?' He raised his eyebrows and looked at me rather sheepishly. 'We started dating.' He smiled. 'Blaire's got expensive taste.' He shrugged. 'I could live with that.'

He turned and faced the body on the floor. 'But when I found out she'd been two-timing me, lying to me, keeping a younger boyfriend on the side—'

'That must have made you furious.' Did I care? No. But since I had nothing else to do – besides getting shot, that is – I was talking.

'You bet. I told her we were through.' He chuckled. 'Can you believe the two of them had the nerve to show up in town today, looking for a handout from me?' He shook his head. 'Couple of jerks.'

'Surely you must have explained all this to Rick?'

'Oh, sure. Not that he'd cared that I'd been duped. Accused me of being an old fool who should have known better.'

Ed crossed his arms over his chest, the gun tilted my way. I inched up against the car. 'He didn't care at all about me – he just wanted his precious money back. The problem was,' Ed said, with a slight jerk of his head, 'I'd spent it all. I promised I'd make it up to him. You know, pay him back over time out of my wages. Out of my flips, like this one.'

'But Rick wouldn't listen?' And I couldn't blame him. Ed Teller was nothing more than a crook. And a killer. Must not forget that part.

'We'd been friends all our lives and he said he was going to go to the police – can you believe it? He was all set to let me, his best friend, go to jail!'

I could but refrained from saying so.

Ed shook his head back and forth. 'I begged

him to let me make it right. But he said no.' Ed's eyes sort of glazed over. 'I saw that rolling pin on the counter. And I hit him on the head with it. But then I wasn't feeling so good. Started feeling kind of sick, kind of funny, you know?'

My mouth was as dry as the Sonoran. I nodded.

Ed chuckled. 'I knew I couldn't drag him outside in the condition I was in. So I emptied the chairs from one of those boxes in your storeroom and hid him inside, figuring I'd come back for him later.'

Ed looked over his shoulder toward the yard. 'I expected I'd bury him out here somewhere. With all the renovating I'm going to be doing, who'd ever know?'

Who indeed? I listened in horror to Ed's confession, partly because of what he'd done and partly because he was only telling me all this because he knew I'd never live to tell anyone.

'Funny, ain't it? All the exertion probably gave me a stroke. I drove myself to the ER.' He smiled evilly. 'Then I realized what a perfect alibi it would make. Nobody would ever suspect me of the murder. Plus, I could come and go as I pleased. Especially in the evening.' He snickered. 'I guess things have a way of working out for the best.'

At the moment, I was going to have to disagree with him there.

Ed sighed and spoke softly. 'He left me no choice.' He swiveled the gun at my head. 'Like you leave me none now.'

THIRTY-SIX

The right leg of the body on the floor twitched and shot out.

Whoa!

I didn't know if this guy was doing the dead man bounce or if he was still alive. All I know is that Ed flinched, Carole Two shot out the open door like a, well, scaredy-cat, and I followed – like a scaredy-human to the Nth power – taking advantage of Ed's distraction.

I had the presence of mind to hit the light switch on my way through the door. The crack of a bullet over the transom let me know that Ed wasn't fooling around.

Old Ed meant business.

I didn't know where Carol Two was heading, but I was heading for the mudroom door that I'd come out of earlier. My purse was in the spare room and I needed to get to my cell phone and car keys.

Then I needed to get the heck out of there!

I half-ran, half-tumbled through the darkness toward the house. I could hear Ed cursing and running behind me. For a guy who'd just been released from the hospital, it sounded like he was making pretty good time.

I felt a hand grab at my hair and I screamed. The tug threw me off balance. I stumbled over the lip of the back porch and went crashing to the ground. My forehead cracked against a cement block and suddenly the stars I was seeing were far closer to the ground than they had been earlier.

Ed's hands latched onto my foot. My hands fished around in the dark, grasping for anything. He was on top of me now, his weight pressing me down, taking my breath away. The cold metal of the gun pressed painfully against my cheek.

My fingers wrapped around a pine two-by-four and I swung with all my might. Ed wailed in pain and I hit him again. I heard a moan, then silence.

I lay there a moment, my heart racing, every bone in my body aching, being crushed by Ed. I arched my back, rolled the man off me and sat up.

Carol Two mrowled from the mudroom door. If she thought I was feeding her now, she was in for a surprise. I headed for the house, stopped midway, ran back and pried the pistol out of Ed's hands. I darted back inside.

I didn't know if Ed was alive or dead. Either way, I didn't want him getting inside the house and coming after me. I raced to the guest room, tossed the warm gun on the bed and fished my cell phone from my handbag with shaking fingers.

I took a deep breath and dialed Information. Yeah, that's right, Information. That might have been a mistake the first time, but not this time.

I took a deep breath as I heard the operator pick up. 'Hi, could you give me the number for a Veronica Vargas, please?' My fingernails clicked atop the dresser as I waited. I knew there was no way Mark Highsmith, Table Rock's lone detective, would accept another call from me tonight. 'And while I'm calling VV, would you mind calling the cops?'

I ignored the operator's confused blubbering and gave him Ed Teller's address. 'Oh, and before you hang up, you might want to call her brother, that's Daniel Vargas. That's right. He's a doctor. I think Ed's gonna need one.' The other guy I wasn't so sure about.

THIRTY-SEVEN

I waved to Clive as he came through the door, a smile plastered on his face. 'Good morning!' Unfortunately, by default, my friendly wave also encompassed Johnny Wolfe, who came in the door with him.

Clive came to the counter, practically dragging his partner in tow. Watching the two of them, the phrase 'kicking and screaming' came to mind.

'We heard all about it,' Clive exclaimed, his voice filled with drama. 'We came to see how you're doing.' He elbowed Johnny. 'And to apologize.'

I wiped my forehead with the side of my arm and tossed an order of beignets in the deep fryer. 'Apologize for what?'

'See?' Johnny hissed at Clive. Both men were sharply dressed in dark suits, obviously a working day at The Hitching Post.

'Oh, stop,' replied Clive. 'Just give her the flowers.'

Johnny Wolfe was clutching a lovely bouquet of red roses with accents of white baby's breath.

'Capture first place at the Junior Olympics?' I quipped.

'Maggie,' scolded Clive.

I lowered my chin. 'Sorry.' He sounded just like my mother. I reached out a free hand and accepted the bouquet. I stuck my nose in a cluster of petals and took a sniff. 'They're lovely. Thank you both.' I made a point of looking at Johnny.

He squirmed. 'You're welcome.' He looked like a doe ready to bolt.

'The roses are totally, totally beautiful,' cooed Aubrey. 'I'll get something to put them in.' She retreated to the storeroom. I hoped she didn't find any more bodies stuffed in boxes back there. I'd sort of had my fill of them.

Dead guys in boxes were definitely off my diet from here on out.

'Maggie Miller!' Mom burst through the door and stuck her hands on her hips. 'What does a mother have to do to get her only daughter to—'

I couldn't help grinning as I arched a brow her way. 'You remember Donna?' I said. 'About so tall?' I held a flat hand about eyebrow high.

'Fine,' huffed Mom, her lavender caftan swirling, 'my only unmarried daughter – to pick up the phone and call her poor, dear mother when she's almost been killed?'

I lifted the piano-hinged counter and gave Mom a hug. 'Sorry, I don't know what I was thinking.' My hand went to my bandaged forehead. I knew exactly what I'd been thinking – how do I get out of here alive? Definitely not, gee, maybe I should give Mom a call.

'Well.' Clive grabbed hold of Johnny's shoulder. 'We really should be going.'

'What? Nonsense,' I replied. 'Come on, sit. I'll bring us all some coffee and beignets.' I turned to my mother. She was still looking put out. I pouted.

'Fine.' She gave in and took a seat. I pushed a couple of tables together.

Dr Daniel Vargas came in while I was preparing the orders for them and a couple more customers. 'Maggie!' he cried, coming through the door. He wore dark trousers and a pale blue shirt. 'I heard all about the attempt on your life last night.'

I smiled. Though I had specifically requested VV's brother, another doctor had come to Ed Teller's house with the paramedics. If you can't count on the Information guy, who can you count on?

'It was nothing,' I said, waving my dripping tongs. 'Oops.' I wiped at his shirt with my rag. 'That'll wash right out.' It was only cottonseed oil, how bad could it be?

'Mr Teller is in intensive care.'

Good. He could stay there for all I cared. 'Is that safe?' Mesa Verde Medical Center had a tough, no-nonsense receptionist but it was hardly a secure facility. Look how easy it had been for Ed Teller to come and go unnoticed.

'There's a police officer on duty outside his room round the clock.'

I breathed easier. With luck, Ed Teller wouldn't be wandering around loose anytime soon.

'What about the young man he sledge-hammered?'

'Also in the ICU.'

I nodded. One dead guy was enough. 'Got time for coffee?' I'd also learned that they'd picked up Blaire near his house and were holding her for questioning. My guess was that she'd be some sort of witness for the prosecution.

'And an order of beignets?' Daniel smiled.

'Deal.' I pointed to where Mom was sitting with Johnny and Clive. 'Why don't you join my mother and friends while I get everything together?'

I carried over two overloaded platefuls of fresh hot beignets sprinkled liberally with powdered sugar. Aubrey carried a tray of coffees.

Daniel rose and took my hand. 'Are you sure you're all right?' He inspected the bandage on my forehead. 'They tell me you refused to stay overnight for observation.'

I nodded. 'I'm fine. Really,' I said, seeing the look of disbelief on the doctor's face.

There was no chance I was going to spend the night under the same roof as Ed Teller, even if it was a hospital roof and separate rooms. I still got the willies thinking about how I'd agreed to spend the night in that killer's house.

The rumble of throat clearing caught my attention and I swiveled my neck around. 'Is this a private party?' asked Detective Highsmith. 'Or can anyone join?' He looked meaningfully at Daniel's hand over mine.

I pulled my hand free. And I wasn't sure why. Maybe it was the way those dumb M&Ms of his were looking at me. Like there might be something more there than candy.

Highsmith tugged at his tie and cleared his throat once again. 'I thought you'd like to know that Brad Smith has been released.'

'He's out of his coma?!'

Highsmith pointed out the window. The reporter sat on the front passenger seat of the detective's sedan.

'What's he doing out there?' I said. 'Tell him to come in.' I motioned for Brad to come inside. 'He's gonna need some help.'

Brad smiled and opened the car door. I still wasn't too sure what to make of the guy. I'd definitely pegged him for a jerk when he'd come to the café practically accusing me of murder.

But then I'd discovered he'd been poking around on his own and almost lost his life trying to uncover the real killer. Brad had done some digging, starting with learning that Ed Teller had been cleared by the hospital days ago to leave. He'd had a minor stroke, nothing more.

It seems Ed had been sneaking out of Mesa Verde when it suited him – for instance, to sabotage my AC unit. Like Ed had confessed, what better cover than a hospital bed? No one suspected he was sneaking out and committing mischief. He'd managed to slip out several times, desperate to find the missing chairs and then later to shut me up. He'd tossed the chairs in the alley, but when he'd gone back they had disappeared. Knowing he might have left his fingerprints on them, he was desperate to find them.

That's why when I'd gone to see him he looked so bad, so clammy. It was all that exertion from running around Table Rock as he tried to cover his tracks.

He'd even discovered Brad following him. Ed had turned the tables on Brad and had run him off the road and into a crevice. Fortunately, Brad had survived the attempt on his life.

As the reporter swung his limbs out the car door, I noticed the left leg of his blue jeans had been cut off at the knee to accommodate the cast on the lower half of his leg. I ran to help him. I retrieved his crutch from the backseat and helped him stand. 'I'm glad to see you're OK,' I said.

'Same here,' Brad replied. 'When I couldn't reach you last night, I didn't know what to think. I was afraid Mr Teller might already have . . .' He paused. 'You know.'

I knew.

I aided him through the door and he joined our little group. Detective Highsmith had helped himself to a cup of coffee and I saw traces of powdered sugar on his lips. I beamed.

'What's so funny?' Highsmith looked irritated. Why? Because I'd caught him actually enjoying life?

'Nothing,' I said. I dropped my hands on the table and turned to Johnny. I smiled. 'You know, I thought you were trying to kill me the other day when you caught me nosing around your backroom.'

Johnny rolled his eyes. 'Please, I was simply trying to get you to leave before you damaged the inventory. Do you have any idea how expensive all those gowns are?'

I lifted my eyebrows. That made sense. 'OK, but what about yesterday afternoon?'

'Yesterday afternoon what?'

'When I saw you at Salon de Belleza.'

Johnny's eyes flashed warning signals but I didn't know why. 'Oh, that's right,' he said loudly, 'you asked me for the name of my manicurist.'

'I did?'

'Let's get something to write on.' Johnny

338

pushed out of his chair and dragged me away from the tables. 'Quiet, Ms Miller.' He looked over his shoulder at Clive. 'It's supposed to be a secret.'

'What's supposed to be a secret?' I asked. 'You and Caitie said something big was going to go down in three days.'

He scowled, tapping a finger against his lips, then answered. 'Fine, I'll tell. But first you have to swear you won't say anything.'

I placed my hand over my heart. 'I swear.' And crossed my fingers behind my back. I knew better than to believe me; why didn't he?

Johnny whispered, his back to the others, 'Caitie's been helping me plan a surprise anniversary party for Clive.'

A surprise anniversary party? 'I thought you were plotting another murder or your great post-murder escape.'

Johnny rolled his eyes. 'Focus. Our anniversary is really a few weeks off, but Clive always figures out when I'm trying to surprise him. This year, I thought I'd plan something early. I figure he'll never expect an anniversary party three weeks before the date.'

I had to admit, it wasn't a bad plan. Though he probably shouldn't have confided in me. I'm terrible at keeping secrets.

He looked pensive a moment. 'I suppose you could come. The party's at our home.'

Gee, such a warm invitation. I was almost insulted enough to say no. But I couldn't let Clive down. He'd be disappointed if I wasn't there. 'Sure, I'd love to. Can I bring anything?'

'Not necessary. I'm having the entire soiree catered. I'm even having a cake made by Markie.'

'Markie?' I rubbed my nose. Powdered sugar always tickles. 'Who's Markie?'

'Markie Rutledge from Markie's Masterpieces, the cake shop over at Navajo Junction. Surely you've heard of him?'

I shook my head.

'Haven't you ever watched BrideTV?'

I could only helplessly shake my head again.

'Well, he's had his own show on there. Plus, he's rated a five-tier cake bakery by *Baking Bridal* magazine.' Johnny flinched. 'Shh, here he comes.'

Sure enough, Clive wrapped his arms around our waists. 'What are you two hens clucking about?' It was irritating to note that Clive's arm could go further around Johnny's waist than mine.

'Nothing,' I replied. 'I was thanking Johnny for the flowers again.' Aubrey had set them in a tall jar on the prep counter near the coffee grinder.

Clive glanced over at them. 'Oh, I see you're using the rolling pin.' He squeezed me tighter then let go. 'You never did tell me how you like it.'

I did a quick scan of the café, spotted zero flies and let my mouth fall open. 'You gave me the rolling pin?'

'Sure, of course,' Clive answered. He was beaming. 'You weren't here so I left it on the counter as a surprise. The door was open but you weren't around. It was a café-warming gift.'

'What was with the threatening note?'

'What threatening note?'

'The one that said "take care."' I wiggled my

340

fingers in the air. 'What was that supposed to mean?'

Clive scratched his head, looking amused. 'It meant take care, don't let anything happen to it like what happened to the last one. I signed it.'

'No, you didn't.'

'Didn't I?' Clive tittered. 'Oh, well, no harm done, right?'

No harm done? No harm done?! I kissed Clive's cheek, then gave it a pinch. 'Nope. No harm done.'

The door tinkled once more and, like a good Pavlovian, I turned to look. It was Trish Gregory coming through the door, looking like an opposing army on the offensive in her Karma Koffee uniform. I frowned and hollered at Detective Highsmith, who was deep in conversation with Daniel. 'What's she doing here?' I pointed a finger at Trish. 'Why haven't you arrested this woman?'

Detective Highsmith turned his chair to face me. 'What for?'

'What do you mean "what for!"' I blubbered. 'The woman destroyed evidence in a murder investigation!'

The detective shrugged.

'Please,' said Trish. 'I didn't know anything about evidence.'

'She's right,' said Highsmith. 'Mrs Gregory had no way of knowing that those chairs might be evidence. Besides, we caught the killer, remember?'

I turned on Trish. 'But you bought the chairs and burned them to the ground. I know. I followed you,' I said. 'I watched you do it!'

Trish's brow shot up. 'You did?' She shrugged. 'I had no idea. Yes, I saw the chairs by chance while shopping at Laura's Lightly Used. Like I explained to the police this morning,' her eyes darted to Highsmith and he nodded, 'when I saw the chairs I figured they might have been the chairs that had been removed to hide Rick Wilbur's body. So I had to destroy them.'

'So you were involved!' I gestured for the detective to haul her away, but he didn't move.

Trish rolled her eyes. 'No, don't you see? I burned the chairs because of bad juju. Who knew what evil might have seeped into those chairs? They couldn't remain. I couldn't let some poor soul purchase them and take them home. They'd be cursed.'

Trish rested a hand on top of my shoulder. 'I had to propitiate the spirits.'

So that explained all that mumbo-jumbo I'd overheard her spouting out at the medicine wheel.

'I can understand that,' said Mom.

I looked at my mother as if she'd gone bonkers. I got the feeling Trish Gregory already was at the deep end of the pool bonkers. In fact, she'd probably been breathing those whatchamacallit ummy-gummy-yer-the-cheffy fumes too long.

'Anyway, I simply came to tell you that the HVAC company will be over to repair your unit this afternoon.' She handed me an envelope.

I turned it over in my hands. 'What's this?' A refund on the rent for all the trouble they'd caused me?

'A bill for the air conditioner and dry wall repair and paint.' She started for the door. 'Don't worry – if you can't pay it all at once we can add a small sum to your monthly rent.'

'What?' My eyes narrowed to deadly slits. 'This is ridiculous. You can't possibly expect me to pay this. It's not my fault Ed Teller tried to burn my apartment down. With me in it, I might add.'

'No, but you did neglect to check the batteries in your smoke detector.' She waved from the door. 'It's in your lease, Ms Miller.'

'You won't get away with this!' I hollered at her backside. 'I'll get an attorney. I'll sue!' First thing this afternoon, I'd turn this whole case over to Andy. He'd know what to do.

Trish turned on her heels. 'Oh, please, Ms Miller. Don't make this difficult. Life is all about letting go. Besides,' she quipped, 'if I were you, the only thing I'd be getting an attorney for is to sue whoever or whatever gave you that haircut.'

I flopped into an empty chair. Who knew life in a small town could be so exhausting? And now, on top of having a business to run, I had a cat. Yeah, that's right, a cat. I couldn't exactly leave Carol Two to fend for herself. Besides, it wasn't her fault that she was a cat and came from a broken home.

Mom planted a kiss on my forehead as she set down her empty cup. She fingered my bangs. 'Don't listen to her,' she cooed, 'I just love what you've done to your hair, Maggie.'

She would. I grimaced and wondered how I'd look in a buzz cut.

The bank had called first thing this morning and told me the problem with the check had been a clerical mistake at their end. That was a relief.

Moonflower had popped in before work and announced that Patti and her sister-in-law were keeping Wilbur Realty going. I guess she didn't want to squash the goose that was laying the golden egg no matter how much she preferred gardening.

Detective Highsmith had told me the police had learned that Joey the Junkman, a local scrap dealer, had found the chairs in the alley behind the café and sold them to Laura. Her clerk, being relatively new, hadn't recognized him.

That left Rick Wilbur's ex, Caitie Conklin. She was just crazy, and ornery. And my next-door neighbor. I'd be keeping a sharp eye on her. I'd be keeping an even sharper eye out for her shears. Who knew the most dangerous weapon to come out of Japan wasn't the samurai sword but the Kamisori scissors?

Aubrey and I replenished the platters of beignets and refilled the coffee cups. Life in a small town might be exhausting, but it had its moments.

I looked at the plain, unadorned paper cup. I really needed to do some branding, some fancy logo like Karma Koffee. Aubrey and I were going to have to do some brainstorming.

I smiled. The first thing I'd do once I did have a spiffy new uniform was to put it on and march across the street to Karma Koffee and rub Trish and Rob's respective noses in it – and I was definitely not going to buy one of their muffins, no matter how tasty they were.

At least, I hoped not. I still think they must be doping them somehow with some hippy-dippy New Age juice. What else could explain this

344

irrational craving I was constantly fighting for Heaven's Building Blocks?

The bell on the door jingled. We'd added the tiny leather strap of brass bells this morning. 'Welcome to Maggie's Beignet Café,' I called out.

A small man entered. He wore a loose-fitted lettuce-green tunic that fell to just below his knees. A pair of rough-hewn leather sandals held long, wide feet. His elongated head was nearly as large as his chest and his eyes stuck out like his designer had made a mistake, leaving his eyeballs too large for his eye sockets. Don't you just hate it when that happens?

We all watched in silence as he approached our group. 'Excuse me,' he said, his voice high and squeaky and tormented, almost as if the language was unfamiliar to his tongue, 'can you tell me the way to the Table Rock Hotel and Convention Center?'

I let out my breath.

Whew.

A sci-fi nut. Looking for the science-fiction costume and gaming convention being held this week at the Table Rock. I'd seen the advertisement in the *Table Rock Reader*.

Thank goodness, because I'd forgotten to hang the No Shirts, No Shoes, No Aliens sign.